Robert Grant

The King's Men

A tale of to-morrow

Robert Grant

The King's Men
A tale of to-morrow

ISBN/EAN: 9783337345075

Printed in Europe, USA, Canada, Australia, Japan

Cover: Foto ©Andreas Hilbeck / pixelio.de

More available books at **www.hansebooks.com**

THE KING'S MEN

A TALE OF TO-MORROW

BY

ROBERT GRANT
JOHN BOYLE O'REILLY
J. S. OF DALE AND
JOHN T. WHEELWRIGHT

" All the king's horses and all the king's men
Couldn't put Humpty Dumpty up again."

NEW YORK
CHARLES SCRIBNER'S SONS
1884

CONTENTS.

THE KING'S MEN.

CHAPTER I.

RIPON HOUSE.

THERE are few Americans who went to England before the late wars but will remember Ripon House. The curious student of history—a study, perhaps, too little in vogue with us—could find no better example of the palace of an old feudal lord. Dating almost from the time of the first George—and some even say it was built by the same Wren who designed that St. Paul's Cathedral whose ruins we may still see to the east of London—it frowned upon the miles of private park surrounding it, a marble memorial of feudal monopoly and man's selfish greed. The very land about it, to an extent of almost half a county, was owned by the owners of the castle, and by them rented out upon an annual payment to such farmers as they chose to favor with a chance to earn their bread.

In an ancient room of a still older house which stands some two miles from the castle, and had formerly been merely the gatekeeper's lodge (though large enough for

several families), a young man was sitting, one late afternoon in early November. The room was warmed by a
fire, in the old fashion ; and the young man was gloomily
plunging the poker into the coals, breaking them into oily
flakes which sent out fierce flickerings as they burned
away. He was dressed in a rough shooting suit of blue
velveteen, and his heavy American shoes were crusted with
mud. His handsome, boyish face wore an expression of
deep anxiety ; and his hands seemed to minister to the
troubles of his meditation by tumbling his hair about the
contracted forehead, while his lips closed about a short
brier-wood pipe of a kind only used by men. The pipe
had gone out, unnoticed by the smoker ; and he did not
seem to mind the fierce heat thrown out by the broken
coals. Above the mantel was the portrait of a gentleman
in the quaint costume of the latter Victorian age ; the absurd starched collar and shirt, the insignificant cravat, the
trousers reaching to the ankles, and the coat and waistcoat
of black cloth and fantastic cut, familiar to the readers of
the London *Punch.* This antedated worthy looked out
from the canvas upon the room as if he owned it ; and the
mullioned windows and carved oak wainscoting justified
his claim, even to the very books in the bookcases, which
showed an antiquarian taste. Here were the strange old-
fashioned satires of Thackeray and the more modern
romances of the humorist Dickens ; the crude speculations
of the philosopher Spencer, and the one-sided, aristocratic
economies of Malthus and Mill ; with the feeble rhymes of
Lord Tennyson d'Eyncourt, which men, in a time-serving
age, called poetry.

Geoffrey Ripon had come to his last legs. And he was
one of the few aristocrats of his generation who had ever

(metaphorically speaking) had any legs worth considering. When O'Donovan Rourke had been President of the British Republic, that good-natured Irishman, who had been at school with Ripon's father, had given him a position in the legation at Paris; but when the Radicals overthrew Rourke's government, Ripon lost his place. And Ripon could not but think it hard that he, Geoffrey Ripon, by all right and law Earl of Brompton, Viscount Mapledurham in the peerage of Ireland, etc., etc., should that afternoon have been fined ten shillings and costs for poaching on what had been his own domain.

His great-uncle looked down upon him with that exasperating equanimity that only a canvas immortality can give—his great-uncle who fell on the field of Tel-el-Kebir, dead as if the Arab bullet had sped from a worthier foe, in the days when England had a foreign policy and could spare her soldiers from the coast defence. And his grandfather, who smirked from another coroneted frame behind him, had been a great leader in the Liberal party under Gladstone, Lord Liverpool, the grand old man who stole Beaconsfield's thunder to guard the Suez Canal, that road to India which he, like another Moses, had made for their proud legions through the Red Sea.

And now Ripon was living in his porter's lodge, all that was still his of the great Ripon estates, with his empty title left him, minus the robes and coronet no longer worn; and his King, George the Fifth, an exile, wandering with his semblance of a court in foreign lands.

The world moves quickly as it grows older, with an accelerated velocity, like that of a falling stone; and it is hard for us of the present day to picture the England of King Albert Edward. The restlessness and poverty of the

masses ; the agitations in Ireland, feebly, blindly protesting
with dynamite and other rude weapons against foreign
oppression ; the shameful monopoly of land, the social
haughtiness of the titled classes, the luxury and profligacy
of the court—perhaps even at the opening of our story,
poor England was hardly worse off.   But then came the
change.   Gradually the bone and sinew of the country
sought refuge in emigration.   The titled classes, after mortgage upon mortgage of their valueless land, were forced to
break their entails to sell their estates.   And at last, when
the great American Republic, in 1889, cut down the Chi-
nese wall of protection, which so long had surrounded their
country, even trade succumbed, and England was under-
sold in the markets of the world.   Then retrenchment was
the cry ; universal suffrage elected a parliament which literally cut off the royal princes with a shilling ; and the
Premier Bradlaugh swamped the House of Lords by the
creation of a battalion of life peers, who abolished the
hereditary House and established an elective Senate.   It
was easy then to call a constitutional convention, declare
the sovereign but the servant and figure-head of the people,
confiscate the royal estates and vote King Albert a salary of
£10,000 a year.

Then Russia took advantage of the great struggle
between Germany and France to seize India, and after the
terrible defeat at Cyprus and the siege of Calcutta the old
King of England abdicated in favor of his grandson George.
But the people clamored for an elective President, and it
was nigh twenty years before the opening of our story that
King George had been forced to seek his only safe refuge
in America.

Thus it was that Geoffrey Ripon had come to depend on

poaching and the garden stuff his old servant managed to raise in the two-acre lot surrounding the lodge. Almost the only modern things in his room were the guns and fishing tackle in the corners and the electric battery for charging the cartridges ; and now he was judicially informed that he must poach no more, the mortgage had been finally foreclosed, and he looked out of his window upon lands no longer his even in name. It is a sad thing to be ruined, and if ever man was ruined beyond all hope, Geoffrey Ripon, Earl of Brompton, was the man ; it is hard to feel you are the last of your race, that you are almost an outlaw in your own land—and Ripon's king, George the Fifth, was suffered to play out his idle play of royal state, in Boston, Massachusetts. Ripon had never been in America. He pushed back his chair from the fire, as it gave out a heat too great for any man to stand. He walked to the window, and stood looking out upon the long perspective of elms, where the avenue stretched away in the direction of Ripon House. As his eye wandered over the broad view of park and forest, a carriage, drawn by four horses, insolent in the splendor of its trappings, rolled toward him from the castle. In that moment it seemed to Ripon that he felt all the bitterness of hatred and envy that might have rankled in the hearts of all the poor wayfarers who had in eight hundred years peered through the park gate and looked at those broad acres that his race so long had held. The carriage rolled swiftly by him, with a glitter of silver harness and liveries ; on one seat were an elderly man and a young girl. As he saw her face Ripon started in surprise. Then, after a moment, he walked to the table and filled his pipe.

" Bah !" he said to himself, " it cannot be possible."

Again he threw himself on a chair by the fireplace, and tried to read the *Saturday Review*. There was a long leader against Richard Lincoln ; but as Lincoln was the one member in the House for whom Geoffrey had any respect, he threw it aside in disgust. He heard a timid knock at the door.

" Come in !" growled Geoffrey, as he turned to light his pipe.

An old family servant, the last survivor of an extinct race, entered with a battered silver tray.

" Please, my lord, a letter from the persons at the castle ; one of them is waiting for an answer."

Reynolds made no distinction between the " persons at the castle" and their servants ; and he always called it the castle, now that Ripon House was the gatekeeper's lodge.

" I suppose," grunted Geoffrey, as he took the letter, " they want to warn me against poaching. So considerate, after I have been fined ten shillings by their gamekeeper."

To his surprise the letter had a familiar look ; it was addressed to him by his title in the ancient fashion, and was in a handwriting which he thought he should have known in Paris. Tearing open the envelope, he read :

" MY DEAR LORD BROMPTON : I hear that you are back to your own estate, and you will doubtless be surprised to learn that I am so near you. Papa telephoned over last week for an estate, and here we are, with a complete retinue of servants and a gallery of ancestors—yours, by the way, as I found to my surprise. I felt so sorry when they called you back from Paris ; I had no idea I should see you again so soon. Papa wanted to look after his affairs in England ; so we have come over again for the winter, and I was delighted to get out of the wild gayety of America for this dear sleepy old country.

" If you have nothing better to do, will you dine with us to-morrow night ? Do not stay away because we are in your old family house. We have no such feelings in America, you know. Richard Lincoln will be here, and Sir John Dacre. Do you know Sir John ? I admire him immensely, you must know.

"Sincerely yours,

"MARGARET WINDSOR."

"P. S. The new minister and legation are not received in society. We missed you so much."

"Maggie Windsor over here," thought Ripon, "with that curious old father of hers, taking Ripon House as if it were furnished lodgings." And he thought of the old house and of his great-uncle who fell at Tel-el-Kebir, and of King George over the sea in America. But he said to himself that Maggie Windsor was a nice girl, as he put out his pipe and went out into the park for a walk.

CHAPTER II.

THE palace of a thousand wings, that nearly two thousand years had gone to build, had been tumbled into ruins in a day, and out of the monstrous confusion no fair structure had yet arisen.

Rich as a crimson sunset, with traditions splendid as sunlit clouds, English Royalty had sunk into the night, and the whole sky was lightless, except where the glory had descended.

The government which had lifted itself like a tower in the eyes and minds of Englishmen for a hundred generations had disappeared, and the ideal government of the people had not yet filled its place.

The British Republic was seventeen years old. For seventeen years King George the Fifth had been an exile in the United States, and the fifty millions of British people had been on trial as self-governors.

Providence had smiled on the young Republic. Its first guardians had been true to their trust ; and like the fathers who laid the deep foundations of American freedom, their souls expanded with the magnitude of duty and responsibility.

The world looked on, sympathized, but for weeks and

months almost feared to speak. But half a year passed, and the dreadful crest of Anarchy had not once been raised.

The French Republic, over seventy years old, strong, unenvious and equitable, was the first to applaud.

The Commonwealths of Germany, thirty-three years old, one after another spoke their congratulation.

The aristocratic Republic of Russia was officially silent. The noble Nihilists, who had murdered four Czars to obtain power, were now constitutionally terrorizing the masses ; but the Russian people had learned from their rulers, and the popular press thundered encouragement to the English Commons.

America smiled like an elder sister, and held out her hand in loving friendship.

From the day of the revolution, the three names which forever belong to the history of British Republicanism were in the front—O'Donovan Rourke, the first President, and his two famous Ministers, Jonathan Simms and Richard Lincoln.

But the story of that first great Administration is read now in the school-books. The sudden death of the President was the first serious loss of the Republic. Had he lived another decade how different would have been the later history of England !

Matthew Gower, the Vice-President, entered on the unexpired term of the Presidency. He was a weak, well-meaning man, and he was jealous of the extraordinary popularity and personal influence of Richard Lincoln, the Secretary of State. When his cabinet was announced, Richard Lincoln, released from his long service in harness, with a deep feeling of relief, went back to his home in Nottingham.

At this time he was forty-six years of age.   He had been
a widower for over twenty years.   At twenty-five he had
married the beautiful girl he loved, and within the year his
wife died, leaving the lonely man a little daughter whose
eyes renewed his grief and love.

This was the tall girl who flung her arms round the neck
of the dismissed minister when he entered his home at
Nottingham.

"No one else, papa!" she cried, as she buried her face
against his heart, sobbing with joy.   "Do not speak to
any one else till I am done with you."

The rest, the love, the peace of home were very sweet.
Richard Lincoln renewed, or tried to renew, his interest in
the work of his younger days.   His daughter loved to go
with him through the town, proud of the famous man who
was hers, heedful of any curious or respectful glance of the
people on the street.

He gave himself up to the new life.   He began to
wonder at and enjoy the beauty, accomplishments and un-
ceasing amiability of his daughter.

Mary Lincoln was a rare type of womanhood.   She had
inherited her mother's grace and lithe beauty of form, and
from her father she took a strong and self-sustained nature.
But there was added a quality that was hers alone—a
strange, silent power of enthusiasm—a fervor that did not
cry out for ideals, but filled all her blood with a deep
music of devotion.   A man with such a nature had been a
poet or the founder of a creed.   But the ideal of a man is
an idea, while the ideal of a woman is a man.   Time
alone can bring the touchstone to such a heart.

It was not strange that under such home influences
public affairs should sink into a secondary place in Rich-

ard Lincoln's mind. He hardly looked at the news-papers, and he never expressed political opinions or pre-dictions. When he did speak of the government, it was with confidence and respect. If he doubted or distrusted, no one knew.

For two years he had lived this quiet life ; but, though he turned his eyes from many signs, the astute and silent man saw danger growing like a malarial weed beneath the waters of the social and political life of his country.

One morning Patterson, his business partner, who was an excitable politician, threw down his *Times*, and turned to Lincoln with an impatient manner.

" We are going to smash, sir, with our eyes open. We are going to the devil on two roads."

" Who is going to smash ?" asked Lincoln.

" The country. See here ; there are two rocks ahead, the aristocrats and the demagogues, and which is worse no one can say. They are getting ready for something or other, and the good sense and patriotism of England stand by and do nothing."

" Has anything particular happened ?"

" Yes ; at West Derby yesterday, the Duke of Bays-water was elected to Parliament, getting a large majority over Tyler, a sound Republican."

" Pooh ! You don't take that as a specimen of all our elections ? The Derby voters are mainly farmers, and the farmers retain their old respect for the lords of the manor."

" And that means something," rejoined Patterson ; " it is not as if those aristocrats had accepted the Republic, which they don't even pretend to do. There are now over forty of them in the lower house."

"Well," answered the ex-Minister, "they have been elected by the people."

"Yes; by the uninstructed people,'' said Patterson, warmly. "The people are talked to by these fellows with empty titles on one hand and by the demagogues on the other, and they think the only choice lies between the two."

"Surely, papa," said Mary, who was interested in the conversation, "the people will not be so easily deceived?"

"Deceived!" interrupted Mr. Patterson. "Why, Mary, here was an election in which the people were led to vote against one of the best Republicans in England, and for a lord who is nearly seventy, who has never done any good for himself or the country—an old pauper, who goes to Parliament for the salary and the chance to plot against the people."

Mary looked at her father as if she wished him to speak.

"These men," he said, "do not regain power as lords, but as commoners. That is good, instead of bad—their withdrawal would be more dangerous. We must remember that those who have lost by the revolution are still as much a part of the English people as those who have gained."

"I don't know about that," said Patterson, stubbornly. "I believe those aristocrats are actually plotting treason; and a traitor separates himself from his people."

Richard Lincoln's silence only stirred up the old Radical. He shot home next time.

"I believe we shall have a lord returned for Nottingham next election."

A slow flush rose in Lincoln's face, and he unconsciously raised his head.

"For the last two years," continued Patterson, seeing

the effect of his words, " only two Englishmen have been heard of to any extent—the demagogue leader, Bagshaw, and Sir John Dacre, the insolent young leader of the aristocrats.''

This time it was the daughter that flushed at Mr. Patterson's words.

" Mr. Dacre is not insolent,'' said Mary, warmly. " I have met him several times. He is a most remarkable man.''

" He couldn't well be insolent to you, Mary,'' the wily Patterson answered, with a smile for his favorite, who usually agreed with his radicalism, " but his tone to the public is a different thing.''

" You extremists are at least responsible for one of these —for the demagogue—'' said Richard Lincoln.

" Yes ; I admit it. The election of Bagshaw for Liverpool was a terrible mistake. But, if we had had our way, the other evil should have lost its head—O, I beg your pardon, Mary ; I did not mean your friend, Mr. Dacre, but the principle he represents.''

Mary Lincoln had exclaimed as if shocked, which brought out the concluding words from Mr. Patterson.

" If one were gone, would not the danger be greater ?'' asked Richard Lincoln. " They keep each other in check. They are useful enemies.''

" Take care they don't some day turn round and be useful friends,'' retorted Patterson. " I believe they did so in Derby yesterday. If they were to do it in Nottingham they would sweep the city.''

Mr. Patterson had scored his mark. The ex-Minister was silent and thoughtful.

" The Republic is like an iceberg,'' he said presently,

"a dozen years above water, but a century below. We shall be able to handle our difficulties—Don't you think so, Mary?" he added lightly, as they went out.

"Papa," said Mary, as they walked across the main street, "I met Sir John Dacre at Arundel House when I was visiting Lucy Arundel last year, and I can assure you he is not an evil-minded man."

"Indeed!" answered the father, rather amused at the relation; "you like him, then?"

"Very much, indeed. He is a perfect old-fashioned cavalier, and the most distinguished-looking man I ever saw, except you."

Her father laughed at the unconscious flattery.

"And the very oldest men are constantly consulting him," continued Mary, who was on a subject which evidently interested her.

There was something in Mary's voice that made her father glance down at her face. But he did not pursue the subject.

The months rolled on in this unrestful peace, and day by day it grew clear that the internal troubles of the Republic were forming a dangerous congestion.

Richard Lincoln again became an attentive reader of the newspapers. No man in England studied more carefully the signs of the times. Daily, too, he listened to the denunciation of the aristocrats by his radical old friend.

"They ought to be banished!" exclaimed Mr. Patterson, one morning. "I said it would come to this."

He pointed to an announcement of a meeting of "gentlemen who still retained respect for their Sacred Cause," to be held at Arundel House the following week, the wording of which was rather vague, as if intended to convey

more than the verbal meaning. The notice was signed :
" John Dacre, Bart."

" Why, that is Mary's friend," thought Richard Lincoln. And when he met Mary, an hour later, he said,
half-jestingly :

" Is your friend, Mr. Dacre, a conspirator ?"

" He is only an acquaintance, papa ; and I hardly know
what a conspirator is. But Mr. Dacre is certainly nothing
wrong. You should see his face, papa."

" Oh, yes ; those dreamers—"

" Papa !" said Mary, almost angrily, " Mr. Dacre is
not a dreamer. He is a leader of men—a natural leader—
like you !"

The eloquence of voice and gesture surprised Richard
Lincoln ; but he was too puzzled by Mary's manner to
reply. Looking at her as if from a distance, he only remembered, sadly, how little of her life he had seen—how
much there was from which he had been left out in the
heart of his motherless girl.

Mary read something in his eyes that made her run to
him and fold her arms around his neck.

" You were thinking of mamma then," she whispered,
with brimming eyes.

" Your face was like hers, Mary," he said, and kissed
her tenderly.

In the growing excitement of the times, father and
daughter were growing daily into closer union. The Parliamentary elections were coming on, and Richard Lincoln
took a deep interest in the preparations. He had been
asked to stand for several places, but he had firmly de-
clined ; nevertheless he had become almost a public character during the campaign. From all sides men looked to

him for counsel. His correspondence became burden-
some, and Mary, having urged him long to let her help, at
last had her way.

In this way it was that she became familiar with the
troubled issues of the time, and learned to think with her
father in all his moods. Their house in Nottingham, with
comings and goings, committees and councils, was soon
like the office of a great Minister.

"This can't last," said Mr. Patterson to Mary Lincoln, one day; "he is needed in London again, and
he will go. I believe they mean to nominate him for
President."

Two days later, Patterson, with all the rest of England,
was allowed to see the secret that had moved the political
sea for years.

The National Convention was held to nominate the
President. The Radical wing (they were proud to call
themselves anarchists) had developed unlooked-for strength,
chiefly from the cities and great towns, and had put forward as their candidate the blatant demagogue, Lemuel
Bagshaw, whose name has left so deep a stain on his
country's record.

On the first day of the National Convention the news of
Bagshaw's strength caused only a pained surprise throughout England. Men awaited with some irritation the proper
work of the Convention. But on the second day, when
the two strongest opposing candidates did not together
count as many votes as the demagogue, there was downright consternation.

Then the Aristocrats showed their hand : they aban-
doned their sham candidate and voted solidly for the demagogue—and Lemuel Bagshaw, the atheist and anarchist,

received the nomination for the Presidency of the British Republic !

The ship was fairly among the shoals and the horizon was ridged with ominous clouds. The petrels of disorder were everywhere on the wing. The Republic was driving straight into the breakers.

A few days later a great meeting was held in Nottingham, at which a workingman proposed the name of Richard Lincoln as their representative in Parliament.

A great shout of acclamation greeted the name and spoke for all Nottingham. Then the meeting broke up, the crowd hurrying and pressing toward Richard Lincoln's house.

Mary Lincoln heard the growing tumult, and looked up at her father alarmed. She had been playing softly on an organ in the dimly-lighted room, while her father sat thinking and half listening to the low music, as he gazed into the fire.

He had heard the crowd gathering in the square below, but he had not heeded, till he started at last as a voice outside addressed the multitude, calling for three cheers for the Member of Parliament for Nottingham. The response, ringing from thousands of hearts, made Mary Lincoln leap to her feet.

Her father sat still, looking toward the open window beneath which was the tumult.

" Father," said Mary, calling him so for the first time in her life ; " they have nominated you. You will not refuse ?"

" No," he said, almost mournfully. " I shall accept —and leave you again."

" Never again," she cried, " my own dear father. I

shall go with you to London. Oh, I am so proud of you !''

And Richard Lincoln accepted the nomination, and was elected. His name rallied throughout the whole country the men who had its good at heart.

But the demagogue was raised to the highest place in the Republic, and his party would have grown drunken with exultation had they not been deterred by the solid front and the stern character of the opposition, the leader of which from the first meeting of the new Parliament was Richard Lincoln.

CHAPTER III.

THE seashore in late November is never cheerful. The gray, downcast skies sadden the sympathetic ocean ; the winds cut to the marrow, and the yellow grass and bare trees make the land as sad-colored as the sea. But even at this season a walk along the cliff upon which Ripon House stands is invigorating, if the walker's blood is young. The outlook toward the water is bluff and bold and the descent sheer.

A neat, gravelled path conforming to the line of the coast divides the precipice from the smooth, closely-cropped lawn which sweeps down from the terrace of the ancient mansion. Ripon House is an imposing, spacious pile. It bears marks of the tampering of the last century when the resuscitated architecture of Queen Anne threatened to become ubiquitous.

A vast plantation of stately trees originally shut out the buildings on three sides from the common gaze, but the exigencies of the lawn-tennis court and the subsequent destitution of the late earl, who renounced his wood fire the last of all the luxuries then appurtenant to a noble lineage, have sadly thinned the splendid grove. Nor is the domain void of historic interest. Here was the scene of the crown-

ing festivity of the pleasure-loving Victorian era when the
nobility of the United Kingdom gathered to listen to a
masque by Sir William Gilbert and Sir Arthur Sullivan in
aid of a fund to erect a statue to the memory of one John
Brown, a henchman of the sovereign.

But what boots in this age of earnest activity more than
a trivial reference to the selfish splendor of a superstitious
past? To-day is to-day, and the nails on the coffin-lid of
the last Hanoverian would scarcely be of silver, so many
hungry mouths are to be fed.

Geoffrey Ripon on the morning following his reflections
was sauntering along the gravel path which bordered the
cliff. He was reading the half-penny morning paper, in
which he had just come upon a paragraph describing the
discovery by the police of a batch of infernal machines sup-
posed to have been sent over from America by friends of
the Royalists. Among the emissaries captured he read the
name of Cedric Ruskin, an old schoolfellow and great-
grandson to an art critic of that surname who flourished in
former days by force of his own specific gravity. Pained
at the intelligence, he sighed heavily, and was on the point
of sitting down upon a rustic bench close at hand when a
melodious, gladsome voice hallooing his name broke in
upon his meditation. He looked up and perceived Miss
Maggie Windsor skipping down the lawn with charming
unconventionality.

"Lord Brompton, Lord Brompton."

He raised his hat and stood waiting for the girl, whose
motions were marvellously graceful, especially if her large
and vigorous physique be considered. No sylph could
have glided with less awkwardness, and yet a spindle more
closely resembles the bole of a giant oak than Maggie Wind-

sor the frail damsels who bent beneath the keen blasts of
New England a hundred years ago. Her countenance disclosed all the sprightly intelligence which her great-grand-
mother may have possessed, but her glowing cheeks and
bright blue eyes told of a constitution against which nervous prostration fulminated in vain. Nor were the bang
or bangle of a former generation visible in her composition. But here a deceptive phrase deserves an explanation.
"Composition" is an epithet which, least of all, is applicable. Miss Windsor's perfections of whatever kind were
wholly natural.

A St. Bernard dog of superb proportions gambolled at
her side.

"I thought it was you," she said. "I am very glad to
see you again."

"And I, Miss Windsor, to see you." They shook
hands with cordiality. "And how do you like your new
lodgings?" he inquired.

"Ah, Lord Brompton, I was afraid you would feel net-
tled that we capitalists should possess your grand old
homestead. My purpose in swooping down upon you in
this unceremonious style was to ask you to make yourself
quite at home in the place. Consider it your own if you
will."

"What would your father say to such an arrangement,
I wonder?" he asked, glancing at her.

"Oh," she laughed, "papa monopolizes everybody
and everything else, but I monopolize him. But you look
serious, Lord Brompton, and less complacent, if I may use
the expression, than when we met last. Dear old Paris.
That was two years ago."

"Ought I to look complacent after reading in the newspaper that my old schoolmate, Cedric Ruskin, has been arrested on a charge of high treason ?''

"Alas ! poor Cedric !—no, that was Yorick. Down, Bayard, down,'' she cried to her dog.

"A great many things may happen in two years, Miss Windsor. When chance first brought us together, I was a landed proprietor, and the heir of a noble lineage. To-day I am a beggar at the feet of fatherless wealth.''

"Excuse me, Lord Brompton, I have a father.''

"Did I say I was at your feet, Miss Windsor ?''

"You are the same clever creature as ever,'' she an-swered. "But I am beginning to believe you are in ear-nest. Is it possible that you are the Lord Brompton who told me once that fate's quiver held no shaft to terrify a philosopher ? ' Dust to dust, and what matters it whether king or chaos rule ? ' Those were your words. I warned you then, but you laughed me to scorn—''

"And now you are deriding me.''

"You are unjust. I met you with a proffer of hospital-ity, but you would none of it.''

"Am I not to dine with you this evening ?''

"True. Then as a further instance that you are still a stoic, come now and exhibit to me the treasures and secrets of Ripon House. I have got no farther than the picture gallery as yet. There is an ancestor of George the Third's time whose features are the prototype of yours—the same dreamy eye—the same careless smile—the same look of being petted. You remember I always said you had been spoiled by petting.''

She led the way across the lawn, with Bayard bounding close at hand.

"I am sure there must be secret galleries and haunted

chambers and all sorts of dreadful places. I telephoned
to Mr. Jawkins to inquire, but he answered, 'Not as I
know of, miss.' I suppose he is so fearfully practical
he wouldn't care if a real ghost met him in a remote
wing.''

"What a pity we didn't live in the last century when
people still gave ghosts the benefit of the doubt," said
Lord Brompton, sadly. "Now we are certain that there
never were any."

"But we may still run across a skeleton in a closet,"
said the girl.

"Oh, yes. But who, by the way, is Mr. Jawkins?"

"Have you never heard of Mr. Jarley Jawkins, the
famous country-house agent and individual caterer?"

Lord Brompton shook his head.

"He is indeed a remarkable man," she continued.
"When we decided to come to England my father telephoned to Jawkins, who immediately sent out a list of
country-seats. We chose this and made arrangements
with him to supply us with guests at so much a head. A
regular country-house party—a duke and duchess, one or
two financially embarrassed noblemen, a disestablished
bishop, a professional beauty, a poet-peer, and several other
attractions. Oh, Jawkins is wonderful. They are all
coming to-day. Won't it be fun? But it may seem rude
to ask you to meet such people? I am sorry. You will
be almost the only guest not hired for the occasion. It
was very inconsiderate of me."

"That's all right," said the young lord. "Perhaps I
may find an opening here. I'm looking out for a job.
Possibly you may not be aware, Miss Windsor, that the
porter's lodge, which I occupy at present, is my sole piece

of property. I will send my card to Jawkins. By the way, does he conduct them in person ?"

" Oh, yes. He comes on the first day to introduce them. Jawkins is a most amusing man. He is enormously rich and a great *bon-vivant.* He has a retinue of thoroughly trained servants whom he dispatches to his customers, and everything he supplies is in the most perfect taste. He has but one weakness : he loves a lord and is the sworn enemy of the new *régime.* Don't you look forward with interest to the feast to-night ? I shall give you a professional beauty to take into dinner ; and of course I shall go in with the man of the highest rank. But here we are," she said, as they reached the upper terrace in front of the house.

" What a superb dog you have, Miss Windsor. What is his name ?" said Lord Brompton, gazing with admiration at the noble creature, who stood on the threshold, panting after his run.

" His name is Bayard."

" Ah, Miss Windsor, I perceive that you still recognize the glamour of a lordly title in the matter of naming your pets. The Chevalier Bayard smacks of royal prerogative."

" Pardon me ; Bayard is named after an American statesman who was contemporary with my great-grandfather. But isn't he a beauty ? He cost $1000. There is not another of his variety in the United States."

" I should like to go to America," said Lord Brompton, pensively, as he entered the familiar library now renovated by the taste of Jawkins. " My views have changed materially on many questions since we last met. I can see that things here are likely to be in a chaotic state for a long

time to come, whereas your institutions have become per-
manent."

" But you ought to wish to remain and help your fellow-
countrymen to better things, Lord Brompton. Look at
that line of ancestors," she exclaimed. " You ought to
do something worthy of them."

The ex-peer shook his head. " I have ambition, I
think, thanks largely to my friendship with you two summers ago ; but the outlook is very gloomy. England is in
the hands of professional politicians. There is no chance
for gentlemen in political life."

" But the King may come to his own again," she murmured, in pity for his mood. " Your title is unimpeached
at his exiled court."

" I have doubts as to the desirability of a return to the
old order of things, even if there were hopes of success.
It is useless to fight against the spirit of the age. The
King is old and fat."

" I saw the King riding in a herdic in Boston a few days
before we sailed," said Maggie. " He was stopping at the
old Province House. Poor sovereign, he looked desti-
tute."

" He is very poor. What was saved from the wreck is
in the hands of Bugbee, the London banker. The court
has since been moved to the South End. But a monarchy
is surely vastly preferable to our present administration.
President Bagshaw is a disgrace to any civilized community, to say nothing of an ideal republic."

" There is the ancestor who looks like you," said she,
pointing to the portrait of a cavalier wearing hat and plume
and long mustaches. " But is there no hope from the
opposition ?" she inquired.

"I cannot yet bring myself to sympathize with the Liberals, although their leader, Richard Lincoln, is a great and upright man. While the King lives I can no more be disloyal to the House of Hanover than my namesake up there could have been to his master's cause. Still, I feel we are living in an age when opinions are no more secure from revolution than dynasties."

"Speaking just now of the Chevalier Bayard reminds me that Jawkins mentioned as one of the guests he had procured for the occasion—"

"Like so much plate or china," interrupted the quondam peer, bitterly.

"Sir John Dacre," continued Miss Windsor, without regard to his petulance.

"John Dacre?" he cried, with interest.

"Yes. Do you know him?"

"Know him ! He was one of my dearest college friends. He is a man of the utmost dignity of soul and consummate breeding."

"Jawkins spoke of him with positive awe as a gentleman of the old school. 'He is a chevalier *sans peur et sans reproche*, miss,' said, he, 'and one of my choicest specimens. He is more precious than Sèvres china ; but at present he declines pay.' "

"St. George and the dragon !" cried Lord Brompton, "what would Dacre say could he hear the comparison ? Jawkins's life would not be worth an hour's purchase. We regarded John Dacre at Oxford as the ideal of a chivalric nature."

"You interest me greatly," said she. "But what has he been doing since you graduated ?"

"We have not met, but I have heard of him as loyal

and devoted to the royal cause when the outlook was darkest. I shall find him the same noble, ardent soul as ever,
I have not a doubt. Like enough his zeal will be the
needful spur to my flagging spirit."

They had been wandering through the spacious mansion
as they talked, but so absorbed were they in the conversation that the changes in the arrangement of the ancient
heirlooms of the once illustrious house of Ripon made but
little impression upon Lord Brompton. Weary at last with
their wanderings the twain seated themselves upon a broad
leather couch, from which they could command a view of a
magnificent stained-glass mullioned window, which dated
back to the days of George the First. The half light of
the apartment was perhaps a begetter of remembrances, for
they began to talk of the past, if indeed so short a period
back as two summers deserves to be so entitled. Through
Lord Brompton's thoughts floated an inquiry as to whether
he was not in love with his companion, for, if not, why this
joyous sense of re-acquisition on his part? He had never
forgotten the pleasant, happy hours passed in La Belle
France, and here they were come again, and he was visiting
side by side with her whose smile had been their harbinger.

" But I am forgetting, Lord Brompton, the object of
our coming here," she exclaimed at last. " I want to
know the secrets of Ripon House. Where is the haunted
chamber ?"

Geoffrey smiled, and rising from his seat walked to the
other side of the room and touched a spring in the wain-
scot. A panel flew to one side and revealed a narrow
aperture.

" Follow me if you have a brave heart," he cried, looking back.

The apartment in which they were sitting was the library and this exit was a curious winding staircase, which gradually grew less dark as they proceeded. At last they found themselves in a sort of antechamber, scarcely large enough to turn about in, formed by a bay or projection. There was an oak seat with the Ripon arms carved on the back. Above it a tiny window, showing the great thickness of the wall, let in a few rays of light.

" Sit down—sh !'' said Lord Brompton, and he put his finger to his lips and nodded toward a low door which was visible a few feet beyond. " It is there.''

" Oh, this is delightful. Is it a real, genuine, ancestral ghost ?''

" In that chamber the Lady Marian Ripon, an ancestress of mine, is said to have died of a broken heart. Her husband, the great-grandson of the Lord Brompton whose portrait you think I resemble, was killed at Teb, and three days after her body was borne to the tomb. This was her private chamber, and here her spirit is said still to linger. It is not a very original ghost, but its authenticity is unquestioned.''

" Have you ever crossed the threshold ?'' asked the girl, with mock solemnity.

" Not since childhood, and then only in fear and trembling.''

" This is beginning to be positively weird and uncanny,'' she murmured, " but I propose to defy the spectre and enter.''

" Have a care—have a care. But you have no key, Miss Windsor.''

She was shaking the handle, which seemed loose and flimsy. " Help me. It is not fastened,'' she cried.

They bent their united strength upon the door, which creaked, groaned, and finally burst open with a crash, causing the dust to fly so that Maggie gave a little shriek of dismay. Complete silence and darkness followed the onslaught, and then with a whisper of " Who's afraid ?" she drew forth a lamp of diminutive proportions and Etruscan design, and turning the crank produced a brilliant electric flame, which permeated the damp and gloom of the ghostly chamber.

Here was, indeed, a monument to decay and mould of the past. A room rife with the cobwebs of ages met their vision where the moth-eaten remains of once gorgeous hangings competed for utter fustiness with the odor of the rotting beams and the dismal aspect of the furniture, some of which had actually fallen to pieces, as though further stability had been incompatible with the long absence of human life. The place seemed almost too desolate for a ghost other than a very morbid spirit in search of penance. In the centre of the room lay in hopeless confusion a pile of all sorts and varieties of garments, many of them of most antiquated description. Plumed hats and velvet knee-breeches of the cavalier period, Jersey jackets and tea-gowns, with Watteau plaits, such as were in fashion when Victoria was queen, were mingled with articles of a more recent date. On the top lay an open volume, the pages of which were brown with dust. Maggie picked it up and read :

> " Howe'er it be, it seems to me
>   'Tis only noble to be good ;
> Kind hearts are more than coronets
>   And simple faith than Norman blood."

" By whom is that, Lord Brompton ? Ah ! I see, Lord d'Eyncourt. His name is on the title-page."

" An eccentric Victorian poet," said the young man, " of much account in his own day, if I mistake not."

" I never heard of him," said Maggie, " but I am little of an antiquarian. It is pretty, though."

" I remember," said he, " that we as children used to act theatricals here in those old clothes, duds we ransacked from the closets."

" But where is the ghost ? I want to see the ghost !" cried the girl, tossing aside the last bit of tarnished finery. " What is this ?" she continued, seizing the end of a beam which had become loosened and projected from the wall.

" You will have the house about our ears if you persist," he cried, as a shower of crumbled stone and mortar followed her investigation.

" Well, it is my house, Lord Brompton ; I have the right if I choose to."

" Why remind me of my misfortunes, Miss Windsor ?"

" Come and help me, then."

" I wish I might be your helpmate forever," he said. She turned and looked at him, slightly disconcerted, and then said : " I was wrong. The women of to-day need no help from any one."

She gave the beam a strong wrench, as though to vindicate her assertion. It yielded and disclosed a kind of box or recess set into the wall. She plunged therein her hand, and drew forth a handsome sword of rich and subtle workmanship and antique design. " There," she cried, " am I not right ?"

Maggie took it to the light. Around the hilt was wrapped a scroll, which she was about to read, when, with a sudden fancy, she paused and said, "What am I doing? These are family secrets, and meant, perhaps, only for your eyes, Lord Brompton."

"Read it, I beg," said he. She obeyed him. In a faint, feminine hand, which resembled a field of corn bowed by the wind, were written these words:

"My grandfather's sword.   MARIAN RIPON."

"The ghost—it is the ghost's own work," they cried together.

"And this sword," said he, "belonged to my name-sake, the cavalier."

"But look—look." Maggie had been staring at the opposite side of the paper.

Geoffrey took it from her hand.

> "Kind hearts are more than coronets
>   And simple faith than Norman blood."

For a moment they looked at one another in speechless surprise.

"Kneel, Lord Brompton," she said at length. He did so, and taking a scarf from among the pile of vestments she girded the sword about him with fantastic grace. "Rise, Geoffrey Ripon, knight, and Earl of Brompton."

"You are forever my sovereign." He kissed her hand. She blushed sweetly, and turning said, "Enough of the past and its customs. We each have a present to face, and mine for the nonce is Jawkins. He must need my directions."

Thus it happened that when Lord Brompton next entered the porter's lodge in which he dwelt, he was girded with the sword of his ancestors.

CHAPTER IV.

JARLEY JAWKINS.

THE library of Ripon House was an apartment panelled in oak, blackened by time and smoke. The high and richly carved mantelpiece bore the arms of the Ripon family, three wolves on a field, or, surmounted by a wild man from Borneo rampant, bearing a battle-axe, gules. Shelves which once were filled with fine books were then empty, the void being covered by old tapestries. The furniture was old and gaunt, save for a few modern soft-cushioned chairs which seemed to have been recently deposited there, and were, by the brilliant color of their coverings, not at all in harmony with the faded tapestries of their high-backed and carven predecessors. On one of the gaunt old chairs Abraham Windsor was seated, holding in his right hand the London *Times*, which slowly issued from a "ticker" upon the table at his side. After looking sharply at the financial news, which just then was being recorded in the "Thunderer," he glanced quickly toward the door, as if he expected some one to enter. Abraham Windsor was a man of sixty, and each year seemed to have left its impress upon the man who had battled through it, so that he seemed his own living history, and by close observation you might read of a youth of scant schooling in books, not spent among folks of gentle breeding, nor protected from the world, but left to shift for itself against the numerous kicks and scanty half pence of the hard world ; then one might discern the period of restless scheming and speculation, and finally the look of successful yet of unsatisfied ambition. Still his face was not a hard and stern one, but shrewd and kindly. He seemed a man who would drive careful bargains, but who was too large-minded and honest to be mean or overreaching. His large head was thatched with thick, bristling iron-gray hair, his face was swarthy and clean-shaven, his black eyes were deep-set and keen, his nose prominent, yet well-shaped, and his mouth firm and resolute, having a humorous curve ; he was plainly dressed in a black broadcloth suit which hung loosely over his bony frame. He threw down the ribbons upon the floor with an impatient gesture, and watched the news of the world, as it coiled at his feet in the white spirals, for a moment ; then he arose from his chair and touched an electric knob. Instantly a stately footman in a dark livery and a powdered wig entered the room.

" Mr. Jawkins has arrived ?" Mr. Windsor asked.

" No, sir. Thank you, sir."

" Has Miss Windsor returned from her walk ?"

" She has come into the house, sir."

" Has Mr. Jawkins sent word when we are to expect him ?"

" Yes, sir ; we are awaiting him every moment, sir. I think I hear wheels now, sir."

" Very well ; ask him to come to me here when he is at leisure."

The tall footman bowed and noiselessly left the room, and Mr. Windsor picked up the *Times* and looked at it for a moment. Presently a short, pudgy man in travelling dress, with thin, smoothly-brushed hair, mutton-chop whiskers and a very red face, was ushered into the room, and Mr. Windsor stretched out his hand in welcome.

" Mr. Jawkins, I believe ?"

" Yes, Mr. Windsor ; I am Jarley Jawkins, very much at your service."

" Glad to see you, Jawkins," said the American ; " take a cigar, won't you ? I will ring for some whiskey and water if you care for a snifter."

" I beg to be excused," replied Jawkins, deprecatingly. " You American gentlemen must have the constitutions of horses ; you seem to be able to smoke and take ' snifters,' as you drolly call them, at all hours, but I really cannot do it, you know. Do you find things to suit you here, Mr. Windsor ? I could have given you many finer houses ; to tell you the truth, I was rather surprised when you chose Ripon House out of my list. There is so little furniture in it that my men have not been able to put in all the necessary articles yet, but it will be wholly in order in a few hours."

" Yes ; your men seem very busy," replied Mr. Windsor. " The upper floors are all ready, but I have been driven into this room on the ground floor this morning."

" Oh ! dear me, what a pity, sir," said Mr. Jawkins, looking around the room. " It is very bare and uncomfortable ; but you will not know the room when my fellows are through with it. You will have one of the finest collections of books here in all England in a few hours. I have purchased the Marquis of Queensberry's collection, and ordered them sent here. Nothing gives so good an effect of color in a room as a library of handsome books, you know. They have turned the *Times* on, I see," he remarked, pointing to the ticker. "I saw in it this morning that Richard Lincoln and his daughter were to be your guests here. Your friend, sir, I suppose? He certainly is not down in my list; great man, sir, but not one of us."

"Mr. Lincoln is one of the men whom I most highly respect in the world," answered Mr. Windsor, curtly. "When do you expect the people in your list to arrive?"

"Oh, they will come at all hours," answered Jawkins. "I must send a lot of traps to the station to meet them. Have you been out to the stables, sir? I have sent you one of the finest studs in all England. Do you hunt, Mr. Windsor?"

"Never," answered Mr. Windsor.

"Since the farmers have taken to shooting the foxes," continued Mr. Jawkins, "the noble old sport has gone all to pieces, even here; but you drive four-in-hand, I hope. I have ordered a beautiful new break for your use. But you will see, sir, all I have done for you. Now, if you are at leisure for the list of the guests whom I have been able to engage. When you have gone over it with me, Mr. Windsor, I think that you will admit that it is a charming country-house party to have got together on such short notice. First, you see, we have the Duke and Duchess of Bayswater. I have engaged them for the first three days of your stay here to give *éclat* to your hospitality, at the price of a diva and her accompanying tenor, I must admit. It is their very first appearance professionally, and I think that I have done very well by you."

Mr. Windsor gave a little groan, which Mr. Jawkins did not seem to notice, however, as he continued :

" I fear that His Grace will not be in the best of spirits at first. He is a grand type of a great nobleman, however, and worth double the money which we pay him. Her Grace is of one of the few families in Great Britain which are found in the Almanach de Gotha. She is like a magnificent old ruin, almost feudal in fact, and as proud as Lucifer. Her stare is said to be withering, and the poise of her head makes a man's tongue cleave to the roof of his mouth."

" And I shall have to take her in to dinner for the next three days ?" groaned Windsor.

" Of course, my dear sir ; but, believe me, you will enjoy it more than Her Grace will," replied Jawkins. " Next comes the Archbishop of Canterbury in point of order on my list, though he is of higher rank than their Graces. Since the disestablishment of the Church, and the forfeiture of the Church properties, he has, of course, been much straitened financially. He must have a comfortable room and a warm fire, and will conduct family prayers. There is some doubt about his coming, though, I see, as he is far from well, but it will be easy to get a prelate at short notice ; I have dozens on my list, ready at call. Next we have Lord Carrington, who is not very good company, but of wonderfully fine family. His ancestors came over with William the Conqueror, but as he has only £200 a year, he was not loath to put himself under my charge. He is exceedingly particular as to his food and drink, and is one of the best card-players in London. He used to make a fine income from his cards ; indeed, he does now in I. O. U.'s. By the way, he inquired whether you played ' piquet ' or ' bezique,' from which I infer that he is looking for an antagonist with ready money."

Mr. Windsor laughed and slapped his knee with his thin, bony hand.

"Ah! the wind sets in that corner, does it?" he asked.

"I am afraid so," answered Jawkins.

"I do not mind taking chances, I admit," said Windsor; "but in the stock-market I am in the position of the banker at the gaming-table. The odds are in my favor. While at piquet this noble lord can get the better of me. Who else have you, Jawkins?"

"I forgot my greatest prize, sir," said Jawkins, handing Mr. Windsor a photograph. "What do you think of her?"

Mr. Windsor looked at the picture with a peculiar smile.

"She is a fine woman, Jawkins. We have as fine, however, in the States. Who is she?"

"Mrs. Oswald Carey, to be sure. Have you never seen her face before, Mr. Windsor? She is considered to be the most beautiful woman in London. Her husband, of course, is left there; he cares only for brandy and soda and baccarat, and would be very much in the way. I believe that he used to have a place under government, but was ousted last year, probably for cause, wonderful as that seems now. But she is a charming woman, and I find that she is the most sought after of any one on my list—that is to say, with the hosts; though the hostesses sometimes object to her, simply from envy of her good looks, for her good name cannot be questioned while her husband is satisfied with her."

Mr. Windsor hummed a little; he was too new to the world of society not to have old-fashioned views on the subject of a woman's fame.

"Go on with the list, please, Jawkins; time flies, and

your presence must be required to arrange the drawing-
rooms.''

" Very well, Mr. Windsor.   Then Sir John Dacre, one
of the biggest men in England ; I never have understood,
sir, how I got him on my list.   He is so proud that I
should have fancied that he would have—saving your presence, sir—have broken stones in the street rather than
bread as a hired guest.   For he is a noble fellow.''

" Some woman at the bottom of it ?'' asked Mr. Windsor, carelessly.

" Something mysterious, certainly, for he absolutely refused to take any fee,'' replied Mr. Jawkins.   " Next
comes Colonel Charles Featherstone, a wild, scatter-brained
soldier, who lost all his fortune in speculation in your
American cotton and grain futures.   He is a great friend
of John Dacre, and they joined me at the same time.   I
am really giving you the gems of my whole collection.''

A flush of triumph spread over the man's round face as
he continued his list.   " Next, I have three of the ' artiste '
class, and here I am not so successful, though to be sure I
pick them up for almost nothing.   There is Erastus
Prouty, who does the satirical ' society ' articles and col-
lects fashionable gossip for the *Saturday Review*, a snigger-
ing, sneering chap, with a single eye-glass and immense
self-conceit.   He called me a cad in his paper once, but I
am above personal feeling, and do not cut the man off from
his income.   Then, you have Herr Diddlej, the great
Norwegian pianist, who will shatter your piano in half an
hour ; and, finally, Sydney, the wit, who, by the way, has
disappointed me greatly, as he has not made a repartee in
a twelvemonth, nor has he set the table in a roar.   I
reasoned with him the other day on the subject, and gave

him fair warning that this visit should be his last chance.
Still, I pity the man ; he is a great *bon vivant,* and if he
should lose his reputation as a wit I fear that he would
have to go to a workhouse or on the London *Punch.*   I
have finished the list.   How does it please you ?''

" I never say that I have made money until the shares
are sold and paid for,'' answered Mr. Windsor.   " Your
list sounds well, but I think I like the old-fashioned way
of asking friends to stay with me better.   Still, your plan
is novel.''

Mr. Jawkins seemed hurt, as an author would who had
looked up from reading the finest passage in his epic only
to perceive that his auditor was asleep and not spellbound.
Jawkins believed in the "*idée*" Jawkins as Napoleon did
in his destiny.

" By your leave, Mr. Windsor, I shall go to my own
room to arrange my toilet, and then I must see about the
disposition of the furniture, bibelots and pictures, and attend to the preparations for the reception of the guests.
You need not meet them until just before dinner, when I
shall be on hand to present them to you.   I cannot be
here after to-night.   I must start to-morrow morning for
Hampshire, where Prince Petroloff demands my services.
You see, I am a hard-worked man, Mr. Windsor.''

" So you are for an Englishman, Mr. Jawkins.   Then
I suppose that it is necessary that you should attend to all
the details of your profession personally.   By the way, my
daughter tells me that she has asked young Geoffrey
Ripon, who used to be on the British Legation at Paris,
where we were two summers ago.   You must arrange for
him at the dinner-table.''

" Ah, the Earl of Brompton !   He is not a client of

mine, but I have my eye on him.　His earthly possessions consist of about five acres of land, a tumble-down hut near by, and a double-barrelled shotgun, and he lost his secretaryship when the new administration made its clean sweep of the offices.　They said he was going to marry a rich girl once, I believe."

" It seems that he did not," said Mr. Windsor, rising from his seat.

Mr. Jawkins bowed and bustled from the room, and Mr. Windsor soon heard his sharp voice ordering the army of workmen in the adjacent rooms with the precision and authority of a field-marshal.

The situation amused and at the same time disconcerted the humorous American, as he settled back in a chair before the great wood fire which crackled in the chimney. Though the chair was soft and yielding he did not look comfortable, for men with long, bony, angular figures never seem to look at their ease.

Abraham Windsor's name twenty years before the date of this story would not have added to the marketable value of the most modest promissory note in the money markets of Chicago, to which city he had come fresh from his father's farm in upper Illinois ; but at this time it was a tower of strength in financial quarters, and men counted his wealth by tens of millions.

He was the Jupiter of the financial world, and men said that when his iron-gray locks fell over each other, as he nodded, Wall Street trembled and Lombard Street crashed ; so that it seemed only from forbearance that he did not sweep all the chips upon the great gaming-table of the world into his deep pockets.　His sudden trip to Europe had caused much discussion.　Some knowing ones whis-

pered that he had bought a controlling interest in the Bank
of England from the assignees in bankruptcy of the Broth-
kinders, with the object of making a panic in trade by a
sudden raise of the rate of discount to six per cent ; others,
that he had come over to unload upon the British public
his shares in the Hudson Bay and Cape Horn Railroad
Company.

He was amused by the wild rumors, for he had, in truth,
come to England with no deep-laid scheme or motive, but
simply because his daughter had ordered his doing so ; for
while Abraham Windsor ruled the shares market and the
world of speculation, a certain young woman ruled him,
and the hard-headed man of affairs, who could outwit an
Israelite banker, was as wax under her dainty fingers. At
the close of the last season at Newport, Miss Margaret had
ordered her father, as she poured out his coffee at breakfast, to engage a country house in England for the winter.
Mr. Windsor looked up from the New York *Herald*, which
likened him to his Satanic Majesty in one column and described his new steam yacht in another, and he said,
" Aye, aye, miss," to her order.

And straightway after breakfast he went to the Casino
Club and telephoned to Jarley Jawkins for his list of estates
to rent in England, for he knew full well that whether Wall
Street or the heavens crashed Miss Maggie's orders were
to be obeyed. She selected Ripon House from Jawkins's
list, and her father hired it, although he had a leaning
toward Windsor Castle, which the Republic wished to lease
for a term of years, or to sell upon easy terms.

Every one in Paris two years before had said that the
penniless young Englishman, Lord Ripon, wished to make
a rich marriage, and that the capricious Miss Windsor,

after having broken, cracked or temporarily discouraged a sufficient number of hearts, was at last ready to accept a lord and perhaps a master. But in the middle of the season the British Legation was recalled, and Geoffrey, after a few words of farewell, disappeared, and from the day of his leaving Paris Miss Windsor had heard nothing of him. She did not know herself whether she cared for him ; he was good-natured and amusing, and she liked to have him talk to her and be her slave, but when he was gone, the world was not a blank to her.

Still, it piqued her that Lord Brompton had effaced himself so completely from her life. " He might, at least, have written to let me know that he lived," she kept thinking. Of course she knew the name of his old estate, and she knew that he owned the porter's lodge and the few acres around it, for he had told her once that he still owned a little box in England, and that when the worst came to the worst he intended to crawl into it and shut the lid. When Jawkins sent his list of estates for rent, and she saw the name of Ripon House on it, her heart gave a little jump. Mr. Windsor had, of course, known of the affair between Lord Geoffrey and his daughter, and had neither approved nor disapproved of it. He knew that, if she made up her mind to marry, he would be consulted only as a matter of form. When she had informed him on their arrival that Lord Brompton was living in the neighborhood, and that she meant to invite him to dinner very soon, the shrewd old man smiled grimly, and acquiesced in her plan.

As her father sat musing before the fire, the door opened suddenly, and Maggie bounded into the room.

" Has Jawkins arrived, papa ?" she asked.

" Yes ; we have just been going over his list of guests together. By the way, Maggie, is your young man to be our guest ?"

" Oh, papa !" Maggie exclaimed, perching herself upon one of his knees and stroking his chin with one of her dimpled hands, " how can you be so ill-bred as to speak of any one as my young man ? Surely I have no proprietary rights over any man, save one very nice old fellow, who is so loyal to his sovereign that he never thinks of complaining of the injustice of taxation without representation."

" You reverse the ordinary process with me ; subjects have been wont to blow up their sovereigns," answered her father, with a chuckle, " and you blow up me. You have not told me about Lord Brompton. It is a long time since you have seen him before to-day."

" Two whole years. He seems so dispirited."

" At not having escaped you ?"

" Oh, you wicked old capitalist ; not at all. At having been so long separated from me. It was very pleasant to see him again. He is such a friend of mine. I should say that he interested me more than any of the others."

" Ah, that unfortunate panorama of others," laughed her father.

" Yes, poor fellows," said Maggie, a little regretfully, " but then I think that most of them had an eye to the main chance, papa. Lord Brompton has not, I know."

Mr. Windsor smiled.

" I hope not, my dear. What is he doing here ?"

" What the world has forgotten to do ; what he can do more graciously than any man I know—nothing," she answered.

"I should think that a young man with the world before him might find something better to do than to mope in a porter's lodge, looking mournfully at the lands which were his father's. What does he intend to do in the world ?"

"Oh, he said nothing of his plan of life," said Miss Windsor ; "but he seemed blue and restless. I think that there is something on his mind."

"These aristocrats, fallen from their high estate, are really in a pitiable condition," said Windsor. "I feel like a cad to have made the arrangement which I have with Jawkins. I wish that I were scot free from the whole business. Poor people, how they must hate me in advance, and what a vulgarian they must think me to be."

"Jawkins says that it is a recognized system, papa, you remember," answered Maggie. "After all, if you wish a great tenor or a violin-player at your parties, you pay them for it. If you wish a duke to awe or a beauty to charm your guests, why should you not hire them ? This is a commercial age. The poor people must live, and if they can only awe or charm, there is no harm in their receiving pay for their sole merits."

"You should have been bred to the bar, Maggie," laughed her father. "You are an eloquent advocate."

There was a rattling of wheels up the driveway, and the great hall doors were heard to open.

"Some of our guests have arrived," remarked Mr. Windsor. "I hope that Jawkins has made all his arrangements for their reception."

Just then the door opened and Mr. Jawkins entered carefully dressed. His manner was quiet and his voice subdued, as if he were whispering in a cathedral, as he said :

" Their Graces the Duke and Duchess have done you the honor of coming under your roof, Mr. Windsor. They are very much fatigued by their journey, and have retired to their apartments."

" We shall meet them at Philippi before the action, shall we not?" asked Miss Windsor.

" Yes, and meanwhile I shall do everything that I can for the comfort of your guests and the arrangement of the house. Believe me, I deeply feel the gravity of the situation," he continued, as he bowed himself out of the room.

" And so do I," said Mr. Windsor to his daughter. " I would rather face an army of irate stockholders than our guests this evening."

CHAPTER V.

WHEN Geoffrey entered that evening the great drawing-rooms of his old home he found that they had been transformed from shabby and musty apartments into beautiful modern salons, which had the air of having been long lived in by people of refinement. There was even a certain feminine touch about the disposition of the bric-à-brac. The handsome pieces of old furniture, which seemed like friends of his boyhood, were still there, retained by the true artistic sense of Jawkins, who knew that no modern cabinetmaker could produce their like ; still everything seemed brightened, as if the old rooms had been touched with sunshine. The walls were hung with good modern paintings and old tapestries ; the tables and mantelpieces were covered thick with curios. To fill a great house with the rare objects of art and luxury that are found in the abodes of those families which have held wealth for generations is an impossibility to the newly rich. Their brand-new mansions, left to upholsterers, resemble great caravansaries, bare, gilded and raw with primary colors. But Jawkins was an artist ; he not only made the houses which he arranged beautiful, but he gave them the

air of having been lived in for years, so that the strangers
within the gates, who had been taught to judge of men's
characters by their dwellings and surroundings, could not
but be pleasantly impressed. Miss Windsor was standing
alone, in a corner of the room, by a little round-backed
sofa, and smiled a greeting at Geoffrey. After exchanging
a few words with his host he walked over to her, and she
stretched out her pretty gloved hand in welcome.

" Well met again, Lord Brompton ; but you are not
wearing your sword."

" ' The Knights are dust,' I fear," he quoted with a
smile. "I was loath to wear it with modern evening
dress. I crave your forgiveness, fair lady."

" As long as you do not have it turned into a plough-
share, or a railway share, which would be more modern,"
laughed Maggie, " I will forgive you."

" Have all your guests arrived ?"

" Of course ; you are the last one, as usual. It has
been rather an ordeal you may believe. Papa was in a
dreadful state about it. The Duke and the Duchess of
Bayswater he was especially in awe of. Dear old souls !
You see them over there, looking like Mr. and Mrs.
Marius in the ruins of Carthage."

Geoffrey, turning, saw a fine-looking old couple. The
Duke still wore the blue ribbon of the Garter across his
breast. He was a mild-looking gentleman, who seemed
to be plunged in deep melancholy. His head was bald
and highly polished, his gray side-whiskers were brushed
carefully forward, and his nose was aquiline. Her Grace
the Duchess surveyed the company with a haughty stare,
which seemed to be a matter of habit rather than of present feeling.

"They were very kind to me when I was a boy," said Geoffrey, with a sigh. "But it is so long since they have seen me that they must have forgotten me. You have a large party."

"Oh, yes ; they have been coming in all the afternoon. I think that it will be very pleasant when we get well shaken together. You see your old friend, Sir John Dacre, over there, do you not ? away over at the end of the other rooms. The fine-looking girl to whom he is talking is Richard Lincoln's daughter."

Geoffrey looked in the direction, and saw the back of Sir John Dacre's head as he bent over to speak to Miss Lincoln.

He made a little start to go over to greet his friend. Miss Windsor saw it, and said : "You will see Sir John after dinner, Lord Brompton ; you would interrupt a pleasant conversation now by being that wretched third who makes a 'company' a crowd ; and at the same time, you would destroy all the proportion of the party by leaving me alone. You must sit on the sofa here by my side, and I will point out all the people to you. You will not sit anywhere near me, you know, at dinner, as you will take in Mrs. Oswald Carey, as I told you this morning."

Geoffrey sat down on the sofa by her and looked about the room.

"I do not see the great professional beauty in this room, Miss Windsor," he said, after he had finished his inspection of the people present, who seemed plunged in the depths of that gloom which always hangs over a party before a dinner.

Richard Lincoln, who had been touched by her Grace's melancholy, stood talking to her. In the opposite corner

of the room sat Mr. James Sydney, the celebrated wit, his
pasty face wearing an air of settled melancholy, while he
gazed vacantly at a curious old Turner, which glowed like
an American sunset against the stamped-leather hangings
of the room.

"Poor fellow, he looks like the clown before he is
painted," whispered Miss Windsor.

Mr. Prouty, the *Saturday Reviewer*, sat on a "conversa-
zione" with Lady Carringford, a commonplace, faded-out-
looking woman of forty, with bleached hair. She did not
seem much pleased by the conversation of the journalist,
and looked furtively across the room as if to hint that she
ought to be relieved, but Herr Diddlej and Sydney did not
see her signals of distress.

Lord Carringford, her husband, a tall, keen-faced man
with blue-black side-whiskers and a furtive eye, was talking with Mr. Windsor, and though he saw his wife's signals, of course, did not pay any attention to them. The
Archbishop of Canterbury, in rusty clerical garb, smiled
benignly at the whole company.

"Mrs. Oswald Carey is far too clever to stay in the glare
of a great room like this," said Miss Windsor to Geoffrey.
"She is one of those women who seek a corner and quiet
and flourish there—not, however, alone. She is in the
smaller room beyond, with Colonel Featherstone, who
must have nearly pulled his great mustaches out by this
time. You know how he twirls and twitches them when
he thinks he is being quite irresistible, just as you are
doing now, Lord Brompton."

Geoffrey dropped his hand from his mustache impatiently.

"Ah, you are always chaffing me, Miss Windsor," he
pleaded.

" I knew very well what you were thinking, sir. That you could cut Colonel Featherstone out in no time. Now, were you not?"

" Not at all. I was thinking of you. Were not my languishing glances turned toward you?"

" Yes, but the languish was all for Mrs. Oswald, and not for me. But it is time to go to dinner now, Lord Brompton. You are permitted to disturb the *tête-à-tête* and Mrs. Carey's peace of mind."

" If you send me away, I suppose that I must obey. A hostess is a despot whom no one may defy."

Miss Windsor smiled pleasantly at the Duke of Bayswater, who just then offered her his arm with great solemnity. Geoffrey bowed to her and the Duke, and walked slowly into the adjoining room.

In a dimly-lighted corner he saw a tall, heavily-built man, with a long red mustache, talking to a remarkably beautiful woman.

" Mrs. Carey and old Charlie Featherstone?" he said to himself, as he stopped to look at them and to await a pause in their conversation before he interrupted them.

" Why, it is Eleanor Leigh!" he exclaimed a moment later, as she turned her head from the shadow of a great Japanese screen, behind which the pair had sought shelter from prying eyes.

" Eleanor Leigh, my old sweetheart, to whom I bade farewell in the dark library of my old tutor's home, seven years ago."

She did not look in his direction, and he had a few moments to observe her carefully.

The slender girl whom he remembered had grown into a superb woman. Her head was poised upon her shoul-

ders like that of a Greek goddess, and around her white
throat gleamed a collar of brilliants.   A tightly-fitting
black gown made by contrast her bosom and arms dazzling
in whiteness.   Her hair was rolled into a large round knot
at the back of her head, and its coils shone red-brown in
the soft glow of the candles.   Her face seemed cold and
calm to him as he looked at her, a faint, mocking smile
played upon her full, red lips, and her delicate eyebrows
were slightly raised.   All of a sudden she turned toward
him, and their eyes met in a flash of recognition.   He remembered those eyes well, but here was something in them
which was not there when his brain last thrilled with their
magnetic glances—a something which he could not understand, but which repelled him.   She raised her hand and
seemed to beckon to him, and he obeyed her command.

" You remember me, then, Lord Brompton," she said
coldly, as she gave him her hand.

" Remember you !" he exclaimed, and was at a loss for
words.   Featherstone, who had withdrawn a step or two,
seemed to see his confusion, and after welcoming his old
friend back to England went away.

Mrs. Carey looked up at Geoffrey with a mocking smile,
as if deriding his embarrassment.   " So we meet again
after all these years, Geoffrey ?"   He looked down at the
floor, confused and shame-faced, as he thought of the
time when he had gone up to Oxford from her father's
house with her image in his heart.   She, too, was thinking of those days of fresh spring-time.   " He is not much
changed," she thought, " save that he looks tired and discouraged ; then his eyes were bright, looking, as they
were, into a world where everything seemed easy and full
of pleasure to him."

"We are both thinking of the old days," she said to
him, as she pulled a rose from her belt, and nervously
crumpled its petals between her fingers. "Ah, how I
wept when you ceased writing to me!"

"I do not imagine that you ever wept any bitter tears
on my account," remonstrated Geoffrey. "I was a mere
boy then; and a girl of eighteen can hold her own with a
man of any age, while a boy of eighteen can no more look
after himself in a love affair than a—"

"Boy of any other age," interrupted Mrs. Carey.
"Ah, Geoffrey, I did weep then more than you can imagine. But I have always remembered you as a dear boy,
who loved me a little and forgot me when he was away.
Men are deceivers ever, and I fancy that I am not the last
woman whom you have loved a little and forgotten since.
But the others are going in to dinner. It is a motley
party, is it not? Just fancy Richard Lincoln's being here,
and the old Duke, and John Dacre, too. Why is he here?
Do you know?"

"I haven't seen him since I first went to Paris," answered Geoffrey, as he offered her his arm.

The pair walked in to dinner in their proper place in the
procession.

"What a beautiful old room this is!" exclaimed Mrs.
Carey as they entered the dining-hall. "Jawkins does
this sort of thing so well! How perfectly he reproduces
the courtly state of the last century when he re-establishes
a house!"

Geoffrey had not been in this room since the day when
he had been called from Oxford by a telegram announcing
his father's sudden death. Then the room had been dark
and there was a hush over it, and the servants had moved

stealthily over the oaken floor, and he had sat by tne window listening to the slow words of the family lawyer, which told him that he was the heir of a ruined estate.

He winced as he seated himself by Mrs. Carey's side, a guest at the great table at which his forebears had broken bread as almost princely hosts. The party had entered, and sat down in silence, and, after unfolding their napkins, looked rather gloomily at each other for a while, but Mr. Jawkins soon broke into an easy conversational canter, and the rest of the party by the time that the champagne appeared with the fish found that their tongues were loosened. The old Duke, who always loved a pretty face and brilliant eyes, got on capitally with Miss Windsor, and seemed to forget his fallen dignity and the mournful face of his consort, as he said pretty things to the beautiful American.

" I had a great curiosity to see Mr. Windsor before I came here," whispered Mrs. Carey to Geoffrey. " He has a strong face, has he not ? They say that he is so rich that he does not know how much he is worth, and that he has made all his money himself."

" I suppose that somebody has got all the money that we people in England have lost or spent," she continued, with a woman's idea of political economy. " Isn't it all dreadful ? I suppose that you are a — What shall I say, a guest ?"

" Why should you not say a guest, since we certainly are at Mr. Windsor's table ?" he asked, as if innocently.

" Ah, you must know what I mean ; one of Mr. Jawkins's list. Just think of the poor Duke and Duchess being on it—the proudest family in England. Did you ever hear of such a thing ?"

" The aristocrats during the French Revolution were reduced to as desperate shifts," answered Geoffrey. " We, at least, are not banished from our country and can earn our living, if we choose, in the old-fashioned way, by the sweat of our brows. I have been digging in my vegetable garden this summer ; you know that I have five acres left, and what with fishing—and don't mention it, pray—a little poaching, I have got along pretty well. I knew Mr. Windsor in Paris, when I was on the Legation there."

" And you were put out of the service by that old brute, Bagshaw. What an odious thing this Republican form of government is ! You know poor Oswald was in the Stamp and Sealing-wax Office. Oswald is a Legitimist, of course, and would not pay the assessment which was levied upon him by the Radical party, and he was ousted last spring."

" Is your husband here ?"

" Oh, dear, no ! They do not wish me if I take Oswald along with me. He is in our lodgings in London. He quite misses the office in the daytime, as he cannot sleep nearly so well at home. Poor Oswald ! Mr. Sydney," she said, turning to that gentleman, who had sat in silence at her side, " I thought that you always kept the table in a roar ?"

" How can a man do that when he is expected to," answered Sydney, gloomily. " I am always saddest at dinner, for I know that I have been asked because there is a tradition in society that I am a wit. If I speak of the gloomiest subjects people snicker ; if I am eloquent or pathetic, they roar. I am by nature rather a lyric poet than a wit—ah, you are laughing, Mrs. Carey, you are laughing. What did I tell you ?"

" But, my dear Mr. Sydney, you are funny, really you are."

" I am funny because I mean to be serious," said Mr. Sydney. " In these days of the decadence of civilization if a man is in earnest, terribly in earnest, people think that he is vastly amusing. I shall try to be funny soon, to earn my wage, and people will think me dull enough then."

The poor man drank a large glass of wine and pointing at the *entrée* upon his plate asked :

" Mrs. Carey, can a man who expects daily to be gathered to his fathers eat a *vol-au-vent* of pigeons *à la financière* ? How can it be expected ? They should not tempt me with such dishes. I know that I ought not to eat them, but I cannot resist. I partake of them and I do not sleep. I have not closed my eyes for three nights."

He began to eat his *vol-au-vent* with the appetite of a boy of fourteen.

" Poor old fellow," whispered Mrs. Carey to Geoffrey. " He knows that he must be amusing on this visit else Jawkins will strike him off his list. It is lucky that I only have to look beautiful. It is no exertion whatever. While poor old Sydney knows that something is expected of him, and as he naturally likes to talk about statistics and his physical ailments, and as he gained his reputation as a wit from a single repartee made at a dinner twenty years ago, he finds it hard to fulfil his part. He is simply funny because he isn't. It's a strange paradox."

" It must, indeed, be a hard task, making one's self a brick without straw," answered Geoffrey. " Think of not having the luxury of being disagreeable—to be always on the rack to perpetrate a joke, Mrs. Carey."

"You did not call me Mrs. Carey when we last met," she said, reproachfully.

"But you were not Mrs. Carey then, and, not being a prophet, I could not very well call you so."

"Do not be flippant. But if we were prophets what a dreadful thing life would be! It did not seem possible seven years ago that Eleanor Leigh would become a pro-fessional beauty, a hired guest, who lived upon the royalty from the sale of her photographs."

"You can congratulate yourself that yours is the only 'royalty' left in the country, Eleanor." He lowered his voice as he spoke her name.

"I will not talk about myself," she said, in a cold, hard tone. "That's a man's prerogative. But I wish you, when we are alone, to tell me all about your life. The lines of our lives, which once bade fair to run along together, have diverged; but fate is strong. We are thrown together again. I know not whether it matters to you that we have met again, but it does very much to me. I wish to know what you have been doing all these years. To-morrow, surely, we shall have a chance to see each other, and till then let us change the subject, for if the walls have not ears, Mr. Sydney certainly has, and very large and ugly ones, too, like a lop-eared rabbit's."

Geoffrey looked with a smile at poor Mr. Sydney's villi-fied ears, and said to himself that the unfortunate wit never could live in much comfort upon the royalties from the sale of his picture. Mrs. Carey looked around the table searchingly. Her quick wit was tickled by the curi-ous incongruities of the scene; by Richard Lincoln talk-ing small nothings to the Duchess of Bayswater across the rich American; by the genial and smirking Jawkins, seated

between Sir John Dacre and that pink of fashion, Colonel
Featherstone ; by Lady Carringford, who was between the
indifferent Colonel and the Duke ; by the three members
of the artiste class, Prouty, Diddlej and Sydney, whom Mr.
Jawkins had placed together with delicate discrimination.
Mrs. Carey gave a little shrug at perceiving that she, too,
was put in the same neighborhood.   Lord Carringford and
the Duchess seemed to be getting along uncommonly well
together.   Sir John Dacre ignored his dapper neighbor,
Jawkins, and was absorbed in conversation with beautiful
Mary Lincoln, who blushed whenever she caught her
father's eye looking questioningly at her.   Mrs. Carey's
glance over the table was at first cursory; she had been so
much interested in meeting Geoffrey that the tide of old
feelings, surging back through her brain, had driven out
all thought of the other people, for in the heart of this
woman of the world, who had lived in ball-rooms and in
the maddest whirl of that most mad and material of all
things, modern society, where love is a plaything and an
excitement only, there had lingered a fond remembrance
of the ardent young lover, whose boyish affection for her,
absence had so quickly cooled.   Through all his wanderings
she had managed to trace him.   The world of society is
small.   She had heard of his affair with Miss Windsor in
Paris two years before ; so her eyes, after wandering over
the table, fixed themselves upon her.   With a woman's
instinct, Mrs. Carey had known that Geoffrey would not
have been so indifferent to her if he had been fancy free ;
when she first saw him, before dinner, her heart throbbed
with passion, and she determined to wind around him again
the chain of flowers which he had snapped so easily when
the great god of modern love, " Juxtaposition," deserted

her. But now she saw that he had long since ceased to care for her. He had called her "Eleanor" once, to be sure; but it was only after she had forced his hand.

She picked up the large bouquet of roses which lay by her plate, and raising them to her face as if to inhale their fragrance, she attentively observed Miss Windsor, for she felt that there must be something between her and Geoffrey; some tie stronger than the memory of a dead flirtation. Her masked battery served her purpose well, for Maggie, presently, after smiling faintly at some remark of Mr. Prouty's, looked quickly over toward Lord Brompton, who was at the time listening attentively to a political conversation between Mr. Lincoln and Mr. Windsor. Maggie only looked at him for a moment, but Mrs. Carey saw that she looked at him with that fondness with which a woman gazes at the man she loves when she thinks that she is un-observed. Mrs. Carey put down her bouquet and turned to Geoffrey.

"Miss Windsor is not a bad-looking girl, is she?" she asked.

"You put me in an awkward dilemma, Mrs. Carey," replied Geoffrey, a little nervously, "in the alternative of criticising my hostess unfavorably or praising the looks of one woman to another. Is that quite fair?"

"Her features are not regular, yet she seems attractive in a way," she continued, not waiting for his answer or answering his question. "You knew her before, did you not?"

"Yes, slightly."

"That is to say, you had a desperate affair with her?"

"It seems to me that you jump at conclusions."

" Not at all. She is interested in you ; I have eyes in my head."

" I should think that you had," laughed Geoffrey, as their glances met.

" And I have noticed that she has been continually looking over toward us. The old Duke has not been lively, you see, and that *Saturday Reviewer* is a disagreeable thing. How she has longed to have you next to her !"

" You flatter me, Mrs. Carey," answered Geoffrey, who was annoyed, as all men are, when they are accused of being too fascinating. " Miss Windsor and I were great friends, nothing more."

" Why, my dear boy, of course you were nothing more. To be great friends is enough ; so you own up to the serious affair ? You think that she isn't watching you—look."

Geoffrey glanced up and caught Miss Windsor's eye. She colored, turned away, and said something to the *Saturday Reviewer*, who had before found his satirical remarks thrown away on his *distraite* hostess.

" See that fine color mounting to her cheeks," said Mrs. Carey.

" She sees that we are talking about her and feels a little self-consciousness. The Americans are not so self-possessed as we are."

" Why do you not marry her ?" she continued, not heeding him. " She has money, is not at all bad-looking. There is nothing else for you to do, and you cannot long go on as you are now, I fancy."

Geoffrey grew red and confused. He tried to make a clever answer. She had such an air of graceful badinage, as she asked the question, that it did not seem to him that he had a right to be angry, and yet he did feel so. It annoyed him very much to be chaffed about Miss Windsor; to have this cold woman of the world suggest to him that he should marry the young American girl for her money.

Mrs. Carey laughed slightly, and seeing that she had pressed her advantage too far, turned to a congenial diversion with Sydney, who had by this time dined well and thoughtfully. She clinked his glass of Burgundy lightly with him in a quaint, old-fashioned way, and Sydney's eyes sparkled; he drained his glass.

Sir John Dacre had seen Geoffrey when the party sat down at the table; but it so chanced that he did not catch his eye until just now. The two men had not met for years, and even now the conventions of society and six feet of mahogany kept them separated more effectually than miles of country. They smiled and nodded, however, and Dacre raised his glass of wine, and the two pledged each other's health in some old comet claret of 1912.

" Who is the man who just smiled at you, Mr. Dacre?" asked Miss Lincoln.

" My dear old friend, Lord Brompton—Geoffrey Ripon you would call him, perhaps. I am downright glad to see him here to-night. Indeed, I came down to this part of the country to see him."

Miss Lincoln seemed chagrined.

" You must be very much attached to him, then, Mr. Dacre."

" Yes, of course I am; and I have not seen him for some years. He has not changed much."

" If he is Geoffrey Ripon, Earl of Brompton, it is to him that this estate used to belong, then?"

" Yes, Miss Lincoln, in his father's day it was a beauti-

ful place ; there were none of these modern gewgaws here.
The old earl would have starved to death rather than have
dined in a room lighted by the electric light. I used to
stay here as a boy ; indeed, I am a kinsman of the family.
I was here last some years before the old gentleman's death.
He lived on here for years without hearing from the outside world.   He even gave up the *Times*, and would not
have anything in the house which was written since the
abdication.   He refused to acknowledge the existence of a
country which had exiled his king."

Miss Lincoln blushed a little as she said :

" Do we not owe our allegiance to our country, Mr.
Dacre, as it is ?   It seems to me that it is our duty to do
what we can for it."

" Ah, Miss Lincoln, I am afraid that we are treading on
dangerous ground.   Your father and I respect each other
as foes, whose swords have crossed, always do ; but it is
not fitting that his daughter and I should discuss this
matter.   Do you notice how intently Mrs. Oswald Carey
watches Miss Windsor ?   I wonder why ?"

" I have noticed it, Mr. Dacre," answered Miss Lincoln.   " Just now she guarded her face with her bunch of
roses, that Miss Windsor might not perceive her scrutiny,
and her look is not a friendly one."

" She is a beautiful tiger," said Sir John, " not a do-
mestic cat, as many women are ; and she means mischief
when her eyes fix upon any one in that way."

Miss Lincoln looked at him in surprise, for he spoke
earnestly, more earnestly than he knew himself ; for something told him that the beautiful woman with the black
gown and gleaming shoulders, sitting opposite to him, was
dangerous to him and his friends.

The dinner was over; the ladies swept from the room, Mrs. Carey following close at Miss Windsor's side.

When the men had returned to sole possession of the dining-room the company separated into little groups. Jawkins fastened upon the Duke, whom Mr. Windsor relinquished with ill-concealed delight. Herr Diddlej sat turning a lump of sugar with brandy in his coffee spoon, and smoking cigarettes, which he rapidly rolled with his yellow-stained damp fingers. Mr. Lincoln sat with Sydney, who forgot his hypochondria over his cigar and became quite amusing, as the smile upon Lincoln's shrewd, kindly face testified, for Richard Lincoln was a flint upon which all intellectual steel struck fire.

Sir John Dacre and Geoffrey grasped each other's hand with a firm grip, and looked into each other's eyes in silence for a moment.

"I came down here to see you, Geoffrey, because I need you."

"You know, John, that I am at your service, now and always."

"It is not my service, Geoffrey," said Dacre. "But later for this. Here comes old Featherstone; we have come down here together. Here, let us get on the sofa; it is the same one we used to sit on when we came here in the hunting season in your father's day."

"I did not have a chance to say anything to you while the ladies were present," said Featherstone, sitting down between his friends. "I am very glad to see you. I had heard nothing about you since you left Paris. They tell me that you are living in the neighborhood."

"Yes, just over there," indicated Geoffrey with his thumb. "You are to stop three days, I hear. You must

both come to see me. You will be my first guests since I
came back to my estate."

" You look as well as ever," said Featherstone. " But
how we have made the running the wrong way, to be sure,
since I last saw you."

Featherstone made a gesture with his left hand, and
looked inquiringly at his friends ; but Geoffrey, though he
noticed the gesture, did not attach any significance to it.

He raised his glass of port over a carafe of water. " The
King," he said.

All three drank, and Dacre whispered, " No more of
this, Featherstone. I shall see Geoffrey this evening ; he
is not one of us yet."

" What an attractive woman Mrs. Oswald Carey is !"
exclaimed Featherstone. " You knew her before, did you
not, Geoffrey ?"

" I was her father's pupil before I went to Oxford."

" And knew the goddess when she was budding into
womanhood. I can see it all. You fell in love with her,
of course, cherished a locket in your left-hand waistcoat
pocket for some weeks after you left her father's tutelage.
I don't blame you. I never saw a woman who made one's
blood course faster."

Featherstone stretched out his long legs and arms and
pulled away at his cigar, a queer smile playing over his
mouth.

" She is a woman whom it is delightful to have been or
be in love with," he continued ; " but to marry—ah ! I
do not envy Oswald Carey. He simply gives his name up
to have a Mrs. put before it. By the way, our hostess is
an interesting girl. I like the old man, too. It is refresh-
ing to see a man who has opened his oyster after living

among such a broken-down lot as we all are. I wish that he could give me a point or two ; they say that he can make a million by turning over his hand. Think of it. There are a lot of fellows who can lose one by the same simple process.''

Geoffrey did not answer ; he felt silent and depressed since the ladies had left the room, and his cigar seemed to him to be altogether too long. It is a bad sign when a man's cigar seems too long to him, and when he tells you that he never knew until lately how offensive the odor of tobacco was to a refined woman you may know that all is up with him. Featherstone, on the other hand, smoked his cigar, slowly and reverently, like a liberty-loving and untrammelled gentleman.

Geoffrey walked out to the great hall, where he found the ladies gathered around the fireplace. Mrs. Oswald Carey sat near the Duchess, and was talking with her. The old lady did not seem pleased with her new companion, and smiled pleasantly at Geoffrey, when she saw him approach. Miss Windsor was sitting in a low chair somewhat removed from the other two. Geoffrey, after a few words of greeting to the Duchess, approached Miss Windsor.

'' You did not linger over your cigar like the rest, I see,'' she said to him, as he sat down by her. '' Tobacco is a woman's most formidable rival, but the charms of Mrs. Oswald Carey are strong enough to draw you in here ! Perhaps you will have a cup of coffee to make up for your deprivation.''

'' Thank you, Miss Windsor ; one lump. But I did not come in to see Mrs. Oswald Carey. I had the pleasure of sitting next her at dinner.''

" We are going to-morrow on a drive to the ruins of Chichester Cathedral. If you have nothing to prevent you, will you not join us?"

Geoffrey accepted the invitation.

" It is a pity that there are so few ladies," continued Miss Windsor ; " we can make up a coach-load, however, and you may drive, if you wish it. Of course, you can then have Mrs. Oswald on the box-seat with you, and then you will be sure to have a good time."

" Oh, Featherstone can drive much better than I," answered Geoffrey ; " I have not driven four-in-hand since I lived in this house. I should much prefer to be upon one of the seats with you."

The men trailed into the hall awkwardly, bringing a fine perfume of tobacco along with them. They stood around for a moment, getting themselves into the position of the social soldier.

Herr Diddlej seated himself before the piano, ran his fingers through his long hair, and was soon weeping over a sonata of his own composition.

Dacre, who was standing apart from the others, before a picture, in a dark recess of the hall, was approached by a footman, who made a quick sign to him, a sign such as Featherstone had made to Geoffrey a few moments before.

Sir John answered, and the servant, in handing him a cup of coffee, slipped a note into his hand. The footman went on handing the coffee, calm and unmoved

Dacre, after glancing at the letter, thrust it into his waist-coat pocket, and furtively glanced at Geoffrey. The latter excused himself to Miss Windsor.

" I wish to have a long and private conversation with you," said Dacre to him, " and when you take your leave

I will walk over with you to your house, where we can talk together.

Mrs. Carey, before the party broke up, excused herself on the grounds of a severe headache and retired to her room. She sat there for some time looking out upon the ocean and the moon-glade, glistening and twisting over the waves like a great serpent. Of a sudden she threw over her shoulders a thick cloak, and, by a dark back passage of the old house, stole out into the moonlight. She felt a desire to walk along the cliff and to soothe her nerves with the deep booming of the waves along its base. And, perhaps, she might meet Geoffrey on his way home, she thought, not forgetting the potency of moonlight and the great Love God, " Juxtaposition."

CHAPTER VI.

THE ROYALISTS.

IT was a clear, cold night as the two strangely dissimilar friends, Dacre and Geoffrey, emerged from the shadow of Ripon Wood and stood for a moment on the cliff path looking down at the unquiet sea, which was still heaving and breaking from the force of the day's storm. From the horizon before them the full moon had risen about two hand-breadths, and the sky was all barred and broken with torn clouds moving rapidly, behind which the moonlight filled the sky. The white light fell on the black sea like spilled silver, and made a glittering road across the waves.

Dacre advanced to the very edge of the cliff and stood with folded arms, looking into the night as if it were a face or scroll to be read. But the eye, in truth, saw not, though the thoughtless sense perceived the shifting clouds and tossing sea. The vision was introspective wholly. It was turned on a wide inner field, where stood arrayed, like an order of battle, a strange array of Principles and Methods and Men.

Dacre was at work—at the work he loved and lived for. The enthusiast, like a general, was reviewing his spiritual and mental troops—proudly glancing along the lines before he removed the screen and called another eye to behold. He had drawn them up, with their banners, to fill Geoffrey, at once, with his own confidence and knowledge—for it *was* knowledge and certitude, not opinion or fantasy, that filled him.

John Dacre was a magnificent dreamer, and he saw and lived among magnificent visions. The spirit that had evoked Royalty and Aristocracy and made them a potent reality for twenty centuries burned in him as purely as in the old poet's picture of King Arthur.

No wrong that is all wrong can live for two thousand years and bind the necks of men. Royalty was the first wave of the rising tide of humanity ; Aristocracy was the second. Both were necessary—perhaps natural. But the waves fall back and are merged when the risen sea itself laps the feet of the precipice.

It is hard to describe Dacre's face at this supreme moment, except by saying that it was visibly lighted with an inner light. Standing in the moonlight, with his pale features made paler, the shadows of the face darker, and his tall form straight and moveless as a statue, from the intensity of his thought, he almost startled the more prosaic Geoffrey, who had lingered to light a cigar before coming out on the breezy cliff path.

"Hey ! old fellow ; what do you see ?" Geoffrey asked as he came up.

But he had to speak again, laying his hand on Dacre's shoulder before he got an answer, though Dacre had noted the question, as his answer showed when it came.

"See ! I see a glorious panorama," and he turned and looked at Geoffrey, still with arms folded. "I have seen the history of our country stretched out like a map upon the sea. I saw thereon all those things which have made England famous forever among the nations—the kings, the nobles and the people, advancing like a host from the darkness to the light."

"Yes, to the light of other days. But you know that has faded," said Geoffrey, as he buttoned his overcoat and pulled down his hat.

"No ; not the light of other days, but the light of to-morrow, which never fades."

"Well, then, I don't understand you, old man ; that is all," said Geoffrey, contentedly, as he paced along, casting a satisfied, thoughtless glance at the shimmering waves below, in some such natural way as a sea-bird flying overhead might have done.

Geoffrey was of a placid and easy, perhaps lazy, disposition ; but his placidity rested like the ice of a mountain lake on deep and dangerous water. It was hard to ruffle him or even to move him ; but when moved he was apt not to return to the position he had left, nor to be quite natural to the new position.

"How far away is your house?" asked Dacre.

"Not far ; there, you see the light over there. Old Reynolds is sitting up for me and keeping the kettle going. He sticks by me through thick and thin. I have tried to make him take a better place, but he will not go."

Dacre was silent, and they walked on, descending from the cliffs and following a path across the wide lawn-like fields, darkened by enormous heaps of shadow from scattered chestnut trees.

An hour before the young men crossed these fields another figure, a woman's, had travelled the same path. She was wrapped in a dark cloak, and though she had lingered and loitered on the cliff-walk, she hurried on the lower ground till she arrived near Geoffrey's lodge.

The speed with which she had walked proved that the woman was young, and when the strong wind tightened the light cloak on the outline of her tall figure, it could be seen, even in the moonlight, that she was lissome and beautiful.

She had, on leaving the cliff path, steered straight for the light in Geoffrey's house ; but when she approached it she walked slowly, and at last stopped in the deep shade of a tree within fifty feet of the lodge.   From this position she could look into Geoffrey's sitting-room, where a fire burned brightly and a light stood in the window facing the cliff.

" I shall wait here," she said, speaking to herself, as if to give herself courage by the whisper ; " no one has seen me—no one but he shall ever know."

But the next moment she almost screamed with terror at a sound behind her.   A bramble cracked, and she saw a man within a few yards of her.   She was terribly fright- ened, and could not speak or move.

It was old Reynolds, Geoffrey's servant, who had seen her on the cliff walk, and had taken a night glass, with which his master often watched the ships, to see if this were not he returning from the house.   Seeing a woman, Reynolds was surprised, for the cliff walk was lonely and not too safe.   He was still more surprised to see her turn into the path to the lodge, and he had not lost sight of her for a moment till she stopped under the tree.

When she turned, even in her terror, she assumed a defiant attitude, and she held it still, facing the man.

Reynolds instinctively knew she was a lady, and with a

touch of his hat, but a doubting sternness in his voice, he said :

"Who are you, please, and what do you want here at this hour of the night—or morning?"

She was reassured, knowing the voice to be that of a common man, and as quickly judging him to be Geoffrey's servant.

"I am an old friend of Lord Brompton's family," she said, steadily enough ; "and as I return to London to-morrow, I have walked here to night just to see where the head of a grand old line is forced to reside."

Reynolds was touched on his tender spot. The stern-ness left his voice, and with bare head he said sadly :

"Ay, ma'am, in truth it is a sad sight to see the Lord of Ripon living in the cottage that was once the home of his groom—for my father kept the gate here for forty years."

"Lord Brompton has not yet come home?" asked Mrs. Carey, for it was she, though she knew he had not.

"No, ma'am ; he hasn't yet come out on the cliff walk. I can see him with this glass—as I saw you," he added, explaining his presence.

Mrs. Carey gave a grim little smile in the dark.

"You would like to see the lodge, perhaps, ma'am, inside as well as out?"

"Yes ; I should like it very much ; but I ought not to venture now. Lord Brompton might return, and I should not wish him to know I had been here for the world. I am overjoyed to know that he has at least one friend who is faithful to him," and she held out her white hand to the old man.

She said this so graciously that old Reynolds was carried

off his feet. This fine patronage sent him back to his young manhood, when he was whipper-in to the old Earl's foxhounds, and heard such voices and saw such upright ladies in the hunting-field.

"Come in, my lady," he said, glancing at the cliff path ; "he cannot reach here under half an hour. You can see all there is to be seen of the poor place in a few minutes."

The old man led, and she followed toward the lodge.

"Have a care of the steps, my lady ; they are the worse for wear."

He entered before her, and threw open the door of the main room. The place was made cheery and comfortable by a blazing wood-fire on the great iron dogs, and a round copper kettle singing and steaming on one side of the hearth.

The lady entered and stood by the table, glancing keenly at every feature. In brief space she had taken an inventory of the room. Old Reynolds passed her and opened a side door which let in a flood of cool air from the field where she had been a few minutes before. The old man stood at the door a moment, watching the cliff path for his master.

"We do not use this door," he said, "for the boards out there are too old to be safe."

Mrs. Carey went to the door, the upper part of which had once contained squares of glass, but was now vacant, and saw that it opened on a short hall-way about four feet deep, with an outer door, also half of glass, which was closed. Through this door-window the old man had looked toward the cliff. Outside was an old piazza, deeply shadowed by overhanging trees.

When Mrs. Carey returned to the table, her eye rested on a photograph on the top of a heap of old letters. She reached her hand for it; but hesitated, glancing at the servant.

" May I look at this ?" she asked, with a sweet smile ; " I know almost all Lord Brompton's friends ;" and she took up the photograph.

One glance was enough ; it was a woman's face, but only some passing woman, whom no one could remember for a month. With a slight smile, she laid it down.

There was nothing more to be gathered, except by closer investigation of the tempting irregularity. She beamed on the old man as she turned to go.

" You will meet his lordship on your way to the house," he said. " He will come by the cliff path."

" Oh, no ; I shall return by the lower walk, which is safer and shorter. What is your name ?"

" Reynolds, my lady."

" Good-night, Reynolds ; and please do not mention my visit to any one."

" Except to his lordship—"

" No ; not even to him, Reynolds. It would only pain him to know that his friends were observing his changed estate. You understand ?"

" I do, my lady, but—"

" But, Reynolds, I ask you to do this for my sake," and again the smile beamed, the white hand was extended, and the subtle seductiveness of beauty had its way once more. Men are never so old, so humble, or so ignorant as to be insensible to the charm. Faithful old Reynolds took the lovely soft hand in both of his, and bent his white head and kissed it.

" Even he shall not know," he said ; and the next moment she was gone—this time not across the moonlit field path to the cliff, but into the dark shadows of the woods on the other side of the lodge.

Reynolds watched her till she was lost in the gloom, and then returned to the lodge, closed the door, and started toward the cliff walk. The old man was strangely excited over this first visit of his master to " his own house," and he could not rest till he had seen the end of it.

But, before he had crossed the first field leading to the cliffs his mysterious visitor had returned to the lodge. She had changed her mind as she walked toward Ripon House, had resolved to see Geoffrey that night, let old Reynolds learn what he might, and she had returned.

She called Reynolds in a low voice once or twice ; then she opened the door and entered the lodge. The place was empty. She went to the side door of Geoffrey's sitting-room through the little hallway and stepped out on the disused piazza, and from there she saw the old servant on his way to the cliffs.

She was about to follow him but she checked herself suddenly.

" No ! this is unexpectedly fortunate. The fates are in my favor—so far, at least. Ah me ! what will they say presently ?"

Turning from the window in a softened mood, she looked at the room with a new look. She saw across the chair, which she knew was Geoffrey's, his old shooting-jacket, and she took it in her hands with a tender feeling, hardly knowing what she did. Holding it within her arms she stood with lowered head and a dreamy look in her eyes. While in this mood her glance fell on the old sword

which lay on the table, still with the slip of paper tied to
the hilt. She took it up and read the scroll.

Holding the jacket and the sword, she sat in Geoffrey's
chair and stared into the fire, with a smile, as if half enjoy-
ing her own audacity.

In a few minutes she heard a footstep, and presently the
old servant entered the outer room, which was the kitchen
of the lodge. She sat still, waiting till she saw him enter
and start at her appearance, and ready to smile his impressionable old soul into quietude.

But the ancient Reynolds unconsciously avoided the
danger. He remained in the outer room, and she heard
him clatter among dishes and throw two logs on the fire.
Then he went off into another room and did not return.

Reynolds, seeing that his master had company, was busy
preparing the one "spare room" of the lodge for a possible guest.

Mrs. Carey grew tired of waiting. She went to the
piazza door, opened it, and looked out. Crossing the
moonlit field she saw Geoffrey, and he was not alone ; but
she did not recognize his companion. The beautiful face
was anything but beautiful just then, and the exclamation
that escaped her was as fierce as the stamp of her foot on
the bare floor.

The two men were so close to the house that she could
not escape by the front door, and she did not know any
other way. Could she instantly find Reynolds she would
then have asked him to conceal her till she could get away
unseen. But Reynolds did not appear.

It was a terrible moment for Mrs. Carey. Discovery in
such a place and at such a time was an appalling thought.
Even with Geoffrey alone she would hardly have known

how to meet the first surprised glance ; but with another, and whom she knew not, the idea was intolerable, impossible.

The men came on slowly ; she heard their voices as they passed near the window.   Then she recognized Geoffrey's companion, and could she have leaped from the piazza and fled, she would have done so.

Of all the men she knew, the only man she feared, or perhaps respected, was Sir John Dacre.   She did not understand him, while he seemed to read her very soul.   His presence robbed her of self-confidence, and made her contemptibly conscious of her frivolity, or worse.   He was like a touchstone to her—and she never cared to be tested.

As the outer door opened and Geoffrey and Dacre entered the kitchen of the lodge, Mrs. Oswald Carey stepped into the little passage opening on the veranda.   She gently lifted the latch of the outer door, but kept the door closed.   She carefully closed the inner door and crouched below the opening.   If discovered by Geoffrey she would confess that fear of Dacre's presence had made her do this thing.

The conversation of the friends had been earnest, it was clear ; and before they had been in the room five minutes Mrs. Carey's fears had given way to her curiosity, and instead of shrinking from the door she raised herself to a kneeling position, so as to be near the opening, and listened with breathless attention.

" The truth is, Dacre," said Geoffrey, " that I am not sure of myself.   I don't know that I have any political principles whatever."

" This is not a question of politics, Ripon," answered Dacre, almost sternly ; " it is a question, it is *the* question of the reorganization of the social life of England, which has been overturned and is in danger of being utterly destroyed.''

'' Well, even for that I am not particularly enlisted. It does not trouble me. Had you not told me about it, I should not have thought that anything very serious was the matter with England, except that we of the titled class have had a tumble and are as poor as the devil. But then some other class has—''

'' Stop, Ripon ! It is unworthy of you to slight the dignity of England's nobility, however poor we may be.''

'' *We !* Why, hang it, Dacre, do I not count myself in ? And I do not speak slightingly. I fear I have no class, and therefore no prejudices. I was too young to be a conscious aristocrat before the Revolution, and now I am too old to be a thorough Communist. But go on, Dacre, I know you have something to propose.''

Even Dacre's enthusiasm cooled for a moment before the odd calmness of Geoffrey, who was, as he himself surmised, a man almost without a class and undisturbed by the hopes, fears or prejudices of those who have one.

Dacre walked to and fro with folded arms, while Geoffrey, slipping into his old jacket, which he had been rather surprised to find wrapped round his ancestor's sword, busied himself with the kettle and a bottle he had taken from a cupboard.

'' Listen, Ripon—'' said Dacre.

'' Hold on, hold on, mine ancient friend,'' said the preoccupied Geoffrey, pouring hot water on the sugar in two glasses ; '' there's nothing like Irish whiskey when you're talking treason.''

" Ah, Geoffrey," said Dacre, sadly, as the friends clinked
their glasses, " men can live treason as well as talk it."

" Is that confession or reproach ?"

" Reproach, Ripon.   The life you live is daily treason
to your country.   You sit idly by while England descends
from the heights of her renown and is clothed in the rags
of the banditti who have obtained power over her."

" Banditti—who ?   The Republicans ?"

" Republicans or Anarchists, whatever they be called ;
the blind and immoral mob that has been misled by
wretches to destroy their motherland."

" Look here, Dacre, do you really mean to say that
Republicanism is immoral and unnatural ?"

" Certainly ; that is just what I mean."

" But look at America—the happiest, richest, most
orderly and yet the most populous country in the world."

" I speak of Republicanism in England, not in
America."

" But where is the difference ?" persisted Geoffrey.
" If the universal suffrage of the people be virtue in
America, how can it be vice in England ?"

" As the food of one life may be the poison of another," answered Dacre.   " Human society has many
forms, and all may be good, but each must be specially
protected by its own public morality.   England was reared
into greatness and flourished in greatness for twenty hundred years on one unvarying order.   America has developed
under another order, a different but not a better one."

" That may be, but in less than two hundred years
America has reached a point of wealth, order and peace
that England has never approached in two thousand."

" America," continued Dacre, " had nothing to un-

learn. Her people had no royal traditions—we have no
democratic ones."

" There is something in that," said Geoffrey.

" There is everything in it. The Americans are true to
their past, while we are false to ours. We are trampling
on the glorious name and fame of our country. We are
recreant to our position, intelligence, to our fathers' memories—or we shall be if we do not—"

" Do not what?" asked Geoffrey, as Dacre paused.

" If we do not unite and have another revolution !" answered Dacre, slowly and firmly.

There was a slight sound outside the room, which made
Geoffrey raise his eyes and glance toward the window ; but
Dacre, now aflame with his subject, stood before him and
arrested his look.

" Ripon, do you think that the nobles, the gentlemen of
England, have lain down like submissive creatures to this
atrocious revolt ? Do you think nothing has been done?"

" In Heaven's name, what can be done?" asked
Geoffrey.

" What did the Anarchists do when they wanted
power?" asked Dacre fiercely. " They banded together
in secret. They swore to be true to each other to the
death. They armed and drilled and prepared their plans.
They watched every avenue, and took advantage of every
mistake of ours. They inflamed the masses against the
Royal Family, the Court, the House of Peers, the landed
aristocracy, and when their hour of opportunity came they
raised the cry of revolution, and the government was
changed in a day."

" Well ?"

" Well !—we have learned their lesson. What they did

we shall do.   We have banded ourselves together.   What is that?"

A noise like a creaking door had struck Dacre's ear, and he stopped.   Geoffrey had heard it, too, and instantly jumped up and walked into the kitchen.   Reynolds was not there ; but Geoffrey heard him at work in another room.   He returned smiling.

"Either an owl or a ghost, Dacre," he said, looking out on the field.   "There is not a soul but old Reynolds within two miles of this place."

Dacre continued to pace the room, and as he walked he said in a low voice :

"I have said too much, or not enough, Ripon.   Shall I proceed?"

"By all means, proceed."

"But you understand—you see the consequence ?   You know enough to know whether or not you want to hear more."

Geoffrey was silent, and sat looking at the fire.   He was moved by Dacre's words ; but he was not filled with any new resolution.   At last he raised his eyes and was about to speak.   Dacre was regarding him intently, and now came and bent toward him.

"Come with us, Ripon," he said earnestly, dropping each sentence slowly.   "We want you.   You are needed. It is your duty."

"I am not sure, Dacre, about that," answered Geoffrey, looking at his friend.

Dacre drew back, with a flush on his pale face.

"I am not sure of that," continued Geoffrey, unheeding the movement ; "but I am sure of you, John Dacre, and I am ready to take your word for it, even when you tell me what is my duty. I am sure that if the gentlemen of England are in a league of your founding, or of your choice, they are banded for no dishonor, but for some noble purpose ; and if you want me I am ready.''

Dacre's mouth quivered as he grasped the hand his friend held out to him. Then he took another turn across the room.

'' Now, go on with your talk,'' said Geoffrey. '' If there is any oath, propose it.''

'' None for you,'' said Dacre.

'' Thanks.''

Dacre then unfolded the plan of the revolution which would restore the House of Hanover, the House of Peers, the titles, and all the old order of aristocratic classification which nearly twenty years before England had put behind her. He wanted to see Geoffrey an actual leader, know-ing the qualities of the man ; and to show him the position clearly he laid the whole scheme bare. It was a terrible enterprise, but on the whole not so formidable as a score of revolutions that have succeeded in Europe since the end of the nineteenth century.

'' You say you will begin with the army ?'' asked Geof-frey. '' How many regiments have you ?''

'' We have eleven colonels in England to-day,'' an-swered Dacre, '' and six of these will be with their regi-ments at Aldershot on the day of the revolution.''

'' How are their men ? Are the subalterns with them ? and can they carry the soldiers ?''

'' Many of the subalterns are not with them ; but there are some exceptions. When the Royal banner is raised and the King proclaimed, depend on it the common peo-ple will respond.''

" How many men of note will be at Aldershot on that day ?" asked Geoffrey.

" Here is a rough plan of the rising and a list of the gentlemen, which Colonel Arundel has drawn up," said Dacre, and he took from an inner pocket a paper containing about forty names, which he handed to Geoffrey, who glanced at it rapidly, recognizing nearly all the names, though he knew few of their owners. Half a score of dukes and earls and marquises headed the list, including old Bayswater and the unfortunate Royal Duke who had chosen to remain in England in poverty rather than share the King's exile in America. Lower down on the list were the names of simple gentlemen like Featherstone and Sydney.

While Geoffrey was looking at the scroll, Dacre had taken up the old sword and read the faded inscription tied to the hilt. Geoffrey saw him and smiled, as he laid the list on the table.

" It is true, Dacre," he said, laying his hand affectionately on his friend's shoulder. " I thought of the words of that scroll to-night when I saw you interested in that girl with the beautiful eyes, who sat beside you."

" Why think of these words ?"

" Because she was a commoner's daughter, Dacre ; but none the less a noble English girl, fit match for any aristocrat in Europe."

" Doubtless," answered Dacre, calmly, looking at the silver hilt of the old sword.

" You have met Miss Lincoln before to-day ? Yes— Miss Windsor told me so."

" Yes ; I have seen her several times at Arundel House."

"Her father is a good man, Dacre. How will he regard our revolution?"

"As we regarded his, no doubt—as a crime."

"God!" thought Geoffrey, pacing the floor, "how strange that two men so noble as these should look upon each other as traitors and enemies!"

"Were it not for Richard Lincoln the Monarchy would have been restored ten years ago. He is a powerful supporter of his class," said Dacre, slowly.

"Dacre!" said Geoffrey, stopping in front of him, "it is we who are class men. Richard Lincoln is a patriot!"

Dacre leaned his chin on the old sword, and looked silently into the fire.

"What will you do with such men as he, should this revolution succeed?" continued Geoffrey. "They will never submit."

"They must," said Dacre, with compressed lips, "or—" The sentence was left unspoken.

Geoffrey saw it was no use to argue. He had cast in his lot with Dacre, and there could be no drawing back.

"Stay with me to-night," said Geoffrey, as his friend was buttoning his coat. "Reynolds has prepared a room for you."

"No; I must see Featherstone, who returns to London early to-morrow. I should like to see you later in the day. I shall come here, I think."

"Yes; it is quiet here. Well, let me walk with you as far as the end of the cliff."

And lighting their cigars the two men struck across the field, Geoffrey having ordered old Reynolds to go to bed.

Mrs. Oswald Carey waited till the old man had left the kitchen and retired. Then she came from her hiding-place and at one glance saw what she wanted—the list of conspirators, which Geoffrey had laid open on the table. Her keen sense of hearing had followed this paper as if it were visible to her eyes, and she knew that it had not been returned to Dacre. With a firm hand she seized the document, and the next moment she had left the room, closing the two doors behind her. She kept close to the wall as she circled the lodge to the lower path, and then she started on a rapid walk for Ripon House.

As Geoffrey returned he was thinking of the list, and he looked for it, with something of alarm at its absence. When he realized that it was gone he walked through the kitchen and called up Reynolds.

" Were you in the room since I went out?" he asked.

" No, my lord."

" Is there any one else in the house ?"

" No, my lord."

" Has there been any one else here to-night ?"

The old man hesitated before he answered this time.

" No, my lord ; no one has been here."

Geoffrey had not the slightest reason to doubt the faithful old man, but had asked the questions for reassurance. As he retired for the night, or rather morning, he said to himself that Dacre had no doubt taken the document, which was too precious and too dangerous to be left in any other hands.

CHAPTER VII.

A FOUR-IN-HAND AND ONE IN THE BUSH.

THE four-in-hand which was drawn up in front of the
great terrace of Ripon House the next morning reflect-
ed much credit upon Mr. Jawkins's *savoir faire*. The
new harness glistened in the sunlight of the bright November morning ; the grooms, in the nattiest of coats and the
whitest and tightest of breeches, were standing at the
horses' heads ; and the horses themselves, beautifully
matched, clean-limbed and glossy, were fresh from a toilet
as carefully made as that of a professional beauty, or even
Mrs. Oswald Carey's own. And that lady stood on the
threshold of the Doric portal, her clinging driving-dress
seeming loath to hide the grand curves of her figure, and
her violet eyes drinking in the day. As she stood there,
she seemed anything but the flower of a moribund civilization, the last blossom of an ancient *régime ;* but there is a
certain force which flourishes in anarchy, a life which feeds
upon the decay of other lives, and grows but the more beautiful for it. Geoffrey looked upon her with a half-repelled,
unwilling admiration, little knowing how near he had been
to her the night before. Then Maggie Windsor came out,
and he tried to look at her instead.

" Remarkably fine horses, those, Mr. Windsor," remarked the Duke, with a gravely approving nod of his polished head. " Remarkably fine horses," he repeated, as if one could not have too much of a good thing from a duke ; and this time he threw in a wave of his patrician hand, gratis. Jawkins looked at him with admiration, and again felt that he was a prime investment. The straw-berry-colored dome of his bald head was alone worth the money, not to mention the strawberry leaves.

" And does not your Grace admire the break ?" asked Mr. Jawkins, with a preliminary bow and smirk. " It is a new pattern ; and the panels picked out in cream color are thought to give a monstrous fine tone to the body. And as for the horses—they're from ex-President Rourke's state stables."

The Duke looked as if he deprecated the introduction of any such recent personage into the company, even by the mention of his name ; and at that moment the Duchess arrived with Sir John Dacre. Sir John did not look much like the member of a coaching party ; a close observer might have noted a slight mutual glance of intelligence passing between his eyes and Geoffrey's. Mrs. Oswald Carey was that close observer.

" A four-in-hand is all very well for those that like it," observed Mr. Windsor to the Duke, " but give me a box buggy and a span of long-tailed horses. Are you off to-day, Jawkins ?"

" Yes ; the Prince has sent telegrams at twenty-minute intervals all through the morning, and in the latest one he began to swear. The Prince is a natural linguist and can swear in fifteen different languages. I must be off to Brighton at once. I will return late at night. I have left one of my young men, who will take good care of you,

you know. Good-by, Mr. Windsor—your Grace, I am your most obedient—'' Jawkins bowed low and jumped into his little dog-cart. By this time the break had got fairly loaded ; the horses were given their heads ; the horn sounded ; and in the wake of the great equipment provided for Mr. Jawkins's clients, Jawkins himself rattled contentedly along to the station.

A fine show made the paint and silver and the flowers and the gay cloaks and furs and the beautiful women among them. What is more dashing and brilliant than a coaching-party ? What more inspiring to the eye, more light and careless ; what fun more fast and furious ? And many a man that morning, who felt his hand clothed with all the might of the people, looked curiously at the equipage of the Yankee millionnaire and envied these gay people, the haughty beauty of the women, the gentlemen with their calm, unruffled exterior, and the light-heartedness, the carelessness of it all.

Now, upon this coach were six people ; and as they bowled along in the crisp November morning they were thinking of many things. Let us fancy, if we can, what some of these gay thoughts were. On the inside seat was Mr. Sydney, the hired wit, the broken-down man-about-town ; his health gone, his future gone, with no family, no friends, no faith in a hereafter and no joy in the present ; and the day preceding, at dinner, he had eaten a *vol-au-vent* which had disagreed with him. Next Mr. Sydney came the Duchess, the gaunt and dignified lady who awed even Jawkins to repose. There was not a night of her life that she did not cry like any schoolgirl whose lover has forgotten her, at the shame of her life, and the bitterness and humiliation of her daily bread. She would rail at the old

Duke, who had come to it so easily, and was willing to prostitute the honors of his race for gross creature comforts, his claret, his cigar; and every morning, when her old eyes opened, she hated the daylight that told her she was not yet dead.

Next the Duchess came Maggie Windsor. Come now (you might say), she, at least, is in her place upon a four-in-hand, with her young life, her happy lot, her pretty, pouting lips and laughing eyes? I do not know; I marked the quiver of those pretty lips, and the flush of her fresh face, as her eyes, no longer laughing, looked at Mrs. Carey, just in front. Beside her sits Sir John Dacre. His lips are closed firmly above the square blue chin, and his eyes, beneath a prematurely wrinkled brow, look straight before him out upon the road. Perhaps you would not call Sir John's face attractive; his expression does not change enough for charm, and there is not light enough in those still gray eyes. As you see it now, so his expression has been these twenty years, from his studious youth at Oxford on. The four horses break into a furious canter down the hill; the coach sways from side to side; and Dacre still looks far ahead and down the road. If there is no light in the eyes, there is no tremor of the lips; just so he looked when at the doorway, all unconscious that Mary Lincoln was looking at his eyes and finding them attractive. Dacre has never thought of women; his life has had but a single thought, a single hope, and that, perhaps, a forlorn one.

In front, on the box-seat, is Geoffrey Ripon, driving, and Ripon is miserable that Maggie Windsor is there, miserable that Eleanor Carey is there, so miserable about either that he half forgets he has promised his life to Dacre, and with him, so close that her full arm touches his, and troubles him as if it had some magnetic influence, sits the beautiful woman whose girlhood he had loved ; she, now knowing this, now conscious of the might of love, and of the power that it gave her womanhood upon this man ; and in her heart the madness of her misery, the scorning of her world, the courage and the passion of despair.

It is a gay coaching party, and many such another rattles through this world with the footmen and the shining trappings and the pomp of paint and varnish.   Oddly enough, no one speaks for moments, while they whirl down the avenue beneath the stately trees.   ‘‘ Where shall I drive you to ?’’ finally says Ripon to the company.

 · ‘‘ Where you like,’’ says Miss Windsor, after a pause. ‘‘ You must know the prettiest place—you have known this country from your childhood.’’

Ripon drove them up to the highest crest of the down, where the long main wave of the green hills stretches eastward along the coast, and the faint blue sea sleeps glimmering in the south.   Still no one spoke ; Dacre’s eyes were lost over the ocean ; even Miss Windsor was grave and silent.   Mrs. Carey tried to point out a sail to Geoffrey ; he could not see it, and she leaned over close to him that he might follow the direction of her eye.   Her breath seemed warm upon his face after the sea breeze.

‘‘ Your eyes are not so good as they used to be,’’ said she.   Geoffrey looked at her, and thought to himself that hers were deeper.   He said so ; but she only laughed the more and looked at him again.   ‘‘ Do you remember our rides in the pony-carriage ?’’   she went on.   ‘‘ Poor Neddy !’’

He did remember the rides in the pony-carriage only too

well ; when he sat beside the laughing girl, and she looked up at him as they drove through the leafy lanes when the shadows lengthened till the sunbeams crept under the old trees and touched her hair with gold. It was in one of these drives that he had vowed that he would always love her. He had broken a sixpence with her in earnest of their betrothal contract. But he did not like to have those drives recalled with Maggie Windsor sitting just behind them. The horses were conveniently restive just then, and perhaps Geoffrey did not put on quite so much brake going down the hill as was necessary. The heavy vehicle went down with a rush ; Geoffrey and Mrs. Carey were not looking at the horses, the Duchess was indifferent, Sydney looked on dyspeptically, and Dacre was looking far ahead, as was his wont. Only Maggie Windsor gave a little scream and grasped the rail.

" It was not so hard to drive Neddy as that four," Mrs. Carey went on. " If I remember aright, the reins were often on the dash-board, and we were not always absorbed in the scenery, I fear." Mrs. Carey sighed, and looked away over the green hills and valleys.

" Poor old Neddy !" said Geoffrey, lightly. " I suppose he carries no such happy burdens now."

" Some people are happy yet," the woman answered. " I told you yesterday I had never blamed you for forgetting me after you went to Oxford. It was true. But I missed you very much." There was a little tremor in her voice as she said this. Geoffrey pricked his horses nervously.

" My heart gave a great leap when you came into the room—it should not leap, being Oswald's," she continued, in a more worldly tone, " but it did all the same. A woman's heart cannot forget its first possessor, you know ; even now that you have lost it—with the rest of your estates," she added maliciously.

" With the rest of my estates," Geoffrey repeated, almost unconsciously. They had crossed the highest hill by this time, and were upon a lower ridge ; before them a long green band of velvety turf stretched away over the billowy downs, the chalk shining through the bare places where the grass was worn away, like flecks of foam. Geoffrey had a sudden thought, and, leaving the road, he cannoned the four noble horses over the close, hard turf.

" Poor fellow !" said Mrs. Carey after a moment. " And are all your estates really gone ? Can you get none of them back ? But where is this—where are you going ?"

" I say," said Sydney, " do you know where you are, Brompton ? This used to be Goodwood Race-course." Goodwood Race-course ; so it was. There was the track, stretching like a band of broad green ribbon over hill and dale ; there was the glorious oak wood to the west, above the smooth bit of grass which used to be the lawn, where the ladies of the reign of Victoria had their picnics and showed their dresses, and book-makers used to jostle ministers in the betting-ring. " Ah," said Sydney, " my father has told me of great doings here—when King George's grandfather was the Prince of Wales."

The break rolled silently over the soft greensward, and Geoffrey feared Miss Windsor could overhear their every word, as Mrs. Carey spoke again.

" This is a glorious day—a glorious country," she said. " Do you know, I have not felt so happy since those old days?" She looked up again, and Geoffrey met the magic of her eyes, and lost himself in them. Suddenly she

turned them from him. " You should be saying all this
—not I," she said.

" When were you married to Mr. Oswald Carey?"
asked Geoffrey, abruptly. He felt that he was slipping
from his moral moorings and wished to lash himself to
them again.

" I have been married four years," she said, coldly.
" But you really must be careful of your driving, Lord
Brompton. I distract you by talking."

" Not at all," said Geoffrey, half troubled that his parry-
ing question had answered his purpose so well. Mrs.
Carey turned round with an indifferent air.

" My dear Duchess, is not the view charming?"

The Duchess made so slight an inclination of her head
that it was hardly an affirmative. She did not approve of
Mrs. Oswald Carey. Not that her approval mattered anything nowadays. But she thought it bad enough to be a
professional beauty and sell one's photograph ; and worse
still to rent one's face out to enliven dining-parties, and
one's neck and shoulders to adorn dinners. True, she
herself rented their great name, their ducal title ; but then
she never could get used to it in others.

If Mrs. Carey noticed the snub, she showed no sign in
her face, but turned to Mr. Sydney. He also had found
the Duchess rather thorny ; and was ready as ever to pay
the homage that one who is only a wit owes to beauty.
And we know that beauty is more queen than ever in this
material age. It is long since our grandfathers first found
the folly of dreams and banished art and poetry from England—with opium and other idle drugs.

" Mr. Sydney, you look as fresh as a daisy. I am so
glad the *vol-au-vent* agreed with you."

" My dear madam, you know not of what you speak. My night was terrible, and no such aurora as yourself was in my troubled dream at dawn." Sydney looked over at the Duchess, fancying this speech was rather nicely turned; but her Grace was quite impassive, and evidently maintaining a sort of conversational armed neutrality.

" Oh, Mr. Sydney, you should have more care of yourself, or I fear the day will come when you will dine no longer, but merely sit up and take nourishment. Now, we expect you to be so funny at luncheon."

Sydney began to be offended, thinking this too flippant treatment of a man of his position. Meantime Maggie Windsor had been asking Dacre about the beauty. " She told me last night she was a very old friend of Lord Brompton's?"

" Yes, I believe she was. I fancy even there may have been some childish love affair between them." Dacre spoke bluntly, as usual. Love affairs had found no place in Dacre's mind; his only thought was his country and his King; and he spoke with little consciousness of the individual human life his words might wound.

" Look there !" cried Sydney, " there is Goodwood House." Geoffrey looked across the park (they had gone down the hill, through the wood, and were now in the open again) and saw a great, rambling house, the central part of white stone, with two semicircular bays. This part was evidently old, but long brick wings were added of more modern construction. " The county has bought it for a lunatic asylum, I hear from Jawkins," said the wit grimly.

" Where is the Duke of Richmond?" asked Geoffrey. " Still in Russia?"

"Giving boxing lessons," said Dacre.

The rest of the ride was made in silence. They went down through a valley naturally fertile. None of the large older houses seemed to be occupied, but were falling into waste. Early in the afternoon they drew up at Chichester Cathedral, among the ruins of which they were to lunch. The grooms took the horses off to an inn in the little village near by, and Jawkins's man proceeded to unpack the hampers.

For some reason, Miss Windsor avoided Geoffrey. The Duchess and Sir John sat silently beside one another; Ripon was left to Mrs. Carey. It was a pretty picnic; but the party did not seem to enjoy it very much. From the Chichester ruin the roof has quite disappeared, but the pointed arches of the nave still stand; and these and the flying buttresses of the choir make a half inclosure of the place, into which the sunlight breaks and slants like broken bars of music through the soft greensward. Here you may lose yourself among the arches and pillars, the broken altars, the overturned fonts, and the old tombs and marble tablets speaking of dead worthies long forgotten. And if you lose yourself with the right person, your loss may be (as these same epitaphs read) her eternal gain.

Geoffrey wandered in here with Mrs. Carey. He had been trying to find Miss Windsor; but he met the other first. He could not treat her rudely, perhaps he did not wish to; but to his speech she answered but in monosyllables or not at all. Finally they sat down on the grass, leaning on an old stone pillar overthrown in a corner, half sheltered by what had been an altar in the old days, before the church was disestablished. Geoffrey did not speak for some time, and when he looked at her he saw that she was crying. Great tears were in her eyes, and as he bent down they seemed tenfold even their usual depth.

"Mrs. Carey! Eleanor!" he cried in despair, "what can be so wrong with you! Pray tell me—please tell me—" She made no answer; her hand was cold and unresisting as he raised it with the soft white arm from the grass; the sleeve fell back, and the setting sunlight showed each little vein in her transparent skin. "Pray, tell me!" Geoffrey went on, and then, more softly, "You know I have never forgotten you!"

Her breast was rising and falling with her weeping; but only a single sigh escaped her lips. At his words a deep sob seemed to break from a full heart; half rising, on an elbow, she placed her hand on Geoffrey's shoulder and drew his head in the bend of her wrist down close to her as she lay. Her lips almost brushed his cheek as she poured into his ear a torrent of words. "I am so miserable! so miserable!" was all he could distinguish. Then she arose, sitting upright.

"Geoffrey Ripon, my life is a lie—a mean, unbroken lie. You know why I married Carey—he could give me position, *éclat*, fashion—fashion, which is all we moderns prize, who have killed our nobles and banished honor from the dictionary. I sold myself to him and I have queened it, there in London, among the lucky gamblers and the demagogues and the foreign millionnaires. All that this world—all that the world can give I have had, Geoffrey Ripon. And I tell you that there is nothing but love, love, love. It is these things that are the lie, Geoffrey— not love and truth and honesty. Oh, forgive me, Geoffrey, but I do so crave for love alone."

Ripon looked at her, speechless. As she spoke the

glorious lips had a curl that was above the earth, and the eyes a glory that was beyond it ; and the grand lines of her figure formed and melted and new-formed again as she leaned, restless, upon the fallen stone. She threw her arm about his neck, and drew him down to her.

" Geoffrey, did you ever love me ? You never could have loved me, when you left me so. See, the broken sixpence you gave me. I have still got it. I have always kept it. " And she tore her collar open, and showed him the broken silver, hanging on a ribbon of her hair about her neck. " Oh, Geoffrey, you never knew that I loved you so ! See—" and she drew out the coin and ribbon, and placed it, still warm from her bosom, in his hand. " Geoffrey, I care for nothing but love—this world is a wreck, a sham, a ruin—all is gone—all is gone but love— dear love—"

She drew him closer to her breast. For a moment Geoffrey looked into her marvellous eyes. Then a faint shadow passed across them, and looking aside he thought he saw Miss Windsor, alone, passing one of the arches.

" Hush !" he cried ; and throwing the ribbon down he rose and stepped a pace or so aside. " Forgive me, Eleanor," he said to her, as she looked at him, " I loved you once—God knows—but now—it is too late. "

CHAPTER VIII.

MRS. OSWALD CAREY rose the following morning before anybody was stirring. She passed down the staircase noiselessly and opened the front door, when, much to her annoyance, she found herself face to face with Mr. Jawkins, who was smoking a matutinal pipe on the front steps.

" Whither away so early, Mrs. Carey ?"

Her first impulse was to tell a falsehood, but the keen, clever countenance of her interrogator convinced her of the futility of such a plan.

" To London," she said, simply ; " can I be of service to you there ?"

" You know I depend upon you to sing ' My Queen ' after the *déjeuner*."

" A matter of imperative importance calls me away. I shall return to-morrow."

Jawkins looked inexorable, and declared that he could not afford to have her go. " You are the lodestone of my organization, the influence by which the various celebrities I chaperone are harmonized. If it is a question of pounds, I mean dollars—this new currency is very puzzling—dictate your own terms. I have a valuable diamond here which once belonged to our sovereign. I shall be happy to

make you a present of it if you will give up your plan.''
He held up the gem as he spoke.

'' What you ask is impossible. There are moments in
a woman's life when even a diamond seems lustreless as
your eyes, Mr. Jawkins, if you will pardon the simile.''
Her sleepless night had made her wrong burn so grievously
that she could not refrain from sententiousness, even in the
presence of this man whom she despised.

The undertaker scratched his head thoughtfully. '' Has
the Archbishop of Canterbury said anything to offend your
irreligious scruples ?''

'' No. ''

'' I trust the prim manners of her Grace have not
wounded your feelings. She has old-fashioned notions
regarding the sanctity of matrimonial relations. She does
not approve, perhaps, of your appearing in public without
your husband,'' said Mr. Jawkins, with an apologetic
smile.

'' I have no feelings. You forget I am a woman of the
world. Besides I am revenged for any coldness on the
part of the Duchess by her husband's affability. I got a
guinea out of the Duke last evening. ''

'' By what method ?'' asked the other, with unfeigned
admiration.

'' He kissed my hand. Perhaps you are now aware,
Mr. Jawkins,'' continued Mrs. Carey, with a captivating
swirl of her swan-like neck, '' that I have established a
personal tariff. My attractions are scheduled. To kiss a
thumb or any but my little fingers costs two bob. The
little fingers come at half a crown. To roam at will over
my whole hand involves the outlay of a guinea. Am I
not ingenious and at the same time reasonable in my

terms, Mr. Jawkins? I will squeeze your hand for sixpence." She laughed charmingly. Go to London she
must and would, but she hoped to accomplish her purpose
by wheedling and to avoid a rupture with the manager.

"Madam," he replied, with polite coldness, "was not
my attitude toward you what may be called fiduciary I
should hasten to take advantage of your offer. But business is business, and I have made it a rule never to enter
into social relations with any of my clients during the con-
tinuance of a contract. Excuse me for saying, Mrs.
Carey, that if you persist in your design I shall feel obliged
to withdraw your back pay."

Pitiful a menace as this may seem to well-to-do people,
it affected Mrs. Carey disagreeably. She was dependent
upon her engagement with Mr. Jawkins for her means of
support. These wages and the royalty she derived from
the sale of her photographs were her sole income. She
could not afford to offend him, and she well knew he
would keep his word. But her desire for revenge would
not brook considerations of policy. Rather than abandon
her plan she was resolved to break with him.

Such was the outcome of her reflections during the moment that she stood smiling at his threat before she made a
reply. She looked at him in a fashion that would have
melted the iron mood of any man but Jawkins. He had
seen beauty world-wide in its most entrancing forms, and
believed himself proof against feminine wiles.

"Is there no alternative?" she asked, beseechingly.

"Mrs. Carey, I will be frank with you. I suspect you
of an intention of going to America for the purpose of
carrying on an intrigue with the late King, one of whose
cipher letters to you has chanced to come into my posses-

sion.   To have you arrested would be very disagreeable to me, and I trust you will not force me to take that step."

Mrs. Carey's surprise was so great that she almost betrayed herself.   This suspicion of his would be an admirable cloak for her real design could she only succeed in representing it to Mr. Jawkins in such a light that he would suffer her to go to London.   Some months previous she had projected a journey to America, and letters had passed between her and the King, but the scheme had been laid aside as impracticable, as she had discovered that the royal family were in reduced circumstances.   It was now well known in London that the King's banker kept him very short.

"Well," she said, with simulated distress, "you have pried into my secret, Mr. Jawkins.   I have never injured you.   What motive have you in standing between me and fortune ?   Why should you begrudge me the *éclat* of wearing the coronet of England's Queen ?"

"I will be frank with you again, Mrs. Carey.   I have rivals in America who would snap you up in the twinkling of an eye.   A royal crown upon the brow of a professional beauty has not its equal on the globe as a great moral exhibition."

"But I would give you the contract," she said.

The manager shrugged his shoulders.

"Is my word of honor of no avail ?" she asked.

"I once lost £100,000 on a similar insecurity, Mrs. Carey."

"You wish to ruin my prospects in life, Mr. Jawkins."

"I am obliged to consider my own."

"You are rich and prosperous already.   I have nothing but my personal attractions, as you well know, and you seek to rob me of the prize when just within my grasp."

" You are unjust, madam." He shuffled his feet uneasily. It was against his grain as a man to see this peerless beauty in trouble and refuse her petition. Her arms apparent in all their white perfection of roundness, her exquisitely poised head and lovely face expressed the poignancy of dismay.

" Is there no security that you will accept, Mr. Jawkins ?"

Jarley Jawkins looked at her, and felt the blood surge in his veins. Mrs. Carey had always exercised a powerful charm over him. He regarded her as the most beautiful woman of his acquaintance. Ordinarily the thought of suggesting anything compromising would not have occurred to him, but her marvellous beauty presenting itself in the same scale with her necessity, blinded him to prudence and every other consideration but passion. It was a contest between the cunning of a luscious beauty striving for a secret end and the self-interest of a mercenary man. The victory was hers, though scarcely by the means she had expected.

" Yes, Mrs. Carey, there is one." He leered at her a little.

" And that ?"

" Yourself." He spoke distinctly and resolutely, for he was a man who faltered at nothing when his mind was made up, but she could see him tremble.

His speech was so astounding that she could scarcely believe that she heard him aright. She felt the blood rush to her cheeks in testimony to the audacity of the insult. Coming from this man such an avowal inspired her with rage and disgust. He, the society costermonger, sighing at her feet! Bah! It seemed too degrading to be true. It could not be true. And yet there he was and a response was necessary. A politic response, too, or all was lost. If she rejected him he would have her arrested. Her mind was made up.

"I know," he continued, as she did not speak, "that my proposition seems at first distasteful, but there is much to be said in its favor."

"Yes?" she queried, looking at the ground.

"I love you. If we fly to America, what is there to prevent our success? We are both clever. I am rich, and you are the most beautiful woman in the world."

"Your offer is so abrupt that I do not know what to answer. Give me time, Mr. Jawkins."

"No, no; now, at once. The steamer sails day after to-morrow," he uttered hoarsely, and he seized her hand and kissed it with passion.

"A guinea," she cried banteringly, and she looked into his face with her beautiful violet eyes, as she had into many another whose love, though nobly born, had been no less scorned in the days gone by.

"Guineas for such as you! You shall have millions. And you will go?"

"Yes," she whispered, "I will go."

He sought to embrace her, but she eluded his grasp. "Not yet—not yet. You must wait." So great was her disgust that she feared lest she should break out in rage and denounce him. Following after her scene with Geoffrey the very intensity of his passion wrought disagreeably upon her nerves. She felt the irony of fate. Yet the reflection steeled her purpose and gave her strength to smile and seem to accept his advances.

She placed her hand, glistening with rings, upon his sleeve. " I will meet you in town to-morrow, anywhere you select."

" No, you must not leave me now."

" It is absolutely necessary. I have my things to get ready."

" My servants will supply all that you need."

" Ah, you do not understand women's needs," she murmured, coquettishly, and she turned to get into the phaeton, which just then had driven up to the door. It had been ordered for Jawkins's morning airing, but it suited her convenience admirably.

He made a movement to follow her, but she turned and spoke to him in French. " Do you not understand that caution is necessary ? We must not be seen together. I will meet you at noon to-morrow in South Kensington Gardens. Adieu." She smiled upon him, and her glance had all the sweetness of that which Vivien bent on Merlin. " To the station !" she said to the coachman.

It took her some time to collect her thoughts and realize the situation. The effrontery of Jawkins seemed so daring that she almost laughed aloud. She had escaped from his clutches for a moment, but it was only a respite, a breathing spell which would soon be over. It would be necessary to provide for the morrow. But that reflection disturbed her little. She was free to pursue the object of her journey and satisfy the desire for revenge which filled her heart. As the train whirled toward London she whetted the stiletto of vengeance upon the grindstone of her wounded feelings. That paper exhibited by Dacre would furnish the needed proof of conspiracy, and then good-by, Lord Brompton, to your cherished schemes for fortune.

It made her wince to think that she had been discarded for an awkward hoyden of a girl, her equal in no particular. So she stigmatized her rival, as she chose to consider Maggie Windsor. "He loved me in the days of my green maidenhood," she said to herself, "but now that I am become the most beautiful woman in England he disdains me." Even Jawkins had spoken of her as the most beautiful woman in the world.

The thought of Jawkins recalled the incident of the morning, which, in the bitterness of her mood, she had forgotten. Somehow or other the idea of quitting the country in his company seemed less repulsive to her than at first. He was rich, and she would no longer be obliged to support herself by a degrading occupation. After the first buzz of scandal and excitement at her elopement the world would cease to prattle, or if it did she would be in America and safe from its strictures. The King was too poor in friends to refuse her recognition at his court. And, after all, there need be no scandal. She would go to America in the rôle of a professional beauty and Jawkins should be her manager. She would keep him at a respectful distance and squeeze money out of him by dint of promises. Once in America she would seek to fascinate the King. She was weary of England. She had exhausted its resources, and it would be amusing to visit the great ideal Republic, of whose magnificent prosperity she had read until her mouth watered. Yes, let this matter of a conspiracy be set at rest and Geoffrey lodged in prison, and she would go. Her glorious eyes sparkled with interest. She would have done with the platitudes and dreariness of private life. A grand career loomed up before her across the ocean, where men lavished millions at the dictate of imagination and put no limit upon enthusiasm. A fig for the dream of an absorbing love, such as for an hour yesterday had flitted through her brain. She would trample on its ashes after she had sated her vengeance.

In this mood she reached London. She took a four-wheel cab and told the man to drive her to Buckingham Palace. Shrouding her features she sank back from observation. Had she not preferred to screen her face she was free to enjoy the emotions of a celebrity. Her photograph was in the shop-window of every picture-dealer in town. Her sympathy with the Royalists had, it is true, lessened her popularity for a time, but supreme beauty is the one attribute which disarms prejudice and converts ill-will.

London at this period, like the rest of England, showed marks of the unhappy condition of its affairs. The thoroughfares, parks and public buildings looked dirty and uncared for. An atmosphere of gloom overhung Mayfair like a pall, as though the very fog had taken advantage of the situation and was clamoring for spoils. It was, in truth, a system of spoils that had been inaugurated in this former stronghold of constitutional liberty. The present government gave every facility to those who advocated popular principles with the aim of feathering their own nests. Under the influence of the social craze all that tended to promote external beauty of architecture or equipment was discountenanced, and a sodden rule of ignorant craft and vulgarity was settled upon the nation. Those at the helm were clever demagogues who were prepared to humor the people, provided they had the control of the public funds wherewith to indulge their licentious tastes. President Bagshaw had converted Buckingham Palace into a barracks, where he sat day in, day out, with boon companions.

Entrance was forbidden to none. The dirtiest scavenger might there at any moment shake the hand of the people's chief representative.

Mrs. Carey alighted, and found herself exposed to the gaze of a group of rough, groggy-looking individuals who were hanging about the entrance to the once famous palace. All the way down Regent Street she had peeped out from the cab windows, hoping to catch sight of familiar faces or fascinating wares in the shopping paradise of the late nobility ; but, though the stores still stood, few passers were to be seen, and the filthy, smoky aspect of the sidewalks told that anarchy was rampant even here. · Revolution is silent in England. The people uprising in their might do not overturn monuments and lop the limbs from statues. They let the dust and the smoke and the fog do the work for them. Only one face was recognized by Mrs. Carey as the vehicle rumbled down to its destination. She caught sight of her husband leaning out of one of the windows of Fenton's Hotel smoking a pipe. The once famous hostelry had become a haunt for pothouse politicians. A sudden impulse of generosity seized her. '' I will invite Oswald to dinner with me to-night,'' thought she.

As she walked into the palace the men made way for her in silence. They removed the pipes from their mouths and stared in mingled bewilderment and admiration. Despite her veil she was too striking looking not to fetter the attention of even the most listless, for the disgust with which these surroundings inspired her and the tenacity of her cruel design gave her a bearing such as Clytemnestra might have envied. She stalked through the corridor and up the stairs, disregarding the gilded hand and tin sign which read, '' To the President's Room. Second Story. Take the Elevator." The idlers in the lobby had recognized her, and a whisper spread until it swelled into a buzz outside that she was the professional beauty.

"Can I see the President?" she asked of a policeman who alone guarded the door of the chief magistrate.

"Name, please," said the functionary, who still clung to this relic of the formality of the past.

"Say a lady," she said, haughtily, and the man, impressed by her mien, threw open the door.

Mrs. Carey found herself in the presence of a large, heavily built man, with a bald head and long, coal-black beard, who was sitting at a desk. He was smoking, and the spacious but bare room was thick with tobacco smoke. A table, on which were empty bottles and the remains of a lunch, stood in one corner. Several men, who also had cigars in their mouths, were sprawling on an enamel cloth lounge in the bay-window which commanded the street. At her entrance these latter arose, and, at a glance from their chief at the desk, shambled out of the room by a side door, casting, however, over their shoulders glances of curiosity and surprise. She waited until they had closed the door, then lifted her veil.

President Bagshaw rose and made a bow, which was an unusual act of homage on his part, for he was a woman-hater as well as an atheist. He even removed the cigar from his mouth.

"What can I do for you, madam?" he asked.

"I have important information for the government." She paused an instant. "Are we quite alone?"

The President went to the side door, and carefully bolted it. Then he resumed his seat, and, resting his ponderous, seamy jaw upon the flat of his hand, waited for her to begin. He was used to all sorts of devices as a prelude to requests for office or emolument, and his expression betokened little interest or expectation. Had not the serious character of the communication she was about to make rendered coquetry at the moment distasteful to Mrs. Carey, she would assuredly have been tempted to tamper with the indifference of this matter-of fact personage, who even already had recovered from the trifling shock to his principles which her entrance had caused.

" I have proofs," said she in a low tone, " of a serious conspiracy among the Royalists."

His countenance changed a little, and a contracted brow of a business man became noticeable. " In what part of the Republic ?" he asked.

" It is a widely concerted plot in which all the leading Royalists in the country are engaged. The King himself is privy to the affair. The outbreak is to occur at Aldershot on the 24th of November. Many of the troops have been suborned."

" Who are the leaders of this conspiracy ?"

" The prime movers are Sir John Dacre and Lord Brompton. It was at the latter's house that I learned the particulars of the affair."

Clytemnestra never plied the sword more ruthlessly than this jealous woman doomed to destruction the man who had spurned her love.

The President was silent a moment. " Have you proofs of what you tell me ?"

She took from her muff Colonel Arundel's letter and handed it to him. " You will find there, sir, a list of the leading rebels and the army officers implicated."

He scanned it eagerly. " H'm ; yes, this speaks for

itself.   And what," he continued presently, with a politician's quick sense, can I do for you in return?"   The idea of being loyal for nothing would never have occurred to President Bagshaw.

"The time may come when I shall ask a favor of the government, but not to-day," said Mrs. Carey.   "My only request is that my name shall not be mentioned in the matter Is that agreed upon?"

"Certainly, if you desire it.   But, madam," continued the demagogue, "the people are grateful to you for the service you have done them."

"You had better ascertain first, Mr. President, that my information is authentic," she said, rising and drawing about her comely shoulders the folds of her cloak, as though to silence the conflicting forces of love and vengeance working in her soul.

The great man opened the door for her himself.   She bent him a stately, solemn courtesy, and covering her face passed slowly down the stairs.

A telegraph company had an office in the basement of the palace.   Here she wrote a message to Jarley Jawkins, which was worded :

"Must postpone journey three weeks.   Leave me alone until then.   C."

When she had dispatched this she bade the driver stop at Fenton's, where she picked up her husband and took him to Greenwich for a quiet fish dinner.   Oswald asked her, in the course of the meal, what business she had at Buckingham Palace.

"I was trying to have you reappointed to your old place in the Stamp and Sealing-wax Office, and I expect to succeed," was her reply.

CHAPTER IX.

"THE COURSE OF TRUE LOVE."

WHEN Geoffrey awakened on the morning after the coaching party, he lay for some minutes dreamily revolving in his head the events of the last two days. He felt that he had reached a crisis in his life, and as he stretched himself on his narrow bed he groaned inwardly at the perplexity and danger of the situation in which he found himself. After his lonely existence he was suddenly in the vortex of the whirlpool. He had promised his life to Sir John Dacre and to his country to be staked upon a hazard, which he thought to be hopeless, and knew to be desperate. He did not think of swerving from this promise, for he felt that he must be true to his order and to high patriotism.

He winced, too, as he thought of the scene with Mrs. Carey in the ruins of the Cathedral. He knew that he could not have averted it, for it had broken upon him with the suddenness of a summer shower. He had entered into a dangerous conspiracy, and had made a deadly enemy on the same day.

He was sure that Miss Windsor had seen the affair in the ruins. He had given the ribbons on the drive home to Dacre, and had taken his place by Maggie's side on the back seat, but she had been cold and constrained, and had answered his remarks with monosyllables. The party was so gloomy that it was a positive relief when a cold drizzling rain set in, and mackintoshes and cloaks covered up the faces of all, and made conversation difficult. But, after thinking of the dark side of the medal, Geoffrey gave a shrug of his shoulders, and cast off for a moment gloomy thoughts, as a duck shakes off water from its oily plumage.

" Mrs. Carey was right," he said ; " love is the great thing, after all ; and I love Maggie Windsor. I have little enough to offer her, not even my life, for that I promised to John Dacre, and the reversion is not worth much, I fear. My title ! Ah, that is an offering indeed ; a title by courtesy, in a democracy which at the same time sneers at and cringes to it. But I love her, and if a man comes to a woman with a sincere love he will at least be heard."

Then the thought of his promise to Dacre filled his mind and heart, and he groaned aloud.

" How can I speak to her of love, when I am on the verge of this emeute at Aldershot ? And yet I cannot give up life without having had the satisfaction of its one joy, its one reality ! I love Margaret Windsor, and there is a chance, a bare chance, of her loving me. Why did she pick out my old house, when she knew that I was living here, if she did not wish to see me again ? Conspiracy or no conspiracy, my poverty, her riches, go hang. I shall ask for her love this very day."

He had finished a very elaborate toilet for him, and Reynolds appeared to summon him to his breakfast, which the faithful servitor cooked and served to him in the old sitting-room. As Geoffrey cracked his eggs and drank his coffee, Reynolds looked wistfully at his master's handsome

face, for he saw a new expression there—a look bright with
hope and the consciousness of an awakened soul—and the
old servant wondered whether the beautiful woman, who
had visited the house two nights before, had changed his
master's face so. He noticed, too, that Geoffrey was
smartly dressed, and that he had tied his neck-tie with
great care, and had put on a coat from one of the crack
New York tailors, so that when the old servitor disappeared
to polish his master's boots he said to himself :

" The young earl is going courting, for a certainty, and
a fine lady he will bring home as his bride. Will she buy
back his house and lands for him, I wonder ?" And
Reynolds smiled to himself as he pictured the head of his
beloved family restored to his own again and Ripon House
under the faithful Reynolds, major-domo.

The dinner at Ripon House after the coaching-party had
been dull indeed. Mrs. Carey had sent her excuses to
Miss Windsor, and the latter, who had seen her head upon
Geoffrey's shoulder in the Cathedral in the morning, was
relieved at hearing them.

For within Maggie's tender heart a love for Geoffrey
Ripon had gained the mastery since the interview in the
secret chamber. Long had that love haunted her gentle
heart, a shade at first, which flitted away for a while, only
to return again and trouble her. But just as she had in-
stalled her love in the innermost sanctuary, fair and god-
like, she had discovered, as she thought, that her idol had
feet of clay ; that the man whose lips and tongue told her
that he loved her on the one day was on the next saying
the same thing with the same lying lips to another woman.

Mrs. Carey had been Geoffrey's first love. Sir John had
told her that, she remembered. " He loves her still and

he pretends to care for me because I am rich," she said to herself as she lay tossing sleepless during the night, a dull pang racking her heart with a real physical pain. In the early morning she arose and looked out of the window over toward Geoffrey's house, down over the lawn and the cliff path and the leafy chestnut trees.

" He is false," she said to herself, thinking of our hero who was sleeping so soundly under the little roof in the valley. " He tried to talk with me on the drive home as if nothing had happened. He is an actor who plays at love, and his eyes and his tongue are under his control as if he were the walking gentleman in the comedy, who kisses the maid while he is waiting in the parlor for the mistress. He does not love Margaret Windsor ; he loves her father's stocks and bonds, and he longs for riches, even with the encumbrance of a wife."

She smiled bitterly as she thought of the breaking up of her dream of love, and she almost cursed the riches which had weighed her down and had filled her with suspicion of all the men who had ever asked her hand in marriage. She had thought that Geoffrey had been prevented from asking for it two years before because he had felt that she was rich and he was poor. When he had bade her farewell in Paris he had hesitated and tried to say something to her, she remembered, but had compressed his lips into a forced smile and taken his leave of her.

As she looked out the window she heard a rumble of wheels and saw the phaeton rolling Mrs. Carey down to the station.

" What is that woman doing at this hour in the morning ?" Maggie asked herself, looking with hot, jealous eyes at the beauty as she sat back in the phaeton. " It is

dreadful to have such a person under one's roof.   I hope
that she is gone and that she will not return.   I suppose,
though, that she is to meet Lord Brompton somewhere."

And so it happened that at the moment that Geoffrey
felt the first pulsing strength of his love for her, and vowed
that he would, despite her riches and his entanglements,
strive to gain her, Maggie was strangling her old love for
him, and her heart was filled with jealous fears ; and the
woman whose wild passion had ruffled the current of their
true love was speeding to London to work their ruin.

Breakfast at Ripon House was a straggling, informal
meal, and the men came down in pink coats.   They were
going hunting on an anise-seed trail, and ordered what
they wished, standing by the side-board and eating.   Maggie, after the men had followed the hounds, left the other
ladies gossiping together in the library before the fire.

She walked down the cliff path which led to the shingle
beach, upon which the small craft of the fishermen in the
little village were hauled up.

Against one of the boats a fisherman, dressed in oil-
skins, was leaning.   He had a paint-brush in his hand,
and he was gazing out ruefully over the bay, which was
lashed into white caps by the strong breeze.   When he saw
Maggie, he pulled at his forelock and set to work vigorously with his paint-brush on the stern of his boat, daubing
with the black paint over the name of the craft.   As the
fisherman obliterated the name, Maggie noticed that his
hand trembled and that he turned his head away from her
that she might not see his face.

" What are you doing, my good man ?" she asked,
coming near him, for she saw that he was in distress.

" Painting and caulking my old boat, miss," answered

the fisherman, blotting out the last letters with a long smear of paint.

" But you are painting out the name ?" said Maggie, inquiringly.

" I have a new name for the craft, miss," he answered, in a hoarse voice : " the ' Lone Star ' ; and I am painting out the old name, the Mary Mallow, which I gave her after my wife ; but, saving your presence, miss, she desarted me these six months ago ; I was too rough and common for her, I suppose."

He put his rough hand over his eyes. " It goes against my heart to paint her name out ; but, as things are now, the ' Lone Star ' is better."

Maggie could not help smiling at the unconscious poetry of the poor fellow and at the likeness between her lot and his.

" I am sorry for you, my man," she said, and she slipped a coin into his hand. " Put in a gilt star on the stern with this. It will be a comfort to you to have your boat smart." The man took the coin and looked at it vacantly. Maggie left him and kept on her way over the beach, past the boats and the drying nets, and the great heaps of seaweed and kelp, to the headland which jutted out into the sea beyond the village. Once there she seated herself in a deep recess of the cliff which commanded a view of the bay.

" And now I am alone, entirely alone, and I cannot be disturbed," she said to herself.

Down below her the breakers rolled in over the seaweed-covered rocks, and dashed into a deep chasm in the rocks, cleft by the attrition of ages, breaking with a dull sough upon the farthermost end of the cleft.

Maggie could see nothing from her perch but the sea, and the opposite cliff upon which Ripon House stood. A few wheeling sea-gulls, and a small fishing-boat, beating out of the harbor, were the only living objects in the view. The waves, crest over crest, hurried toward the headland, and beat into foam at her feet. Her mind was soothed by watching the torn waters, as each wave dashed out its life, in a thousand swirls and white bubbles of foam.

Suddenly she was startled from her reverie by hearing Geoffrey call her name, and she saw him on the rocks below her.

He looked more than pleased at getting so good a chance to see her alone.

"Ah, Lord Brompton," she said, coldly, looking at him, but not inviting him to come up by her. "What has brought you out here?"

"You. I was on my way to make a call upon you, and just as I reached the top of the cliff I saw you on the beach, talking with a fisherman. May I come up to you?"

Maggie glanced down at him, and saw that he was dressed with more than ordinary care; in spite of her hard feelings toward him she could not help smiling at the thought that he had been prinking all the morning to look well when he came courting.

Geoffrey saw her smile, and started to climb up to her side.

"There is not room up here for two, I am afraid," she said in a determined voice.

"I will sit on the sharpest edge of the rock," pleaded Geoffrey.

"It would make me uncomfortable to see you suffer,

just as it would to see anything in pain," she added hastily.
" What did it matter to her," she thought, " whether Lord
Brompton suffered or not ?"

" I would not suffer when I am near you," said
Geoffrey, a little plaintively, wondering why he was treated
so badly.

" If you came you would not be more entertaining than
Heine, would you ?" asked Maggie, looking mockingly
down into his gray eyes.

" Damn Heine," thought Geoffrey, as he lifted himself
up over the rocks. Miss Windsor huddled herself far into
a corner of the niche. There was plenty of room for two
there after all ; yet Geoffrey seated himself in a most uncomfortable attitude, with his stick over his knees, and
looked earnestly at her.

" He has come after the stocks and bonds," said Maggie
to herself, as she steeled her heart against his winning face
and his manly simplicity of manner. She tried to say
something about the sea and the view, but he looked at her
earnestly, and said, in a low, hurried voice :

" Miss Windsor, I have sought you out to-day with a
definite purpose. I sincerely hope that you were not displeased at seeing me. You know why I wish to see
you."

Maggie turned away her head ; there was a sincere ring
to his voice ; could it be possible that he really cared for
her, loved her, Maggie Windsor ? Ah, no ; she remembered Mrs. Carey, and said nothing.

" Miss Windsor—Maggie," he said, " I know that I
have no right to ask you to marry me, save that I love you
with a single heart."

" Oh, Mr. Doubleface," she thought, " how fair you

talk !'' She still said nothing, but tapped the stone in front of her nervously with the end of her little boot.

'' I have nothing to offer you,'' continued Geoffrey, '' except my love and my name ; I do not even know whether I even have a life to give you.''

Maggie was startled by this ; she did not understand it at all.   Geoffrey waited for her to say something, and there was a depressing pause for a moment.

She felt that she had grown pale, and her fingers twitched convulsively at the handle of her parasol.   Here was her lover saying to her all that she had dreamed he might say, saying in an earnest, trembling voice that he loved her ; in a voice so different to his customary tone of banter, that she for a moment almost believed in his sincerity ; yet as she averted her face and looked over the bay she could see clearly in her mind's eye the little picture which had remained in it from yesterday—her lover holding Mrs. Carey in his arms.

'' Lord Brompton,'' she finally said, in a slow, deliberate voice, from which all passion, even all affection was wanting, '' I am sorry that you have spoken to me in this way, very sorry.''

Poor Geoffrey had expected a different answer, and as he sat there looking at Maggie's pale, agitated face, he felt that there was a wall between them, where he had always found a kindly sympathy and an affectionate interest before.   He had expected, perhaps, that she might not care about him enough to marry him, for he was not so young or conceited as to imagine that the priceless treasure of a woman's heart is to be lightly won at the first asking, but he had thought that his sweetheart would sympathize with him at his loss of her ; with the touching pity which at

such times is so akin to love and often its forerunner.
Still he boldly went on with his declaration, feeling that he
did not wish to leave a word unsaid of all that had swelled
his heart with love and hope.   If his love were all poured
out and spurned, would not the chambers of his heart be
swept and garnished for the future ?

Yet what a desolate, haunted chamber it will be, he bitterly thought.

" I could not have told you a week ago that I loved
you, Maggie," he said.   " But I did, though ; only I did
not know it.   I must have loved you since the day I first
met you at the ball.   You remember it, do you not ?
When you first smiled at me I felt that we had always
known each other ; and that evening I was content.   Will
you make me so for all my life ?"   He leaned over toward
her and tried to take one of her hands ; she edged it away
from him, and turned toward him with flashing eyes and
thin, compressed lips.

" It is not possible that I shall ever care for you, Lord
Brompton, in the way in which you pretend to care for
me."

" Pretend to care for you !" he said, angrily.   " What
do you mean by that ?   Why should I come to you with
pretences ?   What should I gain by making a lying love to
you ?"

" Everything," she answered, coldly.

" I do not care to argue this, Miss Windsor," he said,
turning his face away, pained to the heart.   " I am in
such a position that I may not ; but I wished, while I had
a chance, to tell you that I loved you.   Good-by, Maggie,
good-by.   I do not wish to be melodramatic ; but you
may never see me again."

He kissed one of her hands, which lay at her side, and lifting himself from the rock, climbed down the cliff, a mist of tears before his eyes ; and Maggie sat looking over the bay silent and sad, trying to reconcile the evident genuineness of Geoffrey's entreaty with what she knew of him.

Late that evening Mary Lincoln was sitting in her bed-room, in an arm-chair by the fire.   Her thoughts were of Sir John Dacre.

In him she saw the hero of whom she had dreamed during her girlhood ; the young prince clad in golden armor, and in quest of adventures and opportunities for self-sacrifice, who should awake her sleeping heart with a kiss.

The ordinary warm-hearted but pleasure-loving and easy-going man cannot stir the depths of a nature like Mary Lincoln's.   An earnest, ardent spirit, even if it be Quixotic, so that it see before it, like a clear flame, some duty to be done, or some war to be waged, attracts to it the devotion of a strong woman's heart.

Women love adventurous, single-minded men, and will die for them, if need be, gladly and silently ; but such men, intent on their object, seem oblivious to the wealth of love that might be theirs for the asking, were they not too absorbed to ask for it.   And so it was with John Dacre and Mary Lincoln.   He was drawn to her unconsciously by her lovely womanhood ; but his great dream seemed to fill his mind, and that fulfilled, the world had nothing in store for him.   He wished no rewards, no life for himself, but to see his King returned and Great Britain proud among the nations ; yet he liked to sit by Mary Lincoln and ponder his cherished dream.

Of course he would not speak to her of it ; he knew the

danger of his project ; yet she read his heart and knew that he was deep in some adventure which filled his life so that she had no part in it. Still, she saw that she attracted him, even if he did not know it, and they talked together about the glories of the past history of their country, and lived with the great men who, with brain, and sword, and pen had wrought for the honor and fame of their native land.

It was no courtship, no wooing, only a meeting, for a brief space, of two human beings who had been made for each other, but whom fate separated by a rift which could not be bridged. Mary Lincoln knew this, John Dacre did not ; but as he had bade her good-night just before, he felt a sadness steal over his heart, and his voice had trembled as he spoke. Even into the heart of this man of one idea, on the eve of this dangerous conspiracy, all unawares the love god had stolen with muffled feet, so that he did not know his presence. But Mary knew.

There was a little tap at the door, and she heard Maggie Windsor's voice asking :

" May I come in ?"

Mary arose quickly and unbolted the door, and Maggie Windsor entered.

" You will excuse me for disturbing you, will you not ?" asked Maggie, whose eyes were red with weeping, and whose hair had a dishevelled look, as if it had been buried deep in a pillow. " But I felt so lonely and troubled to-night that I have come to talk to you."

Mary leaned over and kissed her with tenderness. " My dear Miss Windsor," she said, " I am touched that you should come to me."

" Oh, please do not call me Miss Windsor, call me Maggie ; I cannot tell you anything if you call me Miss

Windsor. You know I never had a mother ; and there are some things which a girl must tell to some one.''

" Maggie, dear," said Mary gently, " tell me every-thing. It will ease your mind, even if I cannot help you in any way.''

" You cannot help me ; no one can help me," sobbed Maggie, as her friend put her arm around her waist, and gently stroked her hair. " It is only that I love him so, and he is unworthy of it.''

" Do you mean Geoffrey Ripon ?" asked Mary.

" Yes, yes.''

" Geoffrey Ripon unworthy of a woman's love !" ex-claimed Mary. " That cannot be. John Dacre—'' She blushed and turned away her face, that Maggie might not see her as she spoke his name. " John Dacre says that he is the soul of honor and his life-long friend.''

" Oh ! men have such different ideas of honor from ours," exclaimed Maggie. Then she told her friend in broken speech of her love for Geoffrey ; that she had sup-posed that he had not told her he loved her because he felt that he had nothing to offer her ; that she had come to England to see him again ; and then she told of the dread-ful scene in Chichester, and how she had coldly rejected him in the morning because she believed he loved Eleanor Carey, and that he wished to marry for money.

The story seemed shameful to her as she told it : her forwardness in coming to England, and her shattered faith in her lover.

" And yet he seemed in earnest this morning, and he appeared to love me," she said to Mary, when she had told her story, " and when I told him, when he asked me what he had to gain by a pretence of loving me, that he had everything to gain, his face was deadly white and his eyes were filled with tears. Oh, I almost believed in him then, and I should have relented ; I fear I should have been weak enough to have relented if he had not left me ; and now it is all over !"

She burst into tears, and Mary's face was full of sympathy, as she whispered words of comfort in the unhappy girl's ear.

" I own that appearances are against him," she urged, " but they may be explained away. Mrs. Carey is a very dangerous and bad woman ; at the moment when Geoffrey appeared to you the worst he may have loved you the most. Have heart, dear, if he loves you, and if he is a good and true man, as I think he must be, for John Dacre trusts him—"

Maggie raised her head, looked into her friend's eyes and read her secret. Then two hands clasped together tightly, and they kissed and wept together.

" You will see him again," whispered Mary, as Maggie was leaving the room. " You will see him soon, and everything will be right."

" No, I am afraid everything will not," said Maggie ; " but if I have lost a lover, I have found a friend, have I not ?"

And they did not meet soon again, for Geoffrey was dispatched by Dacre upon most important duty—to make arrangements for the concealment of the King when he should arrive in the country to return to his own again. He went into the enterprise heart and soul ; that is to say, with that part of his heart which was left him. Still he feared the end of the affair, and seemed to foresee the ruin to which the troubled waters in which he swam were sweeping the King's men.

CHAPTER X.

ENGLAND was at peace ; but it was the lurid peace before the storm.   All men knew that the days were hurrying on toward an outbreak.   In what shape it should come no one knew, and the mystery deepened the sensation of expectancy and dread.

It had been publicly spoken, in the street, the press, and even in Parliament, that the Royalists were conspiring for a revolution ; and this certainty had sunk deep into the hearts of the people.   Their silence was ominous ; the Royalists looked upon it as favorable.

But there were Englishmen who knew their countrymen better, and who foreboded darkly, though without fear, of the end ; and among these was Richard Lincoln. His heart beat with the popular pulsation, and he knew that there could be but one outcome to such a blind and reckless enterprise.

Mary Lincoln alone perceived how deep was the trouble in her father's soul as those surcharged hours went reeling past.   Deep beyond even his trouble was her own, for though she had not confessed it even to herself, every hope of her life was bound up in the destinies of the Royalist conspiracy.

On the afternoon of November 23d there was an early adjournment of Parliament, and her father came home more depressed than she had ever seen him. Her heart grew cold in the unusual silence.

Mary waited for her father to speak, but the evening wore on, and he had only tried to lead her to every-day subjects.

"Father," she said at last, "there is depressing news. What has happened? Will you not tell me?"

"Yes, there is sad news, dear—gloomy news for some. Those madmen will attempt a revolution by civil war within the next twenty-four hours."

"It is known?"

"Yes, it is all known—and all prepared for."

Mary's face changed as if a white light had fallen on it; her pitiful excitement was evident in the quivering lips and restless hands. She would have cried out in her grief and pity had she been alone; but her father's strength, so close to her, made her strong and patient.

"If it is known," she said, with forced calmness, "surely it will be stopped without bloodshed? They will arrest those gentlemen before they go too far."

Had her father looked into the eyes that spoke more than the lips he might have read beyond the words. But his mind was preoccupied.

"Bloodshed might be avoided by their arrest," he said, sadly; "but the evil would only be postponed, not eradicated. The conspirators have entered the rapids: they will be allowed to go over the falls."

"Oh, father!" whispered Mary, standing beside him and holding his arm, "can they not be warned?"

Richard Lincoln, startled from his own brooding by this

astounding question from his daughter, turned, almost sternly, to speak of the righteous doom of traitors, but he did not say the words.   At last he saw what a less observant eye might have seen long before—the suffering and fear in her eyes, and the lines which concealed anxiety had drawn on his daughter's face.   Without a word she came into his arms and lay upon his breast and sobbed, and no word was needed that was not spoken in the father's gentle hand on her dear head.

The hours of the afternoon went slowly by, and Richard Lincoln was glad to look forward to an unusual evening as the best means of diverting Mary's mind from the subject which filled it.   At seven o'clock a great public meeting was to be held in Cobden Square.   The platform for the speakers happened to be built beneath the windows of Mr. Windsor's city house, and the hospitable American, who was to depart next morning for his own country, had invited a large party to hear the speeches.

Mary was glad when her father told her that he wished her to go with him, for Maggie Windsor was the only one who knew her secret.   As she drove with her father into the square in the evening, the place was bright as mid-day with electric lights.   The crowd was already gathering, and the people were strangely silent.

At Mr. Windsor's there was a large party, and among the guests many of those whom Mary had met at Ripon House.

It was almost a merry gathering.   The genial American gentleman and his charming daughter had conquered even the austerity of the Duchess of Bayswater ; and the Duke conversed with Mr. Sydney, swaying his gold eyeglass on its string with gracious abandon.

Geoffrey Ripon and Featherstone, who were together, saw Mr. Lincoln and Mary as soon as they entered.

" Geoffrey," said Featherstone, in a bantering whisper, " behold our deadly enemy. Do you dare to speak to him ?"

" I should rather not," answered Geoffrey, " but I suppose we must. Heavens ! How pale his daughter is !"

" Come, Ripon. Mr. Lincoln sees us. Here goes to shake hands with the man whom we must send to prison to-morrow—if he don't send us."

Geoffrey Ripon felt more like a truant schoolboy approaching a severe master than he cared to confess even to himself, as he moved through the crowded room toward Richard Lincoln. But when they met there was nothing in the manner of either to indicate any unusual feeling.

Mary Lincoln stood near a window, from which she looked over the still silent but now dense crowd in the square. While she mentally contrasted the two scenes, that within with that without, she turned her head with the consciousness of being observed, and met the quiet eyes of Sir John Dacre, who bowed without a smile.

Mary's strong impulse was to warn him of his danger, at any cost to herself, and she had taken a step toward him, when she was intercepted by Mrs. Oswald Carey. The Beauty was splendidly dressed, and a deep excitement blazed in her eyes.

" We have kept places for you, Miss Windsor and I," said she, with gay kindliness. " Is your father going to speak to-night ?"

" I think not," answered Mary, her old aversion for Mrs. Carey doubled on the instant.

"Then we shall take him too. Shall we go and find him?"

Dacre was still standing by the window, and Mary Lincoln, thinking to bring him to her, asked him if the meeting had opened.

"Not yet," he said, from his corner; "but they are crowding the platform with speakers."

He would have gone to Miss Lincoln, whose earnest nature, as well as her beautiful face, had impressed the single-minded Royalist perhaps more deeply than anything outside the King's own cause. But he did not move, because of his dislike for Mrs. Oswald Carey, founded somewhat on an instinctive doubt of her honesty.

Mrs. Oswald Carey, glancing from Mary's face to Dacre's, quietly resolved to keep these two from coming together that evening if she could prevent it. She now urged Mary to take her to her father while she "delivered Miss Windsor's message," a word adopted on the moment; and Mary had to go with her.

Meanwhile the meeting in the square had opened, and the voices of the speakers were clearly heard in the drawing-room. It would have been a scene of singularly oppressive character even to a heedless observer; but its unexpressed and perhaps unconscious purport was deeply read by many of those who listened from the balcony and parlors of Mr. Windsor's house.

Now and then came from the vast field of faces in the square a rumbling roar that swelled and died like thunder; and then came the single voice of a speaker, stretched like a thin wire, joining roar to roar. All through the proceedings there was never a laugh from the multitude

" Listen :" cried Colonel Featherstone from the balcony, late in the night ; " here is a dramatic fellow."

The man then addressing the crowd was one who had
from his first sentence moved his audience to an extraordinary degree—one of those magnetic voices of the people
which flames the word that is smouldering in every heart.
He had used no cloak for his meaning, like the other
speakers ; but boldly attacked the Legitimists, the Monarchy, the titles and the privileges of the aristocracy.

. " These are things of the past, and not of the future !"
sounded from the deep voice. " The England of to-morrow shall have no aristocracy but her wisest and her best,
shall have no hereditary rights but the equal right of every
Englishman !"

Here followed the thunderous approval of the multitude.

" Listen !" again cried Featherstone from his advanced
place on the balcony. " Listen !"

" Will that crime be attempted ?" cried the electric voice
of the orator. " Yes ! I believe it will be attempted."
Then there was a low murmur among the mass, and a
changing of feet that made an ominous, scuffling sound.
" What then ? Then it will be every man's duty to strike
down the enemies of the people—to destroy them, so that
we and our children shall not be destroyed. We do not
appeal to the sword, but the sword is ours, and we can use
it terribly. Their blood be upon their own heads who
dare to lay their hands on the charter of the people's
rights !"

In the wave of tremendous applause that followed these
words Mary Lincoln looked at Dacre, who had turned from
the window. His face, always severe, was now set in fierce
sternness. Again she was on the point of going to him to

speak the warning that was burning her heart, but she saw
Dacre suddenly draw himself up proudly, as if he had been
challenged.   She followed his look and saw her father
meet Dacre's glance as sword meets sword.

Every line in Richard Lincoln, from bent brow to
clenched hand, seemed filled with the meaning of the
orator's ominous words.

The two men, standing almost within arm's reach,
looked for one earnest moment into each other's eyes and
hearts.   What might have followed, who can say, had not
the engagement been broken from without.   Mary Lincoln
passed between them, and laying her hand on her father's
arm spoke to him, asking to be taken home.   The father's
eyes fell to. the troubled face, and without speaking he
went with his daughter.

Mary and her father were hardly missed out of the bright
party ; but one face became smoother when they had departed—the Beauty's.   The gloom of the public meeting
brought out the brilliant elements of the gathering with
rare effect.

From group to group flashed Mrs. Carey, and her lips
and eyes were less eloquent than the clinging touch of her
arm, which was almost a caress, as she left or tried to leave
her impression of sympathy and admiration on one after
another of the Royalists.

Two men she avoided, instinctively and deliberately—
Geoffrey Ripon and Sir John Dacre.   Calculating, cool,
unprincipled as she was, she feared to meet the eyes of
these two men, whose very lives she had undermined and
sold.

It was eleven o'clock and most of the ladies had gone,
when the beautiful woman, attended by Featherstone, drew

her soft cloak round her in her carriage and gave her hand, without a glove, to be kissed by the big colonel, bending in the doorway.

" Your driver knows where to go ?'' asked Featherstone, closing the door.

" Oh, yes ; straight home,'' answered Mrs. Carey, smiling ; '' good-night.''

She lived in a quiet street on the south side of Regent's Park, and thither she went. But when she reached Oxford Street she rang the carriage bell and changed her course.

" Drive to Clapham Common,'' she said, curtly, '' and as fast as you can.''

It was a dark night, with a drizzling rain, and as the cab rattled along the empty streets she lay back with closed eyes, evidently thinking of no unpleasant things. It was over five miles to her destination, and more than once on her way her thoughts brought a smile to her lips, and once even an exultant laugh.

On the Battersea side of Clapham Common, in one of those immense old brick ·houses built in the time of Queen Victoria, with trees and lawns and lodges, lived a man whose name was known in every stock exchange and money market in the world—Benjamin Bugbee, the banker.

From his devotion to the House of Hanover, in its glorious and its gloomy fortunes, and from his intimate business relations with the royal family, Bugbee had received the romantic title of " The King's Banker,'' a name by which he was recognized even in other countries.

Bugbee was a small, bald-headed, narrow-chinned old man, with an air of preternatural solemnity. From boyhood up, through all the stages of life, he had been noted for the mysterious sobriety of demeanor which now marked him as an angular, slow-moving, silent and unpleasant old man.

The devotion of Bugbee to the House of Hanover was clear enough ; but the springs of it were quite unseen until some years later, when they were laid bare by a rigid Parliamentary inquiry. The astonishing truth was that this silent and insignificant old man, since the year of the King's banishment, had controlled with absolute power one of the greatest, if not the greatest, private fortunes ever accumulated in any country—that of the royal exile, who was known to his devoted followers as King George the Fifth.

It is true that the poverty of George, in his residence in the United States, was of world-wide notoriety. The shifts of the " Court" in Boston for very existence, and the extraordinary measures adopted from time to time by royalty to make both ends meet were a scandal in the ears of kings and courtiers everywhere.

Nevertheless, George was one of the richest men in the world—or at least he had been while on the throne, and he would be again should he ever become the reigning monarch of England. The enormous wealth which had begun to accumulate in Victoria's frugal reign had grown like a rolling snowball for over a hundred years. For the latter half century the royal investors had, wisely enough, avoided all national bonds except those of the two old republics, France and America ; but in the great cities of the earth, and notably in those that stood the least chance of bombardment or earthquake, the heir of the Hanoverian line was one of the largest owners of real property.

George's royal grandfather was a generous and almost

extravagant monarch ; but his enormous private wealth was sufficient even for so luxurious a prince. The inheritance which had made his reign stable and pleasant he secured for his son, strictly stipulating that it was to be enjoyed by him or his heir while reigning as monarch of England.

Fatal words these of King Edward's will, for they secured the lifelong poverty of the grandson whose welfare he had at heart. During the few years of George's reign the royal coffers overflowed with gold. Bugbee, the King's banker, was exhaustless as an ocean of wealth.

But the revolution that banished the King and his noblemen, among them those who had been executors with Bugbee of King Edward's will, left the solemn little banker absolute master of the royal fortune—until George or his heir came back to reign as King of England.

For twenty years Mr. Bugbee had been in possession, or rather dominion. The poverty of the royal exile in America was well known to him ; but to the demands and petitions of George and his " Court" he turned a deaf ear. His conscience, he answered, would not allow him to touch one penny of the treasure, which could only be legally drawn by a reigning King of England.

In the early years of the King's exile, Bugbee had sent considerable sums to his royal master, which he alleged were from his own purse ; but though he had since continued these, the annual amount had been reduced to a beggarly allowance.

Still the old banker was the most trusted agent of the Royalists ; and weak George himself regarded with a vague respect, almost like fear, the inflexible integrity which controlled the conscience of this most devoted subject.

Mrs. Oswald Carey did not hear the city clocks, which

"clashed and hammered" the midnight hour, as her cab rolled up the tree-lined avenue of the pretentious house of "The King's Banker."

The driver rang the bell ; and as the door almost instantly opened, Mrs. Carey, from the cab, saw several men in the wide hall, some sitting and others standing, like men in waiting.

A tall flunkey took the card, closed the door, and Mrs. Oswald Carey had to wait in the cab a full minute. Then the door opened, and down the wide steps of the porch hobbled Mr. Bugbee, with gouty, tender feet, the top of his bald head shining under the lamp.

"I had almost given you up," was his greeting ; and as he helped the Beauty from the cab there was an unquestionable welcome in his gratified smile. That they had met before, and intimately, was evident in the manner of the reception. The truth was that Mrs. Oswald Carey and her husband were old connections of the banker, the husband through monetary difficulties and the wife through complications of her own, in which old Bugbee had, for some reason or other, assisted her more than once. She knew that her husband was in the old man's power, but she never pretended to know it. On his side, old Bugbee was a foresighted worker. For years past he had seen that the day of the King's return would come, and for that day he meant to be prepared in more ways than one. In his cunning old brain he had some plan laid away in which he had provided a part for this beautiful and utterly unprincipled woman.

"Am I too late?" asked Mrs. Oswald Carey.

"Only too late for supper," was the dry answer of the old banker, but the tone was pleasant.

· Through the hall, where those in waiting stood respectfully as she passed, the banker led her to a small, luxuri-
ously furnished parlor on the ground floor. As she threw
aside her wraps and sank into a soft chair, old Bugbee
opened the door of an inner room, and turned to her :

" These are your apartments," said he.

The Beauty looked around, but said nothing, only nodding her head.

" You are very tired ?" questioned old Bugbee.

" No ; not very. But I should like some supper—and
a glass of wine."

Mr. Bugbee touched a bell and gave an order.

" It is almost midnight ?" she asked.

" It is after twelve—ten minutes. The morning of the
great day has come."

And the old banker looked into the eyes of the young
Beauty, and almost smiled in response to her low, derisive
laugh.

" He came to-day, then ?" she asked.

" Yesterday," corrected Mr. Bugbee ; " at noon, he
landed from my steam-yacht, in the very heart of London.
So much for the international police."

" Do they know ?" said Mrs. Oswald Carey. " Does
Sir John Dacre know ?"

" Sir John Dacre helped the King into his carriage when
he landed. He knows that he is here, and expects to
meet him at Aldershot to-morrow."

While pretending to move and speak as if quite at ease,
Mr. Bugbee was obviously nervous and unsettled. Mrs.
Carey observed this, but without appearing to do so.

" Where is your husband ?" Mr. Bugbee asked quietly,
with his face turned from Mrs. Carey, whose side view he

had before him in a low mirror. He saw her move in her chair, and slowly look him all over, and then glance down as if considering her answer.

"He is on the Continent—at Nice, I think."

She had dined with him that day, but did not know that from the dinner Oswald Carey had come straight to Mr. Bugbee's house to keep an appointment with the wily "King's Banker," who wished to know how the Beauty had spent the day, and whom she had seen.

"What a liar she is!" muttered old Bugbee, but he smiled at himself in the mirror, as if approving his superior astuteness.

"Then there is no danger of his making a noise about your absence from home to-night. Some husbands would be alarmed, and might apply to the police."

Mrs. Carey looked up to see if Bugbee were serious ; and then she laughed heartily and rather loudly, while he held up his hands with an alarmed expression.

"Hush !" and the frown of the old man was something to remember. "They observe as much formality as if he were in Windsor Palace."

"Well—he will be there to-day, will he not ?" and Mrs. Carey looked innocently at the banker.

He came closer and bent his broad, bare poll to her as he spoke :

"No ! He will never see Windsor again."

"But the Royalists—will they not raise the King's flag to-day ?" Still the guileless surprise in her face, which had its effect on old Bugbee.

"Yes ; they will strike to-day at Aldershot—and they will be defeated."

"How do you know ? Have they not plenty of men ?"

" Men ? Men are only in the way. They have no money. ''

" And the King ? Will he be taken ?''

" He will not be there, '' and Mr. Bugbee drew close to the Beauty again.

" Where will he be ?'' she asked.

" Here—with you ! You will save him by detaining him.''

She sat still, and looked at him with a steady stare. She knew quite well what purpose the old banker had in mind, and what she had come there for. But she meant to play her own game, not Bugbee's.

Her own game was to get the old King under her own influence, whether he went to reign in Windsor or to rust in America. She knew his character well, and she had little doubt of her power if she could only get the reins. From that position she knew enough, too, to overcome all scruples of conscience in the King's conscientious banker.

Bugbee was playing against two possible results—the success of the King or his death. Either was ruin for him. Investigation would follow, whether George were a king or a corpse. So long as he remained in exile the Republicans would never attempt to confiscate the private fortune of the banished monarch ; while, on the other hand, the royal exile would not venture to appeal to the courts against his banker, thereby exposing his enormous wealth to the cupidity of the Republicans.

" You have gone too far,'' said Mrs. Carey, steadily looking at the banker ; '' I shall do nothing of the kind. My reputation—''

" Shall be quite safe—your husband being at Nice,'' and old Bugbee's was the guileless face now.

" Humph !"

" No one else will miss you for two days."

" Ah ! for two days. And then ?"

" Then you go home ; you have been visiting your American friends, or any other friends out of London."

" Yes ; that is all very well," Mrs. Carey said quietly. " And he—the King ?"

" He will return to America at once, leaving this house in two days, when all is quiet, to go on board the steam-yacht which brought him over."

Mrs. Carey said nothing more for nearly a minute.

" Where is that yacht now ?" she asked at length.

" In London ;" and the old banker dovetailed his fingers and stood with a smile as if ready for all questions.

" And for my services—my assistance in this game of yours—"

" Pardon me," interrupted Bugbee, sententiously, " it is not a game of mine. It is my plan to save the King from certain destruction."

" Well, whatever it is," said Mrs. Oswald Carey, impatiently, " for my part of it I shall have—what ?"

" Ten thousand pounds," answered old Bugbee, dropping the words slowly.

" When ?"

" When the King is safe—when he is gone. In two days' time."

" That will not do !" and there was a ring of purpose in the Beauty's voice that made the old banker's heart beat quicker, and made him keenly attentive. She repeated : " That will not do ! He may not go to America, or he may not remain here. He may be captured, or he may be killed. He may go to Aldershot to-morrow, despite all your plans. You know he intends to go. But I—I shall have risked everything, whether you win or lose, and at your bidding. Oh, no, my dear Mr. Bugbee, it will not do at all.''

'' What do you want, then ?'' asked the old man.

'' I want the money now, and I want just double the sum you have named.''

'' You cannot have—''

'' Then I shall go home ;'' and Mrs. Carey rose and began to arrange her cloak, but keeping her eyes on old Bugbee's face. Both were playing for the same stake, though only one knew it. Mrs. Carey read the old banker's purpose, but Bugbee had no idea that she had any outlook beyond the purchase money—twenty instead of ten thousand pounds. He was secretly not displeased at the demand, which seemed an indication of her sincerity.

'' You shall have the money,'' he said, having pretended to consider. '' I shall write a check now.''

'' I want the money ; I do not want a check.'' And she remained standing.

Old Bugbee smiled as he went out. In a few minutes he returned, and finding her still prepared to go, took the cloak from her, and placed in her hand twenty crisp Bank of England notes.

The entrance of the tall flunkey prevented Mrs. Carey from speaking her pleasure, but she looked it at the banker.

'' You are wanted, sir,'' said the erect flunkey.

Old Bugbee hurriedly left the room, and as soon as the door had closed, Mrs. Oswald Carey ran to a large mirror, where she smiled at herself, and concealed her treasure in her dress.

Then she went into the rooms which the old banker had said were hers ; and some minutes later, when the banker returned and she came toward him, he smiled approval at the few supreme touches that had made her beauty positively radiant.   Her dress was cut low and square, and a soft gauze of exquisite texture covered her bosom.   This had been concealed throughout the evening by a skilful arrangement of rich lace.   There was a single red rose in her hair.

" You are to present a petition," old Bugbee said, as if giving instructions.   " Have you thought of it ?"

" Trust me," she said, smilingly.   " I am ready."

Leaning on the arm of the King's banker, Mrs. Carey ascended the wide stairs and on the first floor entered a small parlor.   Through an open door she saw, in a great room beyond, three men, two of whom were bowing obsequiously, as if taking their leave.

The third person was the King.

Mrs. Oswald Carey smiled inwardly as she took in the points of this extraordinary figure, which was so like, yet so absurdly unlike, the prints with which all the world was familiar.

King George the Fifth was dressed in a splendid court suit, his breast blazing with orders, and his coat and waistcoat literally covered with gold embroidery.   He was a short, heavy man, about fifty years of age, with a large, oval head, made still more large and oval by a great double chin, and by the soft fatness of his cheeks.   His hair had been red, but was almost gray, and he was bald on top. He was closely shaven, showing a heavy, sensual mouth, out of all proportion to a small and rather fine nose.   But his eyes gave the expression, or want of expression, to his face ; they were set very far apart, and they were small, round and prominent, with white eyelashes.

Had his legs been proportionate to his body he would have been a large man ; but they were very short. As he stood, in laced coat, breeches and buckled shoes, he was laughably like a figure on a playing-card—the figure in profile.

When the two men had backed out, the banker led Mrs. Carey into the presence. Then both intruders bowed reverentially. The King had sat down and he remained seated, paying not the least heed to the courtesies, but closely regarding the lady, whose extraordinary attractions had struck him at first sight.

Mrs. Carey advanced timidly and sank kneeling at his feet ; and still the royal eye graciously scanned the beautiful petitioner. Once she raised her face to speak, but meeting the gaze of the King her suffused eyes sank again.

" She is quite overcome, Bugbee," said the King in a husky voice, as odd as his appearance.

" The sight of her King has overpowered her, your Majesty," answered old Bugbee, in a low tone of solemn awe.

" Come now," said George, encouragingly, and he touched the soft chin in raising her face : " Speak ! What may we do for so fair a subject ?"

" Oh, my King !" exclaimed the Beauty, clasping her hands, " I come with words only for your own ear."

An unquestionable frown shadowed Bugbee's face at the audacity of the woman. George's little eyes rested on the face of the speaker, as if he had not comprehended. The old banker remained standing in his place.

" I am bound, your Majesty, only to speak my message

to you alone.'' She was so evidently excited and her pleading was so eloquent that the King was at once deeply interested.

George had raised her by taking her hand, and now he looked vaguely from her to old Bugbee.

'' It is a message.   You said a petition,'' said the King, dubiously, to his banker.

'' Your Majesty, I thought—''

'' Leave us, Bugbee,'' interrupted George, with a wave of his hand, not looking at the banker.   '' Let us hear this fair messenger.''

Old Bugbee bowed and backed till he reached the door, hardly knowing whether to be pleased or indignant.   He ought to have made the woman explain her plan to him before she entered the King's presence.   Now he must wait, while she was free to act as she chose.

When the door closed on the banker Mrs. Carey's whole manner changed.   She drew near the King and excitedly laid her hand on his arm.

'' Oh, your Majesty !   I have come to save you !   You are betrayed !''

'' Betrayed !'' repeated George, trying to grasp the idea, while his little eyes were quite expressionless.

'' Betrayed !'' sobbed Mrs. Carey, '' and all is lost except your Majesty's life and liberty.''

'' How do you know this ?   Why does not he know ?'' and the alarmed George nodded at the door.

'' I do not know, your Majesty.   I only know that I know it, and that I have come here to save you at the risk of my life ; but what is my life to the precious life of my King ?''

'' Betrayed !'' repeated George, as if the meaning of the

word were slowly coming to him out of a fog. " But to-morrow—to-day—my men will proclaim the restoration."

" Oh, my King ! to morrow—"

" To morrow I shall be King !" re-echoed George, while his glance wandered round the room, as if seeking to escape from the bore of excitement. " Betrayed ! No, no ; my men—"

" Your men, Sire, to-night will be dead or in prison," said Mrs. Carey, with increased firmness, reading the puerile nature and seeing the value of emphasis.

· " I am to join my gentlemen at Aldershot at noon," muttered the King.

" No, no !" cried Mrs. Carey, and her beautiful hands clasped his arm beseechingly. " Your Majesty will be lost if you attempt to go—all who go there will be lost."

There was a depth in her voice at these words that carried conviction.

" Your Majesty must escape from England to-night !"

" Impossible !" cried George, with some dignity, but more irritation.

" Oh, listen to me, Sire !" she sobbed, " and do not despise my words because I am only a weak woman."

Here the small eyes of the King rested on her again, and the royal hand soothed her back to calmness by stroking her beautiful hair.

" Everything is known," she continued, " except that your Majesty has landed. If that were known all were lost. President Bagshaw has surrounded Aldershot with soldiers. There are twenty to one against the Royal-ists."

" But the King's name will change them ;" and as he spoke George seemed really to believe his words. " When

Colonel Arundel proclaims me King, as Dacre says he will—''

"Oh, Sire! Sire!" sobbed Mrs. Carey, now really touched by the vivid picture that appeared of her own treachery; "even that is known to the President—and all the soldiers who are to kill Colonel Arundel have already received his instructions!"

This precise and terrible statement staggered George, and a look of simple alarm came into his eyes.

"Then what is to be done?" he cried, in a bewildered way.

"Your Majesty must escape this night—this hour. You are not safe one moment in London; you know not who might betray you. The steam-yacht which brought you to England lies ready this moment to receive you."

George tried to think; but he could not. He walked about nervously.

"Let us have Bugbee here!" he exclaimed, with a burst of relief.

"No! I implore your Majesty! Do not trust any one —even him. He may be true as steel—I do not doubt it. If he be true he will not object to your escape. But not knowing all, he may advise delay—and delay is destruc- . tion."

"What shall I do, then? Tell me, tell me, child. What shall I do?"

There was a pitiful confession of weakness in the words and manner of George as he spoke. He had come to a woman, unmanned, and set her mind above his—had placed himself in her hands. And never were woman's hands readier for such a gift. He felt their caressing care before she spoke ; already the renunciation was beginning to bear fruit for the weak one.

"You will call Mr. Bugbee here, Sire, in a few moments, and tell him without a word of explanation that you are going on board the yacht to-night."

"But it is so strange—"

"Kings have a right to strange fancies," she said smiling, but speaking with a firm tone. "You will simply tell him, Sire, that you wish to go directly to the yacht—now."

"Yes, I will do that," said George ; and with royal brusqueness he said, "call him here !"

"I will send him, Sire—for I am going now," and she spoke slowly and sadly.

"You are going ? No ! You are not going until I am quite safe—until I have gone on board the steamer." George's tone was deeply earnest, and there was actually a kind of wail in his petition.

"I came to save my King ; and now he is safe, my duty is done."

Still he urged his deliverer not to leave him till he had left the land ; and after much entreaty she consented to ride with the King to the vessel, and thence to be driven to her home. It was half an hour later when she descended to her parlor, and found Mr. Bugbee impatiently awaiting her, as she had expected. With lightning words she explained the situation, and bade Bugbee order his private carriage.

"But this false alarm will be known to-morrow," cried Bugbee, wrung with wrath and perplexity. "He will learn that it is all a lie, and then—"

"There is no false alarm, man !" hissed the Beauty in the banker's ear. "It is all true—every word !"

"How did you learn it ?   Who is your informant ?"

"President Bagshaw.   Is that sufficient ?"

The old banker gazed on Mrs. Carey with a dazed look, which gradually faded into one of intelligent admiration.

"I begin to understand," he said, slowly.   "But why not have told me ?"

"Because *I* wanted to save the King this time," answered Mrs. Carey.   "You don't object, do you ?   I assure you it does not interfere with any plan of yours."

Mr. Bugbee could not see that it did, nor, even if it did, could he see how he could help it now.   He had not gauged this woman rightly.   She had outwitted him, and he saw it.

"You will order the carriage at once, won't you ?" said Mrs. Carey, taking up her cloak.

"Yes, at once," and Bugbee rang the bell.   "But he returns at once to America ?" he asked in a low voice.

"That is his purpose—and mine," said the Beauty.

In less than half an hour Bugbee departed in a fly in hot haste to prepare the yacht for the royal guest ; and some minutes later George the Fifth handed Mrs. Oswald Carey into the banker's closed carriage, and the pair were driven off to London.

CHAPTER XI.

THE RAISING OF THE FLAG.

MR. WINDSOR's guests had all departed, the lights were out in the rooms so lately filled with the pleasant discord of animated voices, and the kindly old American host had gone to his rest with the satisfaction of believing that his last night in England would be enjoyably remembered by his new friends when he and his daughter were far on their voyage home.

But Mr. Windsor knew, a few weeks later, that beneath the smooth surface of his farewell party, as he had seen it, ran a secret current of fatal force and purpose. He had entertained unaware on that night nearly all the Royalist leaders, who had taken advantage of his invitation to meet in a place where suspicion of their movements could not follow.

The gentlemen left Mr. Windsor's house not in groups or even pairs, but singly. It was remarkable that none of them had a carriage, and that after leaving the house every one turned and walked in the same direction.

About an hour after the last guest had gone, in a large house belonging to a banished earl, where Featherstone had resided for the past two weeks, there was a full meet-

ing of the Royalist chiefs, including those who had been at
Mr. Windsor's, and many more. They had come singly
from many quarters, but all on foot, and they had entered
by a door on a quiet side street. There were perhaps forty
men in all.

Here were old and dignified noblemen, more than one'
of whom wore threadbare coats and other signs of actual
poverty ; and here were young spirits aflame with the hope
of action. Here a lot of antiquated baronet-squires flock
together, and yonder stands a knot of grizzled colonels with
the professional air of men awaiting orders. Here is the
old Duke of Bayswater, listening through his eyeglasses,
while Geoffrey Ripon and Featherstone have a quiet jest
with Mr. Sydney.

Shortly after midnight—at about the same moment that
Mrs. Oswald Carey received the bank-notes from Mr.
Bugbee—the hum of conversation ceased in this meeting
of the Royalists, and all eyes were turned toward a table in
the centre of the long drawing-room, where stood John
Dacre, who had just entered the room, his hands filled
with papers.

Dacre was in the uniform of a staff officer, and on his
breast he wore the battle-cross he had won in his first campaign, and also some gaudier honors awarded him for
loyalty and devotion to the cause of the King.

The strong light of the chandelier showed the tense lines
of his finely-cut face, which was white with excitement, and
his eyes burned beneath his brows with a flame too strong
to be subdued by any outer light.

Before he had uttered a word he had in some way im-
parted to many of those around him something of his own
exaltation and intensity of spirit. He laid on the table the

papers he had carried, and looked round the room with his face proudly raised.

"Gentlemen!" he said, holding his voice from an exulting cry, "our campaign has begun. We are no longer without a leader. Our monarch has come to claim his throne, and, if necessary, to win it by the sword. This night King George sleeps in London. To-morrow he will sit upon the throne of England. GOD SAVE THE KING!"

But, though death might be the consequence, a brave cheer burst from the hearts of some of those who heard—some, but only a few, and among these were Geoffrey, Featherstone, and the grizzled colonels.

To many others that cheer seemed as deadly an outburst as the roar of artillery. For a moment all stood as before ; then they broke and mingled, talking excitedly, and a goodly number edged toward the door, and soon made their way out of the house.

But at least twenty men remained, while Dacre issued orders, handed instructions already written, or verbally repeated important words to the officers who should the next day head the revolution.

"Colonel Arundel," said Dacre, addressing a white-haired but erect man of sixty years, "to you belongs the first word of the restoration."

The old colonel walked to the table opposite Dacre and bowed, as if awaiting instructions.

"At the hour of noon to-morrow," continued Dacre, speaking to Colonel Arundel, "the King's banner will be raised at Aldershot, and at that hour you will proclaim to the brigade under your command the restoration of the Monarchy and his Majesty's presence in the camp." The veteran withdrew with a proud smile.

"Colonel Featherstone, Sir James Singleton, Lord Arthur Towneley, Mr. Blaney Balfour;" as Dacre read from a list, the gentlemen named drew near the table. "You are of the royal escort; you will await the arrival of the King at Aldershot and accompany him to the camp."

When Dacre had issued all the prepared orders for the outbreak, the meeting broke up.

As Geoffrey walked with Dacre to their quarters, the streets of London were deserted and quiet, as if no danger lay hid in the clouds of the morrow. Dacre was filled, body and soul, with the assurance of a glorious success; but cool-headed Geoffrey felt none of his enthusiasm, though his step was light and his voice as full of cheer as his friend's mood required. But when they met a burly, quiet policeman on his beat, who placidly wished them, "Good-morning, gentlemen," Geoffrey could not restrain a burst of hearty laughter—which, however, he did not explain to Dacre.

Geoffrey slept soundly for a few hours, and was up early to keep his appointment with Dacre. He could scarcely credit his senses to find himself on such an errand, as he strode through the already busy streets, meeting the quiet folk at their early occupations, while he was bent on civil war in two hours' time, with his overcoat pockets heavy with loaded pistols!

Dacre and he breakfasted in a private room at the old Army and Navy Club almost in silence. They had met at the door, coming from opposite directions, and greeted each other with a firm grip of the hand. Under a large overcoat Dacre wore his old staff uniform, and he smiled proudly as Geoffrey took off his outer coat and showed his ancestors' silver-hilted sword buckled high round his body, so that it should not strike the ground or be seen below the coat.

As they drove to the railway station it was a dull, drizzling morning. At the station they saw many of those who had attended the meeting the previous night ; but, by arrangement, the conspirators did not recognize each other, even by a sign. When they arrived at the Aldershot Station there was no indication of anything unusual. A few orderlies from the camp came and went, but this was an every-day sight.

The Royalists dispersed at once, some walking, some in the common camp omnibuses, and some in cabs. The point of assembly was in the officers' lines of the infantry camp, where Colonel Arundel, who was acting brigadier, had provided a large mess tent for their reception—and on this morning, by his arrangement and for their guidance, no other tent but this in the camp was marked by a flag.

On arriving at the tent, Dacre and Geoffrey found only two of their fellow-conspirators, both youths, awaiting them. But it was very early, not 9.30, and the hour of meeting was 11. The next man to arrive was Mr. Sydney, who, fearing a shot from his old enemy, the gout, more than a bullet from a Republican rifle, stepped gingerly from the omnibus that dropped him near the lines. As Geoffrey shook his hand, a pang went through his conscience for ever having made a jest of so simple and brave a heart.

By ones and twos, as the hours passed, the Royalists came to the rendezvous. Not once had they met with question or opposition. The sentries, as they passed, stood to "attention," evidently regarding them as officers belonging to the camp.

The mess tent was well removed from the regular roads of the camp, and only a few soldiers passed near it all the morning.

Once, while Geoffrey stood at the open door, a mounted artillery officer rode past. He was a young man, with a strongly-marked, stern face, and as he passed the tent it seemed to Geoffrey that he cast a sudden, keen glance within. At first, Geoffrey was so convinced of this that he turned to speak to Dacre ; but glancing after the officer, he saw him stop and speak to a man who was coming toward the tent, and whom Geoffrey recognized as one of the military men of the previous night's meeting. After a few words they saluted like friends and separated.

"You know that officer, sir?" asked Geoffrey, as the old soldier came to the tent door. "I thought he looked this way in an odd manner as he passed."

"Oh, yes," answered the other ; "that is young Devereux, the clever fellow who has invented the tremendous gun, you know, and revolutionized the old tactics. An able fellow, sir—and a colonel at thirty-six. I knew his father forty years ago at Woolwich, when we were cadets."

"You think I was mistaken, then, in fancying that he looked this way?" asked Geoffrey.

"I should say so—bless my soul ! I should hope so, too. That's the cleverest fellow in the whole service ; and we don't want to meet him at the very start."

"Perhaps he may be with us?" suggested Geoffrey.

"No ; it isn't likely. Devereux is with nothing but science and discipline. But if he were with us he would be better than twenty regiments."

"And against us?"

"Ah ! there are circumstances that alter cases. With

us he would be free to act on his own devising, for we should make him commander of the forces. Against us he is only a subordinate, controlled by some stupid major-general.''

Eleven o'clock came, and there were twenty-seven men in the tent. Besides these were the several officers of the regiment in camp, who were in their quarters ready for the signal.

At the door of the mess tent rose a tall flag-pole, with halyards attached, which entered the tent. To these, by the hands of Dacre, was fastened the Royal Standard of England, to be given to the breeze at the sound of the noonday gun.

At half-past eleven the bugles of the infantry regiments were heard sounding for a general parade ; and in a few minutes the scarlet lines were seen on the parade ground, forming, wheeling, and marching into brigade formation.

The commanding officer and the colonels of six out of seven regiments would call on the troops to cheer for King George when they saw the royal banner at the mast. Inside the mess tent there was a scene of quiet preparation, which had its ludicrous as well as pathetic features. Many of the Royalists had come in military uniforms of various kinds and countries. As the hour drew near they laid aside their overcoats, and composed an odd group for a military critic. The Duke of Bayswater wore an old red tunic of the yeomanry cavalry, which he had commanded in his county half a century before ; Mr. Sydney a lancer's fatigue jacket, which he had worn as a lieutenant in King Edward's time ; there was one in the tunic of a captain of French artillery, and several others wore continental uniforms. Every one was armed in some way or other.

As the infantry brigade wheeled into line on the parade-ground a distant trumpet sounded far in the rear.

"Dacre, what is that trumpet?" asked Geoffrey, in a low tone.

Dacre looked at his watch as he listened. He did not reply, but shook his head and smiled at Geoffrey.

"That is an artillery trumpet," said the old officer to whom Geoffrey had spoken before, and who now came quietly to Dacre. "It came from the direction of Colonel Devereux's battery—though I remember distinctly he told me that this was not a field day."

It was clear to Geoffrey's eye that Dacre was suffering under some heavy fear or despondency that quelled his excitement. There was a look in his face of tense expectancy that was pitiful to his friend.

"The King was to have been here at eleven," said Geoffrey to him at last. "It is now twenty minutes to twelve. Can anything have happened, Dacre?"

Dacre looked at him reproachfully; but only shook his head, without a smile. Geoffrey walked to the door, and turned suddenly, almost with a shout.

"Here's Featherstone!" he cried. "He was in the King's escort; he has news."

The Royalists crowded around Featherstone as he entered, but their eager eyes found no reassurance in his face, which was pale, and, still more unlike Featherstone, full of anger and gloom.

He did not reply to the hail of questions which met him, but looked around for Dacre, and went to him.

"The King?" asked Dacre, sternly.

"The King has disappeared," answered Featherstone, "and no one knows where he has gone."

There was a dead silence in the tent ; not a man moved. Dacre looked at his watch. It was ten minutes to twelve.

" He may be on the way here by another route," suggested the old Duke.

" What have you done to obtain information ?" asked Dacre.

" At eleven o'clock the escort waiting at the station in London telephoned us that the train had gone and the King had not arrived. We waited ten minutes and then I telephoned direct to the house of the King's banker and received in answer these words : ' The King left here at two o'clock this morning to go on board his steam-yacht. He has sailed for America.' In reply to my questions, no reason was given for his going, as no one there knew, and Bugbee had not returned since the King's departure."

Featherstone folded his arms and looked at Dacre, on whom again all eyes turned. He held in one hand the royal banner, fast to the halyards, and in the other hand his watch.

At this moment the artillery trumpet heard before sounded much nearer, and it was answered, apparently, by other trumpets at different points of the camp.

" Gentlemen," said Dacre, drawing up his tall figure with superb pride, and looking calmly round the tent, " in two minutes it will be noon—the hour of our movement. Yonder rides the brave man who will proclaim the Monarchy, and it is too late now to warn him or his fellow-officers and patriots. We may draw back ; but they will go on. The world will be the witness. If the King has been false to us—and we do not know that he has—we shall be true to our cause and to ourselves."

There was a pause. Dacre's eyes were on the dial in his hand.

"Gentlemen!" he cried, as he placed the watch in his pocket, "it is twelve o'clock! Shall I raise the King's flag?"

"Ay! Up with it!" rang out the brave shout.

At that instant the noonday gun boomed, and had the Royalists listened they might have heard the rumble of artillery and the rattling of cavalry surrounding them in a vast circle. But had they heard it they would not have been stayed. To withdraw now, to sneak away from the very brink of danger, would be worse than death. They must go on to the end. The world's eyes were on them, or would be to-morrow; the world is always looking at yesterday.

Like bees from a hive they swarmed, a handful of men, from the door of the mess-tent, drawing their swords to conquer a kingdom for a king who had run away. There was a noble despair in their hearts.

"Up with the King's banner!" shouted Featherstone, and Dacre went to the mast and drew up the flag.

"God save the King!" shouted every throat, as the heavy folds went upward.

But there was a hitch in the halyards, and Dacre's excitement did not allow him to remove it quickly. The royal banner stopped on its way aloft—stopped at the half mast —and there ominously remained for a full half minute before the lines were cleared and it soared to the masthead.

On the parade-ground seven regiments of infantry had wheeled into line, and presented arms as the commander rode to the front of the brigade. When the noonday gun boomed, a thrill went through the scarlet ranks, for even the linesmen knew that a tragedy was about to be enacted. The word had been passed through the camp that the Royalist traitors would at that hour declare themselves.

Never was drama seen upon the stage in which the actors approached the tragic ending so fatuously, so deliberately.

Colonel Arundel, riding in front of the staff, halted and faced the brigade. The troops presented arms ; the band played the national anthem, '' God Save the People !'' When the music had ceased the eyes of Colonel Arundel were turned to the flag-pole at the mess-tent. His heart leaped within him when he saw the lines shake, and then, true to the moment of time, up went the flag of the King.

'' Soldiers !'' shouted the old commander, baring his white head and pointing to the royal banner ; '' behold the flag of your King and country ! King George has come to claim his own again, and he is now in personal command of this camp. God save the King !''

The whole brigade stared at the flagstaff where the big banner of King George had stopped at the half-mast like a mourning emblem. A round of suppressed laughter came from the troops—a sound that sent a shudder through the old colonel's heart, which no violent outcry could have done.

The vibration of the commander's voice was still in the air when a horseman dashed down to the head of the brigade, a man with a face of terrible power and purpose. It was Colonel Devereux. He faced the brigade like a man cast in iron, so still he sat for half a minute. He was an electric centre, reaching the eyes and nerves of every man in the brigade.

'' Present—arms !'' and the brigade sprang into motion beneath his thrilling voice.

" Men !" he said slowly, but with a force that sent his voice to both flanks of the brigade, " the command of this camp has this day been given to me by the only power on earth able to give it—the President of the British Republic."

" And I, sir—what am I ?" indignantly demanded Colonel Arundel, but in a voice too low to reach the soldiers' ears. Insulted as he was he would have no altercation in front of the troops.

" You, sir !" answered Colonel Devereux, and his voice rang like a trumpet, " you are a traitor to the people !"

While this scene was in action, an insignificant movement took place on the inner flank of one regiment in the brigade. A sergeant and six men were detached, and the squad marched at a quick step along the rear till they came to the centre, when they wheeled to the front, passed through the formation, and halted directly in front of Colonel Arundel. The grounding of their arms completed the terrible charge of the new commander.

" Soldiers," cried Colonel Devereux, turning to the brigade, " behold the death of a traitor !"

The sergeant gave the word to his men in a low voice, and seven rifles were levelled at Colonel Arundel, who sat still in his saddle, hat in hand, as he had saluted the King's flag. One swift turn of his head now and he saw the great emblazoned banner in the air ; the next moment his breast was torn to pieces, and the old man fell forward as his horse swerved, and then the body tumbled from the saddle and lay in front of the brigade.

" Colonel Gardener, take command here," said Devereux to an officer in the horror-struck staff ; " and you, gentlemen," designating three or four of the staff by a motion of his hand, " follow me." He wheeled his horse and rode straight for the mess-tent, where the royal banner was flying.

A young artillery officer, with one Gatling gun and a dozen troopers, were galloping toward the place from another direction. They reached the tent at the same moment as Colonel Devereux.

" Halt !" he shouted to the gunners, and the mounted party stopped as if turned to stone.

" Haul down that flag !" he ordered Dacre, pointing with his naked sword.

" Never !" answered Dacre, standing at the foot of the mast.

Colonel Devereux gave a stern command to the officer of the gun ; the piece was trained on the flagstaff, and next instant, with a hellish roar, its sixty bullets tore the flag-pole into shreds, and the enormous banner cumbered the wet earth.

Before the discharge Geoffrey had bodily seized Dacre and dragged him out of range. Better, perhaps, had he left him to his fate, for death at that moment, with his duty done, his sword in hand and his flag above him, would have saved him the deeper agony of shame and disappointment, which walked with him like shadows henceforward to the grave.

The officer in charge of the gun ordered his troopers and drivers to ride across the fallen banner ; and the hoofs and muddy wheels rent it to pieces and befouled it in the mire.

" You are a coward !" cried Dacre, and rushing to the front he crossed swords with the mounted officer, wounding him in the arm. Next moment he was stretched senseless on the ill-fated flag, a gunner having struck him down with the stock of his carbine.

The others yielded without a word. The artillery officer, his hand dripping blood, took their swords one by one and flung them contemptuously on the flag, beside John Dacre's senseless body.

As they were marched off, surrounded by a cavalry guard, to be taken to London, Mr. Sydney, seeing that the Duke of Bayswater could hardly keep up, gave his arm to the infirm old man.

"This is a grim joke," said Sydney; "I wonder what they will do with our friend Dacre."

"Thanks," said the poor old fellow, leaning heavily on Sydney, and putting up his collar to keep out the rain. Then he turned a last look at Dacre, still lying as he had fallen. "If he is dead, I suppose they will bury him like a Christian gentleman, as he was." And, raising his hat, the courtly old man saluted the fallen soldier.

Featherstone handed Geoffrey a cigar, and lighted one himself as the procession started.

"I wonder where King George the Fifth is about this time," he said, with a forlorn smile.

"No matter where he is," answered Geoffrey, in a voice of settled belief; "one thing is certain: Monarchy is dead forever in England—and it is time!"

CHAPTER XII.

THE news of the suppression of the conspiracy and the arrest of the ringleaders caused great excitement over England. Enormous crowds paraded the streets of London demanding the exile of all persons who had formerly borne titles. The King was hung in effigy and his lay figure cremated in the public kiln at Lincoln's Inn Fields. Socialism became rampant. ˙ A rabble of the lowest orders of the people invaded Hyde Park and the other public gardens, making day and night hideous with their orgies. The famous Albert memorial statue was blown to shivers by dynamite at high noon, and unbridled license became the watchword of the masses. Such anarchy had never been known in England. Even the government, who at first were inclined to suffer the demonstration against the Royalists to gather head, grew alarmed. Absolute revolution was imminent, and resolute measures had to be taken. Nor did the public temper cool until threescore of the most wretched of those who live in the foul dens of the great city lay dead along the streets of Kensington and Belgravia. The military were forced to shoot them down to stem the tumult.

Comparative quiet was restored at the end of ten days,

and then the government ventured to bring the prisoners
to London under a strong guard and lodge them in the
Tower.   Twenty thousand people, it is estimated, dogged
the footsteps of the troops who escorted them, and it was
only the points of bayonets and the muskets ready to deal
death at a word that secured their·safety.   The conspirators marched two and two with lancers carrying loaded
carbines on each flank.   There were sixteen in all.   John
Dacre and Geoffrey Ripon were side by side.   Neither of
them had much hope of escaping the fury of the mob.
The Duke of Bayswater and Colonel Featherstone rode a
little in advance.   The poor old duke's hat had fallen off,
and his bald head was a shining mark for missiles.   An
egg had struck his pate and made an offensive daub.

The streets through which the procession passed were
lined with spectators.   From Government House, President Bagshaw and the leading members of the party in
power looked down upon their victims, and the windows
of Whitehall across the way afforded a view to the friends
of the opposition, among whom sat Richard Lincoln and
his daughter.   The great commoner would have preferred
to avoid the spectacle, but Mary had expressed a desire to
see the prisoners on their way through the streets.   She
looked pale and stony-eyed as she sat watching for them,
and her father sighed as he observed her, for he knew her
secret.   His brow was anxious.   These were troublesome
times and a source of concern to all who loved their country.   He knew the government to be composed of men
who thought only of their own interests.   This semblance
of authority was the sole bar that prevented the insubordi-
nate masses from overriding law and decency.   How long
would President Bagshaw be able to withstand the popular

clamor for a liberty that was akin to pillage ?   This foolish conspiracy had biassed thousands of order-loving citizens against conservative measures.   His own party were reduced to a pitiful minority, and the conduct of the Royalists had caused a reaction which threatened to engulf the constitution and the laws.   And, as if that were not enough to sadden the soul of an honest man, his only daughter loved the traitor whose mad enthusiasm had precipitated these ills upon the country.

It was Mary's voice that interrupted his revery.

" They are coming, father."

Lincoln looked out, and as far as the eye could reach the streets were black with a sea of heads.   The glistening of bayonets, the waving flags, the uniforms, the mad shouts and derisive groans, and above the tumult the drums beating in full rhythm, made an exciting scene.   But all was lost upon Mary.   Her eye had singled out John Dacre, and she was gazing down at him in speechless agony.   He appeared to her wan and sick.   His clothes were torn and covered with mud.   But he bore himself as ever, erect and dignified.

As though by instinct, he looked up to the window, and their eyes met.   He raised his hat with the courtly grace of a gentleman, forgetting for an instant the situation and the consequences that may accrue to her he saluted.   The glance of the crowd followed his gesture, and many caught sight of the pale girl and beheld her throw a rose to the handsome prisoner.   It fell wide of him for whom it was meant ; indeed, he did not see the flower fall.   It dropped among the crowd, and would have been trampled in the mud beneath the feet of those who hated her lover had not Geoffrey Ripon darted from the ranks and snatched it up to his infinite peril, for the trooper at his side struck him with the butt of his carbine. ".See," he said to Dacre, who was stalking on in unconscious revery ; " see, she has thrown you a rose. Be of good cheer, man." And Geoffrey could not help thinking that if the one he loved had dropped a rose at his feet, how slight a thing his present plight would seem.

But Richard Lincoln saw her action, and, with a start of anger, he said, " That man is a traitor, Mary. And yet you are my daughter."

Those of his friends standing near had failed to notice her throw the rose, nor did they now heed the blush which mantled her face as she looked up at their leader.

" I know it, father ; but I love him," she whispered, and she would have fainted had not Lincoln supported her with his strong arms and led her from the room.

There was another also who watched the prisoners with eyes of recognition. Mrs. Oswald Carey had left her lodgings early in the morning so as to secure a good position from which to view the procession, and from a coign of vantage close by the houses of Parliament was feasting her gaze upon the victims of her treachery. A long cloak covered her figure, and her face was muffled. Only her beautiful eyes were visible. Owing to the bitter feeling prevalent against the Royalists, she feared to show herself, for she had been so intimately associated with the dissipations of the nobility, the people would have stoned her. She felt proof against discovery in her present garb, and had waited for hours, hedged about by the rabble, for a glimpse of Geoffrey Ripon.

Her revenge had been swift and equal to her expectation. Its sequel was yet to follow. As she gazed at the

face of the young man, which exposure had rather enno-
bled and made more handsome, strange feelings were
awakened within her. She scarcely knew whether she
were sorry to see him there in peril of his life, or that she
would be pleased to know that he had paid the penalty of
treason with his head. Her love and hate were so intermingled that she could not distinguish which had the upper
hand. He passed close to where she was standing. But
even had he been able to recognize her, he could not have
suspected that her perfidy was the occasion of his misfortune. She had guarded her secret carefully. President
Bagshaw had been true to his word. No rumor of the
means by which the conspiracy was unearthed had reached
the public ear.

As she made her way home through the crowded street
after the procession had passed, reflection as to what would
be Geoffrey's fate absorbed her thoughts. In the present
state of the public temper it was not likely that he would
escape death. To be shot for high treason seemed the
logical sequel to his escapade. Well, if it must be so, she
preferred to see him on the scaffold rather than in the arms
of another. She would wait until all was over, and then
find in America solace for her disappointment. She had
played her cards well. The King was madly in love with
her, and she had no fear of his sailing away without her.
If so, there was Jawkins still. She had lulled the manager
into such a feeling of security that he had run up to Scot-
land to undertake an important contract. An American
billionaire, having rented the Trossachs for the season,
had engaged him to superintend his arrangements. Titled
people were at a premium since the discovery of the conspiracy, and Jawkins could command his own prices. His

reply to this patron, " I will provide you with a pair of peers if I have to filch them from prison, but they come high," was illustrative alike of the energy and the business sagacity of the man. The poor old Archbishop of Canterbury, who had escaped from Aldershot scot free, was being hurried from one corner of England to the other to supply dinner requirements. Jawkins had caused her some trouble at first, it is true. Upon the receipt of her telegram at Ripon House he had hurried up to London, and ferreting out her lodgings accused her of wishing to give him the slip. She had assuaged his feelings by lunching with him at a public restaurant and permitting him to engage their passages to America for a fortnight later. Had it not been for the King's arrival she would have kept faith with him.

The trial of the prisoners was set down for one week after their consignment to the Tower. It was to take place in the House of Parliament, and the indictment against all was for high treason. The attorney-general, James McPherson, was to conduct the case for the government, and the accused retained the services of Calhoun Benjamin, a great-grandson of the Benjamin for some time a famous lawyer in the reign of Victoria. It was not permissible for any member of either house to appear as counsel. The constitution required that the joint bodies should adjudge the cause. Still, after the formal arguments any member was at liberty to rise to a question of privilege and address the assembly. Such was indeed the usual custom.

Mary Lincoln doubtless had this in mind when she whispered to her father the evening before the trial, " You will speak for him, will you not, father ?"

" I cannot tell," said Richard Lincoln. " Why should

I, Mary? His desert is death, and I should not know what to say in his behalf.''

"But if all of us were treated according to our deserts, how few of us would escape scathing. Only you, father; I know of no one beside.''

The patriot looked down at the pale girl sitting at his feet and stroked her hair. Her eyes were filled with tears, and she gazed at him imploringly. He knew her secret to the uttermost now. She had told him, all the evening of that dreadful day when London saw her throw down a rose to her country's traitor. Still, if it were to do again, would she not do it? Her love was stronger than her sense of shame.

Richard Lincoln sat and gazed into the fire. These were indeed troublesome times, but a light seemed breaking just below where the clouds lowered darkest. A week had seen a great change in public sentiment. Debate in Parliament had been fierce and bitter. At the head of his party he had striven to show that those who held the reins of power abused and deceived the masses, and that true liberty lay not in ignorant usurpation of right, but intelligent recognition of a lawfully constituted authority which regarded all alike. At first his purpose had been misinterpreted, but as by degrees the true significance of his words were grasped by the popular mind, groans gave place to silence, and sullenness to cheers. He had not hesitated to wield the axe of reform with a yeoman's hand, and the flying chips told of the havoc he was making among the dead wood of ignorance and craft. It was his aim to demonstrate that a demagogue in the seat of power is no less a menace to the happiness of the people than an aristocrat.

Yet in the face of his triumph arose the shadow of this strange, unnatural love ; for it seemed unnatural to him that his only child should have given her heart to one whose ambition it was to destroy that which he had helped to establish and bring back the frippery of an unhallowed past. He had found it difficult at first to conceive it as possible, but her confession, and more eloquently still her pallid cheeks, left no room to question the truth of this misfortune. And to-morrow he would be called upon to doom to the scaffold the man whose being had become so much a part of hers as to have led her to play the traitor also. As thus he pondered the breaking light seemed to fade from the sky, and the clouds lowered gloomy and impenetrable.

"Father," said Mary again, "I am sure you can save him."

Lincoln shook his head. "Not even if I would, girl," he replied, sternly.

"You, too, desert me," she murmured. She covered her face with her hands for a moment, then with a sudden impulse she stood, tall and resolute. Her eyes flashed fire. "If it is wrong to love a traitor, let it be so. I cannot help loving John Dacre, and I should like to die with him."

Richard Lincoln gazed at her in amazement. There was pride, too, in his glance. He saw in her transfigured face a repetition of his own youth when the spirit soared impatient of restraint and knew not yet the curbs that check the extravagance of ardent natures. In those early days he had struck out for the ideal right, even as her heart in the fulness of its love poured out its tide of passion. He held out his hands to her, and his lips trembled.

" My child, my child ! would to God I could save your
lover. You are dearer to me than all the world beside.
Do not spurn your father's arms. His breast is your
rightful place for comfort now."

She suffered him to clasp her in his embrace. " I will
be brave," she whispered, looking up into his eyes.
" Kiss me ; I will be brave, and—and when he dies let me
die, too."

" My child !" murmured Lincoln again, and there was
terror as well as pity in his tone. He held her close, and
her head rested on his shoulder. " All may yet be well,
my dear one," he said tenderly.

Before daybreak the next morning a stream of people
was pouring up from the city and winding its way through
Cheapside and Fleet Street and the Strand to the judgment
hall in the Houses of Parliament. By the time the guard
from the Tower reached Westminster, vast multitudes lined
the sidewalks and formed so dense a mass in the square in
front of the gates that progress was well-nigh impossible.
The populace was orderly, however, and fell back before
the horses of a troop of cavalry, with no further demonstration than a sullen murmur.

The prisoners were brought before the bar of the Commons, and the Upper House entered immediately after to
take their seats. It was an impressive scene. One might
have heard a pin drop as the officer of the Crown rose to
read the indictment, and again when, as he sat down, the
hoarse voice of the clerk called out the names of the
accused, shorn of all titles, to rise and answer to the charge
of high treason against the Republic of Great Britain and
Ireland.

" What say you, John Dacre—guilty or not guilty ?"

" Not guilty."

Dacre's glance moved gravely around the vast hall and met the gaze of a thousand eyes without flinching. Fate willed that it should distinguish a pale, lovely face amid the press that lined the galleries, and linger thereon a moment as though loath to turn aside ; but even while he gazed, the drapery and shoulder of another woman were interposed between his sight and the delicate features of Mary Lincoln, and shut her from his view. " What say you, Geoffrey Ripon ? Are you guilty or not guilty ?"

It was these words that had caused the stranger to lean forward and crane her neck—a beautiful neck that, muffled as she was, did not wholly escape the admiration of her neighbors. Her eyes sparkled with a light cold and malicious as the gleam which emanates from a blade of steel. As the lips of young Geoffrey Ripon flung back a clear denial of the charge, a hope was in his heart that the sweet maiden of his fancy might be among the hundreds looking down. She was not there, but her rival, Mrs. Oswald Carey, sat and watched each shade of his expression.

And now the witnesses were summoned and confronted the prisoners. The proofs were ample and overwhelming. It almost seemed mistrusting the intelligence of the judges to dwell upon the evidence, to quote the opening words of the attorney-general, and as a consequence the argument of that official was a model of conciseness. Then the time was come for the defendants' counsel. Mr. Benjamin arose and spoke for an hour. His speech was painstaking, but not particularly impressive. In conclusion he said that rebellion had often been punished before without the shedding of blood. He instanced Jefferson Davis, the great Secessionist, and the clemency of the American peo-

ple. Mr. McPherson in reply adduced the Irish rebels
executed by the government of Victoria, and thereat a
shout arose which shook the walls of Parliament and was
echoed by the crowd outside. Even the prisoners glanced
at each other with downcast looks. The perspiration stood
out in beads on the bald head of the Duke of Bayswater.

" It is all up with us," whispered Ripon to Dacre.

" My God and my King ! It is a noble cause to die
for," answered the cavalier, and his proud face looked
beatified.

There was a dread and awful silence as the attorney-
general finished his last words. The hour for judgment
had arrived, unless it were that some senator or commoner
wished to speak for or against the prisoners. A bitter and
illiterate friend of the government saw fit to spring to his
feet and enter upon a violent harangue. Clemency would
be misplaced in the present juncture, he said. Death for
one and all was the proper measure to be meted out to
Royalists and traitors. His truculent words seemed to
please the audience, and he sat down amid a tempest of
applause. For an instant there was no movement on
either side of the house, and then Richard Lincoln, the
leader of the opposition, arose and stepped out into the
aisle, so as to command his hearers. A flutter of expectation, a murmur of surprise, spread through the assembly,
and as he opened his mouth to speak, every ear was alert
to catch his words.

" I rise," he said, " to speak for the people, the great,
true-souled people. They have, it seems to me, no representative here, or I have failed to interpret aright the language of my predecessor. Are the people merciless ?
Have they no heart ? I know that the contrary is true.

It is no argument with them that others have preferred cruelty to mercy, and vengeance to justice. I stand here to-day, for the people and for justice.''

He paused, and as no sound expressed one way or the other the feelings of his auditors, he spoke once more :

'' Let these men live. Fine or imprisonment will accomplish all that you desire, save the satisfaction of revenge. Capital punishment in this age of the world is an ugly smear upon the escutcheon of constitutional liberty. Let these men live, and your children's children will write you down in their books as worthy of remembrance. They are guilty, but blood will not atone for wrong-doing. Let them live, I say, in the name of justice and the people.''

He finished and sat down. Not much of a speech in the way of argument, some will say. It is the manner more than the matter of words that sways men's hearts. No cheers were heard, it is true, but his hearers sat upon the benches thoughtful and silent. The Speaker of the House glanced about him, but no one rose to contradict the testimony that had fallen from the lips of Richard Lincoln.

And now the judges arose and left the hall. For four hours the assembly and the crowds in the streets waited in patience. Before the fifth had elapsed the usher's rod announced that a verdict had been reached. The silence was breathless. The Speaker took the scroll from the hands of William Peters, the leader of the House, and read aloud that John Dacre, as the master spirit of the late rebellion at Aldershot, was sentenced to be shot to death at noon of the next day, and that all the other leaders were to be imprisoned for the term of fifteen years.

There was a roar and a rush as the people rose to escape

from the galleries, and few observed a slender girl slip from her seat to the floor.   A woman with beautiful eyes, whose face was otherwise veiled from view, stooped to her succor, then gave a shrill cry.   Mary Lincoln lay lifeless. Mrs. Oswald Carey, whose shriek it was that made this known, was not one to believe that a woman can die of a broken heart.   But if even such a result of her treachery had been foreshadowed to her, she would not have faltered.

CHAPTER XIII.

AN UNFINISHED TASK.

IMMEDIATELY after the sentence was pronounced the prisoners were led back to the Tower. They were chained together by twos, and Sir John walked with Geoffrey. During the entire walk from St. Stephen's, along the river embankment, neither of them spoke to the other. For Geoffrey, at least, it was a subject of life-long regret that he had not done so.

It was part of the policy of Bagshaw's government thus to march them through the streets, a spectacle, like a caravan of caged beasts, for the populace. Geoffrey thought to himself, curiously, of the old triumphs of the Roman emperors he had read about as a schoolboy. Then, as now, the people needed bread and loved a show. But the people, even then, had caught something of the dignity of power. Silently they pressed upon the sidewalks and thronged the gardens by the river. Not a voice was raised in mockery of these few men ; there is something in the last extremity of misfortune which commands respect, even from the multitude. And, perhaps, even then the first-fruits of freedom might have been marked in their manner, and magnanimity, the first virtue of liberty, kept the London rabble hushed.

Geoffrey's eyes were turned within as he walked, as if he were thinking, but of thoughts far distant, far back in the past. Dacre held his glance still high and forward, fixed and straight upon the road before him. Only once, when they passed the Temple gardens, did Geoffrey's eyes stray outward ; it was when he marked the windows of his old study in the Inner Temple, where he had studied to be a barrister in days gone by ; then his look grew introspective as before.

When they came to the gate of the Tower the soldiers divided and drew apart in two lines, between which the prisoners passed into the great courtyard. A squad of the Tower garrison—no longer in the gay livery of the King, but in the plain black coat and helmet of policemen—stood before the door. The banner of the British Republic—the red and white stripes, with the green union and the harp—floated over the loftiest tower of all. The prisoners were then separated, and each was led to a different cell. Then for the first time Geoffrey thought of Dacre ; but he was already under a special escort and being led away ; it was too late. The last that Geoffrey saw of him he was walking erect, with his silent lips still closed, steady like the course of some strong stream above the fall. As he watched him, Geoffrey heard the distant murmur of the people beyond the gates.

Geoffrey well remembered the room that was his prison. He had been taken there as a sightseer when a child. It was in the Beauchamp Tower ; and—strange coincidence—there was the bear and ragged staff of Warwick, still visible, cut deep into the old stone walls.

So, thought he, it had all ended. History repeats itself, but in strange new forms that seem as if they half mock, half follow, the old. Then, the King was wrong; was now the people in the right? They brought him some food; and after eating he threw himself on the ground and tried to sleep. But his sleep was troubled with his dreams of waking: now he heard Margaret Windsor's broken words again; now he was in the great hall of St. Stephen's speaking; then he heard again the echo of the gun that shot down the royal flag, and then the silence of the people, forever estranged, more dread, more terrible than any words of enemies or noise of battle. Again he thought of Dacre and his look when all was lost: a look unchanged, unmoved; a look less of despair than the majesty of certain fate—a fate not new nor sudden, but chosen of his own calm will. A man of stone, thought Geoffrey; the incarnation of one thought; hardly human in his conscious strength. And yet, as Geoffrey saw him in the darkness of the night, his heart went out to him, and he felt that he loved this man as he had never loved a friend before.

The dawn came, and its gray damp breath broke through the iron bars. It seemed all unreal in the daylight. Old stories of escape passed through his mind: how men, in childish stories of history or romance, with some rude instrument of iron, had carved their will and way through walls as thick as these. But how idle they seemed! How futile, how vain to make with his two hands a way through stone, or burrow like a mole into the earth! And yet those legends seemed no less a dream than this of his.

There was a strange silence as the morning grew on; he wondered if the world outside were all asleep. He had foreseen it; and yet he had not quite foreseen this; some glorious end, in a battle, perhaps, fighting out in the free country, beneath the sun. Again his thoughts turned to his friend, and he felt a strange assurance that Dacre had foreseen it all along, but not held back his steps one whit for that. And there was Maggie—in America—could she, and her life, be in the same world with this? Yet it was natural enough, and such things had always been, only he had never truly pictured them. The day seemed endless. If he could only hear something of the others, and not be so terribly alone. If he could but learn where they were— where Dacre was. He heard a dull sound like the noise of distant firing, but more like thunder, coming heavily through the ground. Geoffrey ran to the window, drew himself up, and looked out through the bars. There was a sea of upturned faces, all pale and with one fixed look, a myriad times repeated, pointed to the base of the Tower below his window where he could not see. Then he fell back upon the ground, burying his face in his hands.

Dacre himself had slept that night a dreamless sleep, as he had slept any night before in the years since he had seen his path and chosen it. At noon the people came to his cell and led him out. Numbers of men were standing in the corridor and on the stairs ; he looked on between the lines and walked to the door. Then he begged that his handcuffs might be removed. As he paused a moment, Richard Lincoln stepped forward and ordered that it should be done. Then he fell back, bowing once to Dacre. Richard Lincoln had come there from the death-bed of his daughter to do this last service to the man that she loved. Then Dacre passed on, out of the great door into the full light of the noon. There in front of him was a great concourse of people, the multitude Geoffrey had seen from his window. Dacre looked out from the prison gate with his fixed, clear eyes, but the road was growing very short before him now, and still his glance went on beyond—beyond the company of soldiers standing thirty yards in front, the butts of their rifles resting on the ground.

"John Dacre, you are found guilty of high treason to the people. Have you anything to say?" It was Bagshaw, the President, who spoke, in his capacity as general of the army.

Dacre made no reply. He was thinking of the treason of his King, and not of his own. And there in front of him were the people—the people, in might of numbers, in the majesty of strength, ten thousand to his one. But as he looked upon them their ten thousand faces were turned on his, their hearts within their eyes ; and Dacre might have noted that in all of them there was not one but spoke pity—pity, in their silence, for himself. Then he turned aside from the door, with his back to the prison wall. " I am ready."

" John Dacre—you have nothing to say?" said the President again. " You may yet save yourself. Where is the King?" Dacre turned his glance upon him, slowly.

" I am ready," said he again. He seemed to overlook the President as he spoke, and he never looked at him again.

"Give the order to make ready!" said Bagshaw, angrily, to the officer in command, and the slight click of the rifles followed his words.

The narrow courtyard was as still as if deserted, though it seemed you could almost hear the breathing of the multitude that thronged the streets. But to die thus, penned in a narrow courtyard, passively, vainly, shot like a dog.

A low murmur began to come from the people, indeter-
minate, inarticulate ; it came to Dacre's ears like the hum
of distant battle, and perhaps he saw the battle, and the
royal standard, and that last unworthy King for whom this
thing was done. Then came Bagshaw's voice again :
" Where is the King ?"

" Silence, sir !" thundered Richard Lincoln, and Bagshaw slunk back a pace or two, like a chidden dog.

" The King is dead," said Dacre, so clearly that all the
people in the street heard him, but no one made a sound.
Then he threw back his coat, as if to bare his breast to the
levelled muskets ; and as he did so the withered rose dropped
out and fell into his hand. It was Mary Lincoln's rose
that he had thrust there on the day before. And as he
looked at it the false bonds of his faith fell from him like
the fetters of a dream, and he looked upon the multitude
and saw that theirs was the right, and he knew that his life
was thrown away ; then first he remembered she had loved
him, and he saw what might have been. He saw the poor
image of a king--the King who had deserted his own cause
and left him in his loyalty alone ; he saw the throng of
humanity standing silent there before him, and the sweetness and the virtue of the life which he had put behind.
Then for the first time his firm lips trembled, as he lifted
the poor rose to his lips, and kissed it once, in memory of
her whom he was leaving, as he thought. But Mary
Lincoln was dead ; and as he turned his face upward, he
seemed to see some vision in the sky, and they say that a
great glory shone into his face.

" Fire !" came the word, and the sheet of flame leaped
out toward him, and he fell ; and the rose-leaves, scattered
by a bullet, lay about him on the stones.

CHAPTER XIV.

GEOFFREY's jailers were lenient to him after that first day. He was removed to a room with carpet and furniture ; his table was well served ; he was allowed to walk about in the courtyards ; books and pen and ink were given him— everything but newspapers. The fact was that Bagshaw felt he had gone too far. The vindictiveness, the cruelty of the populace, was already a thing of the past—of that past when they had not yet learned their power. The people were good-natured, impressionable, forgiving ; and that low murmur from the street on the day of Dacre's execution, the third time the President had sought to make his prisoner betray the King, had well-nigh driven Bagshaw from his office. It was Richard Lincoln who had saved the government that day, by his stern rebuke to the President ; the latter liked him none the better for that.

Geoffrey felt this change of sentiment in the manner of his keepers ; and when he remembered that first terrible day, it was but to hope that his fears had been exaggerated. Undoubtedly John's sentence would be commuted to imprisonment like his own.

But the more convinced Geoffrey became of this, the more his mind turned to the other persons of those event-

ful days. The King had not come—that was the grim fact
—the King had not come to claim his own ; had left his
honest gentlemen to fight or fall without him ; and no
one, even now, could tell how different the event might
have been that day had George the Fifth but proved his
own cause worth defending. Geoffrey, Dacre, none of
them had had news of the King since the day of Aldershot.
Up to the very stroke of noon, as Geoffrey remembered,
Dacre had expected him. But they had waited in vain.
And now the White Horse of Hanover, and with that the
Norman Leopard, was a thing of the past. From his
window Geoffrey could see the red, white, and green
tricolor in the Tower yard. He inclined to think the
King was dead.

Geoffrey had never been by conviction a Legitimist ;
hardly even had he been one by affection. Dacre's mag-
netism, Dacre's nobility of purpose had overcome his
earlier judgment ; for the one effort he had lent his life to
his friend, to stake on a cast of the die. Now that they
had fairly thrown and lost, he returned to his former judgment. But with the cause that they had lost had gone his
own future.

He did not care so much for this, since that last scene
with Margaret Windsor. What future was there for him
now ? Stone walls do not a prison make ; he might as
well be here as penned up, useless, in his four acres about
the lodge at Ripon House. His friends—what friends had
he ? Dacre, Sydney, Featherstone—they were walled up
with him. And Geoffrey, walking in the Tower yard,
would look up to the scattered windows, and wonder
which of them was his friend's ; and if he noticed a dull
red stain on the stones at the base of the wall, he thought

it was some old mark, dating from Cromwell or the Roses. Still, Geoffrey was a young man, too young to have wholly learned to be a fatalist ; but the more he thought of escape, the more hopeless it seemed.   With a confederate, a friend outside, it might perhaps be possible.   But what friend had he left in the wide world ?   Geoffrey racked his memory to think of one.   There were some two hundred men he knew at his club in the West End—but which one of these, who had not been at Aldershot, would leave his snug rubber at whist for the Tower ?   There was Jawkins—if Jawkins could be brought to think it worth his while.   Mr. Windsor—the shrewd American was with his daughter in America ; and the daughter deemed him false, and had forgotten him.   False !   There was Eleanor Carey ; she had loved him ; would she not seek to save him ?   The woman whose maidenhood he had loved ? He had not heard of her since the night before Aldershot ; but this was rather a hopeful sign than otherwise.   The more Geoffrey thought, the more he felt assured that here was the one person in the world that might be trusted to remember him.

So, when Geoffrey had been in prison some three weeks, and one day the turnkey came and said that some one wished to see him, Geoffrey thought of Mrs. Carey at once.   His heart beat high with hope as he followed his guide through a labyrinth of stairs and passages.   He even forgot to look closely at each door, as he was used to do, to find some sign of Dacre or his friends.   Eleanor ! was on his lips to cry as the jailer opened the door of a distant room and bade him enter.

In the centre, by a table, was standing an old man, dressed in black, with a white head bent well forward upon his shoulders. It was Reynolds, no longer dressed like a servant, but disguised in a suit of broadcloth, such as was worn until recently by the oldest gentlemen. The old man bent still lower, took Geoffrey's hand and kissed it.

"Thank God!" said he, in a whisper, "dear young master, you are alive, at all events." Reynolds still used old-fashioned forms of speech.

It was a strange thing to Geoffrey to be still called young. He felt as if he had seen a century at least—the twentieth. He looked at Reynolds with a slight but de-- cided feeling of disappointment. He had hoped for Mrs. Carey.

"Yes, Reynolds, I am alive, and glad to see you," he added, as he saw the tears in the old man's eyes. "Sit down." Geoffrey pushed a chair toward him; but the old man would as soon have thought of sitting down in the presence of the King. "And how is Ripon House?"

"Ripon House, your lordship, is much the same. I think I may succeed in letting it to one of your lordship's old tenants." Geoffrey looked up, surprised; then he remembered that by Ripon House Reynolds meant the lodge. "With your lordship's permission I can get thirty guineas a year for it," Reynolds added.

"By all means, Reynolds," said Geoffrey. "But, Reynolds, I must have no 'your lordship' any more. That is done forever. I was foolish ever to have consented to it."

"Yes, ·your lordship," replied Reynolds, simply. "I knew your lordship would consent, so I have brought the first quarter's rent in advance." And the old man laid eight five-dollar gold pieces on the table. Geoffrey grasped his hand.

"Thank you, Reynolds," said he. The old man was more embarrassed than if he had kissed him.

"Your lordship—your lordship is—" Reynolds stammered, and Geoffrey interrupted him.

"None of that, remember;" he lifted a finger pleasantly. "But I asked you about Ripon House."

"The old castle (it was not half so old as the lodge) is shut up, earl," said he. "The American is in his own country."

"Reynolds, do you know what became of the King?"

"No, your lord—Earl Brompton."

"Or who it was that betrayed us? Some one must have carried all the particulars of the plan to Bagshaw."

The old man did not answer for a moment.

"Reynolds, have you seen Dacre?"

The question was sudden. "Does—does not your lordship know—" he faltered. Geoffrey sprang from his chair.

"They shot him."

Geoffrey sank back to his seat. The old servant walked to the window, pulling out his handkerchief. Outside was heard the measured step of the turnkey pacing to and fro.

"Reynolds, will you carry a letter for me?" said Geoffrey at last. "Think before you answer. You are no longer in my service, you know. I can no longer pay you."

"I am always in the earl's service," Reynolds interrupted.

"Thank you, Reynolds. The letter is to Mrs. Oswald Carey. You remember her?"

Reynolds started. "Forgive me, earl—but does your

—your honor know—'' The old man spoke in much trouble ; Geoffrey looked up in amazement.

'' Oh, forgive me, Earl Brompton—but—I once told a lie to you. That night—you remember that night when Sir John met your lordship in his room, and I said afterward there had been no one there ?''

'' Yes,'' said Geoffrey. '' What then ?''

'' There was some one there. A lady was there. Mrs. Carey.''

A terrible light broke upon Geoffrey. It was she that had taken the paper ; it was she that was the traitor who had been the cause of Dacre's death. And his old love for her had killed his friend.

'' There is no one left''—the words broke from his lips with a sob—'' no one but you, Reynolds.'' He groaned aloud with rage and sorrow as he saw the part this woman had played. She had come between him and the girl he loved ; she had betrayed the loyal cause ; she had struck down Dacre, with her lying lips, her lovely eyes. And he had almost loved her.

'' I have a message for your honor.'' Reynolds spoke humbly, timidly, as if his master blamed him. '' The young American lady—Miss Windsor—before they went away, she desired me to write to her.''

Geoffrey looked up, as if a ray of light had entered the prison window. '' Wait,'' he said, simply. The old man stood at the window, while Geoffrey drew a chair to the table, sat down, and tried to write. Many a letter was begun, half finished, and then torn into fragments. When at last a note was done and sealed, Geoffrey turned to Reynolds.

'' You will send it to her ?''

" I will take it to her in America," said the old man ;
and he hastily thrust the note into the breast of his coat, as
the turnkey entered. Geoffrey thrust one of the gold
pieces into the jailer's hand as he led him away.

" You will be taken to Dartmoor Prison to-morrow,"
said the jailer, as if in reply. Geoffrey looked over his
shoulder to see if Reynolds heard ; but the old man was
busy in buttoning up his coat, and did not look his way.

The day after these occurrences the French mail steamer,
putting in at Cork Harbor, took on board several passengers. Among them was old Reynolds. It was Christmas
week, and the ship was full of Americans, running home
for the holidays, with the usual retinue of English and
French servants, among whom Reynolds passed unnoticed.
There were but two people in all the West that Reynolds
cared to see ; in Maggie Windsor and her father the old
man had a strange confidence ; but as for these people,
their evident prosperity made him sorrowful, their wealth
offended him.

As he sat upon the deck that evening, his old cloak
drawn about his shoulders, a lady passed up and down
before him, arm-in-arm with a gentleman whom he had
never seen. There was a grace, a certain sinuous strength
about the woman's figure that was strangely familiar to
him. He tried to think where he had seen such a form
before ; and, do what he would, his memory would not
stray from the library in the old lodge at Ripon House.
The man with her was middle-aged, or perhaps a little
older ; he had a red beard of some three weeks' growth,
not long enough to hide the contour of his fat double
chin. His small eyes had a way of turning rapidly about,
but not resting anywhere, as if he feared a steady glance

might lead some one to recognize him. Reynolds wondered who he was.

The night was mild for the season, and there was a
bright moon. All the other passengers were below in the
cabins, the sea was calm, and the strains of an orchestra
were heard from the great saloon, where the passengers
were dancing. There was an electric light behind where
Reynolds sat, and pulling the evening paper from his
pocket he tried to read. He had his own reasons for not
caring to go below ; apparently so had the other two, for
they still walked the deck in front of him. Once, as
they passed him, they stopped for a moment, and the
light fell full upon the woman's face. It was Mrs.
Carey.

The paper fell from the old man's hands. Their eyes
met for a moment, then the woman turned away.

Reynolds was thunderstruck. Could that be Mr. Carey
with her ? he thought. He had never seen Carey, but he
fancied not. Her husband must be a younger man.
Reynolds hoped she had not recognized him. He hated
the woman now ; he felt a fear of her, well grounded, after
all that had happened.

For several days after this the weather was bad, and Mrs.
Carey came on deck without her companion. Reynolds
avoided her, and she did not seem to notice him. Yet she
had a fascination for him, and he would slyly watch her
from the corners of his eyes, as one looks upon some brilliant serpent. This was the woman who had wrecked his
master's life—who had betrayed the King. Reynolds
wondered where the King was then. He fancied, with
Geoffrey, that he must be dead.

On the fourth day they made the lightship anchored off

the Banks, and stopped for news and letters. Reynolds
bought a paper ; Mrs. Carey had a telegram, which he saw
her reading with evident interest.   His newspaper, which
was a mere résumé of the telegrams received in the ocean
station, had a long despatch about the so-called meeting at
Aldershot.   It said that George of Hanover was believed
to have fled to America, but that it was not the policy of
the government to pursue him.

"You seem interested in your paper, Mr. Reynolds,"
said a voice at his shoulder.   The old servant stood up,
and touched his hat, from habit.   It was Mrs. Carey.   She
was dressed coquettishly in a sea-green travelling dress
that showed her beautiful figure at its best ; her hair was
coiled above her fair neck in two glossy red-brown bands.
Reynolds looked into her deep eyes and hated her.   He
cared more for his master than for any woman's eyes.
"How did you leave poor Ripon ?" she asked.

"My master is in Dartmoor Prison," said Reynolds,
sadly.

"Your master is a crazy fool," said the beautiful
woman, spitefully.   Reynolds made as if to go, but she
detained him.   "Why are you going to America ?"

"I have a message from Lord Brompton to the King,"
said Reynolds.

For fear that she might in some way thwart him, he did
not tell her his real errand.

Mrs. Carey laughed scornfully.   "No need to go so
far," said she, and she beckoned with her hand.   The
stout man with the reddish beard came up, like some huge,
dull animal called by its mistress.   His sensuous, fat face
was pallid with seasickness, and as he looked at Mrs.
Carey there was a senile leer in his eye.

" King George," said she, " this is a servant of Lord
B·ompton's."

The decks were almost deserted, and no one was near
enough to overhear them.

The old man's mouth opened ; but he could only stare
vacantly.　He stammered some incoherent syllables, and
tried to bend his knees, but they knocked together, trembling.　He doffed his hat, and, with the sea-breeze blow-
ing his thin white hair about his temples, stood looking at
the King.

" I am sorry for your master," said the man with the
beard.　" But—it was useless.　Was it not useless, my
dear ?" he added, turning to Mrs. Carey.

She laughed contemptuously, but made no reply, and
the two resumed their promenade upon the deck.　Reynolds watched them a long time sadly.　She seemed to
have complete control over the man, and Reynolds noticed
that he even brought her a footstool, when she sat upon
her sea-chair upon the deck.　No one among the passengers seemed to know him or notice him ; but many an
admiring glance was turned upon Mrs. Carey.　" Curse
the jade !" said Reynolds to himself.　Now, indeed, he
saw that it was all true, and felt for the first time that his
master .would never come back to Ripon House.　But he
could not understand it.　To say that the sun fell from the
heavens would be but a poor simile to describe the effect
this interview produced on the old man's mind.　He sat
like one dazed through the rest of the voyage.　And King
George, passing him, saw the old man sitting there, and
felt ashamed, abased, before the look of the old servant.
Only Mrs. Carey had a proud sparkle in her evil eyes, and
gloated in spirit at the message that the man would take to

his master back in England. And when, on the fifth day, they landed in Boston, she got into a carriage and drove off with the King, and Reynolds saw her wave her jewelled hand at him from the window.

He himself asked for the house of Mr. Abraham Windsor. Mr. Windsor, like most rich Americans, had a winter house in Boston, a plantation in Florida, a palace in Mexico, a shooting-box in the mountains of Montana, and other arrangements for circumventing the American climate ; and Reynolds was driven to a great stone house, with court and gardens, fronting on a park. He asked for Miss Windsor ; the servant looked at him curiously, but bade him wait.

Reynolds was tired with the voyage and the bustle and hurry of arriving ; and this great city, this great America, so fine, so bright, so rich, made him sad and depressed. What likelihood was there, he thought, that this gay, luxurious American would think or care for his poor master over in Dartmoor Jail ? But, as he looked up, he started with astonishment. Hung upon the wall was a water-color, beautifully done, of the great avenue leading up to Ripon House. He heard a rustle at the door, and, turning hastily around, he saw Miss Windsor. She was more beautiful than the other, was his first thought ; and making a step forward, he bowed humbly, not daring to take the hand she frankly extended to him.

" Mr. Reynolds !" she said, sweetly. " I am so glad to see you !" This was well—she remembered him, at all events ; and, therefore, his master.

" My lady," said he respectfully, " I have made bold to bring you a letter—from England."

"From England?" she said, feigning surprise; but a quick blush mantled her cheek.

"From the Tower of London," said Reynolds, gravely.

"From the Tower?" she cried; "is—is your master in prison?"

"My master is now in Dartmoor Prison, if it please you, my lady," said Reynolds. "He was sentenced for fifteen years—for trying to serve the King."

He drew forth the letter, carefully wrapped in a double envelope. She took it from him quickly, and tore the covering open. This is what she read:

"MY DEAR MISS WINDSOR: When I see you again—as I hope, if the fates so will, I may—you, I hope, will be married, and I shall be getting to be an old man. Fifteen years is much to take from the sunny part of a man's life; and I can hardly look for much but shadow after that. I have thought much of you, since I have been here, and of our last meeting. And I have but one thing to tell you—what, perhaps, it would have been better for me to have told you long since—and to ask for your forgiveness for myself. I should not like to think that you were thinking ill of me, all these years that I am to stay within these walls.

"Eleanor Carey—at whose feet, as I now know, you must have seen me that day at Chichester—was the woman I loved when she was a young girl, beautiful, as you know; lovely, as I then thought. She was Eleanor Leigh then. Eleanor Carey pretended on that day that she had never ceased to love me. My noble friend John Dacre had formed a plot to restore the King of England, and this woman was one of us. It was she who made a breach between us that day. It was she who went the morning before to my house, and, overhearing Dacre's talk to me, stole a paper containing the names and plan of our conspiracy. It was she who of all our friends was the only traitor. She murdered my dear friend as truly as if it had been her hand that dealt the blow. He was shot in the Tower court below here, with his back to the wall, by a company of soldiers. And, as I now believe, it was Eleanor Carey who in some way met the King, and kept him from us on that day.

"I tell you all this that you may believe, in spite of all you may have seen that day at Chichester, Eleanor Carey is not the woman I love.   You did not believe this at Ripon House.   Margaret, will you believe it now?

"Yours, forever,
"GEOFFREY RIPON."

"Fifteen years!" said Maggie, meditatively, after she had read the letter, with varying waves of white and red in her face, not unremarked by Reynolds, as he stood with his hat in his two hands.

"Fifteen years!   Papa!"

The door of an adjoining room opened, and Mr. Windsor appeared.

"Yes, my dear."

"Papa, this is Mr. Reynolds."

"Mr. Reynolds, I am very happy to make your acquaintance."

"Mr. Reynolds was Lord Brompton's servant—at Ripon, you remember?"

"Oh! Reynolds, I am glad to see you."

"That will do, Reynolds; you can go."

"Papa, I have a commission for you in England."

Reynolds's face fell.   "Any—any message for my master, my lady?"

"No.   Oh—stop—yes.   You may tell him," said Maggie, with a heightened color, smiling, "you may tell him I am about to be married."

CHAPTER XV.

LOVE LAUGHS AT LOCKSMITHS.

IN the centre of its wide waste of barren hills, huge granite outcroppings and swampy valleys, the gloomy prison of Dartmoor stood wrapped in mist one dismal morning in the March following the Royalist outbreak. Its two centuries of unloved existence in the midst of a wild land and fitful climate had seared every wall-tower and gateway with lines and patches of decay and discoloration. Originally built of brown stone, the years had deepened the tint almost to blackness in the larger stretches of outer wall and unwindowed gable.

On this morning the dark walls dripped with the weeping atmosphere, and the voice of the huge prison bell in the main yard sounded distant and strange like a storm-bell in a fog at sea.

Through the thick drizzle of the early morning the convicts were marched in gangs to their daily tasks, some to build new walls within the prison precincts, some to break stone in the round yard, encircled by enormous iron railings fifteen feet high, some to the great kitchen of the prison and to the different workshops. About one third of the prisoners marched outside the walls by the lower entrance, for the prison stands on a hill, at the foot of which stretches the most forsaken and grisly waste in all Dartmoor.

The task of the convicts for two hundred years had been the reclamation of this wide waste, which was called " The Farm." The French prisoners of war taken in the Napoleonic wars that ended with Waterloo had dug trenches to drain the waste. The American prisoners of the War of 1812 had laid roadways through the marsh. The Irish rebels of six generations had toiled in the tear-scalded footsteps of the French and American captives. And all the time the main or "stock" supply of English criminals, numbering usually about four hundred men, had spent their weary years in toiling and broiling at " The Farm."

Standing at the lower gate of the prison, from which a steep road descended to the marsh looking over " The Farm," it was hard to see anything like a fair return for such continued and patient labor. Deep trenches filled with claret-colored water drained innumerable patches of sickly vegetation. About a hundred stunted fruit trees and as many bedraggled haystacks were all that broke the surface line.

As the gangs of convicts, numbering about twenty each, marched out of the lower gate on this dull morning, they turned their eyes, each gang in the same surprised way as that which preceded, on a small group of men who were working just outside the prison wall.

To the left of the gate, on the sloping side of the hill, was a quadrangular space of about thirty by twenty yards, round which was built a low wall of evidently great antiquity. The few courses of stones were huge granite boulders and slabs torn and rolled from the hillside. There was no gateway or break in the square ; to enter the inclosure one must climb over the wall, which was easy enough to do.

Inside the square was a rough heap of granite, a cairn, gray with lichens, in the centre of which stood, or rather leaned, a tall square block of granite, like a dolmen. So great was the age of this strange obelisk that the lichens had encrusted it to the top. The stone had once stood upright ; but it now leaned toward the marsh, the cairn having slowly yielded on the lower side.

Around this ancient monument were working four men in the gray and black tweed of the convicts ; and it was at their presence that the gangs had stared as they passed.

One of these four men was young, one middle-aged, and two well down the hill of life, the oldest being a tall and emaciated old man of at least seventy years. They were four political prisoners—namely, Geoffrey Ripon, Featherstone, Sydney, and the old Duke of Bayswater. There was a warder in charge, who addressed them by numbers instead of names. He called Geoffrey '' 406 ;'' Featherstone, '' 28 ;'' Sydney, '' No. 5,'' and the old Duke, '' 16.'' The prisoners recognized their numbers as quickly as free workmen would have answered to their names.

'' No. 5,'' said the Warder, sharply, a bearded man, with the bearing of an old infantry soldier, '' you must put more life into your work. You have been fooling around that stone for the last ten minutes.''

'' No. 5'' raised himself from the bending posture in which he had been, and looked at the officer with a gentle reproach.

'' It is a heavy stone, and I have been thinking how it

can be moved," said "No. 5," and he smiled at the officer. He was not the Sydney of old, but a woe-begone creature, obviously sixty years of age, on whose thin frame the gray clothes hung in loose folds.

The officer thought "No. 5" was making fun of him, and he became angry.

"No use thinking," he shouted; "move the stone."

"No. 5" tried again, but his starveling strength could not shake a tenth of its weight.

"Here, you, 16," cried the officer to the old Duke; "bear a hand here. Your mate says he can't move that stone."

"No. 16" and "No. 5" applied their united force to the stone, but it remained as before. The two poor old fellows regarded it with perplexity while furtively watching the officer. It was pitiful to see the expression of simulated mortification on their faces, which was meant to placate the Warder.

"Let me assist them," said Geoffrey to the officer, and he got a good "purchase" on the block and easily heaved it from its bed.

"No. 16," the old Duke, bowed his thanks, and "No. 5" pressed Geoffrey's hand. The officer, more rough than cruel, turned away to hide a smile at the courtesies of his charge. Soon after, he gave them instructions about the work, and left them, going down to "The Farm" to superintend the making of a new drain.

"This is heavy work, Duke," said Geoffrey to the old man; "but we ought to be thankful for the sentiment which sends us to do it instead of the criminals."

"I suppose so," said the Duke, in a desponding tone; "but it is not pleasant to think that after a century and a half the tomb of political prisoners in Dartmoor should be repaired by the hands of political prisoners."

" Not pleasant, but natural, Duke," said Mr. Sydney ; " so long as there are principles, there must be men to suffer for them."

" Whose monument is this ?" asked Featherstone ; " I am all in the dark—tell me."

Geoffrey, who had been employed in the office of the Governor of the prison, and who had, on hearing this old monument was to be repaired, volunteered on behalf of the three others to do the work, now told the story of the old monument as he had learned it from the prison records which he had been transcribing.

" In the wars of the Great Napoleon," Geoffrey said, " the French prisoners captured by England were confined in hulks on the seacoast till the hulks overflowed. Then this prison was built, and filled with unfortunate Frenchmen. In 1812 the young Republic of America went to war with England, and hundreds of American captives were added to the Frenchmen. During the years of their confinement scores of these poor fellows died, and one day the Americans mutinied, and then other scores were shot down in the main yard. This field was the graveyard of those prisoners, and here the strangers slept for over half a century, till their bones were washed out of the hillside by the rain-storms. There happened to be in Dartmoor at that time a party of Irish rebels, and they asked permission to collect the bones and bury them securely. The Irishmen raised this cairn and obelisk to the Americans and Frenchmen, and now, after another hundred years, we are sent to repair their loving testimonial."

" It is an interesting story," said Featherstone.

" A sad story for old men," said the Duke.

" A brave story for boys," said Mr. Sydney ; " I could lift this obelisk itself for sympathy."

They went on, working and chatting in low tones, till an exclamation from Sydney made them look up. Sydney was on top of the cairn, scraping the lichens from the obelisk. The moss was hard to cut, and had formed a crust, layer on layer, half an inch in thickness.

" What is it, my dear Sydney ?" asked the Duke.

" An inscription !" cried Sydney, scraping away. " An inscription nearly a hundred years old. I have uncovered the year—see, 1867."

" Ay," said Geoffrey, " that was the year the Irish were here."

Featherstone had gone to Sydney's assistance, and with the aid of a sharp flint soon uncovered the whole inscription. It ran thus :

SACRED TO THE MEMORY OF THE

FRENCH AND AMERICAN PRISONERS OF WAR,

Who Died in Dartmoor Prison during the Years 1811–16.

Dulce et decorum est pro patria mori.

Underneath were the words, " Erected 1867."

Very tender and true was the touch of nature that made these four prisoners, now looking at the ancient letters, akin with those who slept below, and with those who had so lovingly preserved their memory. The sudden uncovering of the inscription seemed to give a talismanic value to the words. The centuries cleared away like the mist from the moor, and the four Royalist prisoners saw the brave Americans carry their dead comrades to their English grave ; they saw their set faces as they faced the armed guards and invited their own destruction ; they saw the Frenchmen who had followed Napoleon from Egypt to Waterloo laid here by their younger fellows who still dreamt of future glory under their world-conquering Emperor. And when all this phastasma cleared away came another picture of the Celtic patriots raising the cairn and cutting the sweet old Roman words on the monolith.

" May they rest in peace !" said the old Duke, taking off his convict's cap.

" Amen !" said Sydney.

" How this day's work would have suited John Dacre," said Featherstone with a deep sigh ; and the name brought tears to the eyes of the four prisoners, who went on with their labor in silence.

But interesting as was this employment to the Royalists, it was on quite another account that Geoffrey had, while acting as clerk in the Governor's office, secured this work for them. The truth was that he expected to hear from friends outside who might help them to escape. A letter which he had received from his old servant Reynolds had puzzled him exceedingly with its repeated regrets for the difficulty of getting admission to the prison. But at last the idea struck Geoffrey that Reynolds was hinting that he should seek employment outside the walls. The restoration of the old monument soon gave the opportunity, and Geoffrey had seized it.

He had said nothing of all this to the others; for he might have quite misinterpreted Reynolds's letter, and he did not wish to raise vain hopes. There was not the least sign as yet that he had been right. The old high-road across Dartmoor, it is true, passed the spot at which they were working, skirting the very prison wall; but it was an empty and desolate path.

That day and the next they labored at the cairn, until at last the stones were sufficiently removed to allow the monolith to be raised by a derrick into an upright position. They had just rigged the derrick and the old Duke and Mr. Sydney were standing at the wheel ready to turn, while Geoffrey and Featherstone mounted the cairn to arrange the rope. The Warder sat on the low wall with his back to the road and the prison.

As they stood on the cairn, Featherstone saw an old man on the road driving a donkey-cart. The harness had given way, and the old man was busy repairing it, standing behind the Warder. Something in the old man's attitude rather than appearance induced Featherstone to look at him again. His raised hand seemed to purposely arrest attention.

Featherstone looked too long and too sharply, for the Warder observed him, and turned to see what he looked at. The old man on the road saw the motion, and, instantly dropping his hand, went on with his mending, meanwhile addressing the donkey with reproving words.

The Warder looked for a moment, then turned his attention to the workers at the cairn.

"Heave on that handle, you, No. 5; don't let your mate do all the work. Come, now—heave!"

And the two decrepit old men "heaved," as he called

turning the handle of the windlass, until their old joints cracked.

"That'll do ; slack away !" and they rested panting, while the rope was fixed for another grip.

"Geoffrey," whispered Featherstone, with his head bent beside the stone, "look at that old fellow on the road. I am sure he made a signal to me, and stopped when he saw the Warder looking."

When Geoffrey had arranged the rope he looked toward the road, and almost shouted with joy and surprise to see faithful old Reynolds, with both hands raised in recognition and a wide smile on his honest face. Fortunately the Warder was at the moment encouraging the Duke and Sydney to "heave" on the wheel.

Geoffrey quickly recovered, and turned his attention to the rope.

"Try and find what he wants," he whispered to Featherstone. "It is my old Reynolds. Careful !"

While he whispered there was a crash on the road that made the whole group start. The harness had wholly given way and the shafts had come to the ground.

The old driver was in a sad plight, and he looked helplessly at the wreck of his team. He turned wistfully to the Warder and asked him to send one of the prisoners to his aid.

"Here, you, No. 16," shouted the Warder to the Duke ; "lend a hand here on the road ; look alive, now." The old man went toward the wall, as if nothing could surprise him, no indignity arouse a spark of resentment. He tried to hurry to win the Warder's approbation ; but in doing so he stumbled in climbing the low wall, upon which he turned to the officer with a look of apology.

Geoffrey took advantage of this moment to offer his services. He leaped from the cairn, and asked the Warder to let him take the place of the old man.

"All right—go along. Here, you, No. 16, scramble back to your work. If you don't look out you'll lose your good-conduct marks."

Mr. Sydney gave the Duke a look of sympathy and a smile of cheer as he took his place on the windlass again, and Featherstone looked down from the cairn at both his old friends with actual tears in his eyes.

Meanwhile Geoffrey had gone out to Reynolds, and in bending to the shaft gave the old man's hand a grip of welcome and gratitude. Reynolds moved to the other side of the cart, and stooping out of sight of the Warder took a letter from his pocket and showed it to Geoffrey. Featherstone, from the top of the cairn, saw the movement and made a brilliant stroke.

"Look out, down there!" he shouted to the old men, "my hand is caught in the bight!"

There was a brief excitement in which the Warder joined, while Featherstone played his part to the life. When it had passed the cart was raised, and Geoffrey had the letter in his stocking.

Reynolds gave Geoffrey a look that was better than words, and then he thanked the Warder and went off with his donkey.

"Bravo!" whispered Featherstone as Geoffrey joined him; "that was done in a way to make the professionals envious."

For the rest of the day Geoffrey felt like a man made of India rubber. He leaped up and down the cairn like a boy, and he whispered all kinds of encouraging words to

the old men at the wheel. He felt the letter in his stocking all the time, and wondered why he could not read it by
very insight. He turned a hundred times in alarm to see
if the Warder's eyes were on its hiding-place. Who had
written it? Was it a plan of escape? Perhaps it was only
a word of empty sympathy; but no, Reynolds was a practical man.

Oh, how long the hours were, till at last the prison-bell
rang at six o'clock, and the gangs all over the farm formed
into little squads and marched toward the prison, the
warders drawing after them the light iron bridges of the
canals, which were locked on one side every night. By
this means " The Farm," which was intersected by a score
of these wide and deep trenches, was impassable; and as it
hemmed in one side of the hill on which the prison stood,
with a guard tower on either end, it was a greater safe-
guard even than the wall of the prison.

The four political prisoners marched into the yard.
The Warder, before locking them up, made each one raise
his arms and stand to be searched. He then ran his hands
lengthwise over the whole man, mainly to see that no
weapons or tools were concealed. As his hand passed over
the letter in the stocking Geoffrey closed his eyes in the
tense pain of anxiety. He did not breathe till he stood in
his narrow cell and had closed the self-locking door with a
bang. Then he sat down on his hammock and hugged
himself with joy.

When all was quiet on the long corridor and the prisoners were eating their meagre supper Geoffrey drew out his
letter and broke the outer cover. It was addressed in a
hand he had never seen before—a plain, business-like
hand:

"To Mr. Geoffrey Ripon, or any of the Royalist prisoners."

"No more titles," mused Geoffrey with a smile; "there is something American in the 'Mr.'"

This thought naturally led him to think of one in America whose handwriting he had blindly and unreasonably hoped to see in this letter. Now, with a sigh, he saw that it was not for him alone, but for "any of the Royalist prisoners" as well.

The letter was written on small sheets, joined at the top by a thin brass holder. From the first word it was a plan to escape from Dartmoor and from England. It showed that everything had been carefully examined and considered by those outside before they had attempted to communicate with the prisoners; and all that remained must be done by those within the prison. The letter ran thus :

"We have arranged everything but your actual getting out of the prison and crossing the marsh at the foot of the hill. ['The Farm' was here meant.] This marsh extends between two guard towers, and is nine hundred yards long. It cannot be crossed at night, for the warders withdraw and lock on the prison side the swinging bridges of the numerous canals. These canals are seven feet deep and fourteen wide, and the banks are soft peat. It would be dangerous to try to swim them. You must procure a long plank or beam, and carry it from trench to trench. You can get such a plank, which two men can carry easily, at the new tool-shed which the convicts are building against the outer wall of the prison to the right of the lower gate.

"We cannot do anything to help you out of the prison till we hear from you. You must escape by the lower side of the prison and cross the marsh, for the town and warders' quarters extend on the other three sides. In the old tool-shed against the outer lower wall, where you leave your tools every evening, there is a small portable steam-engine. Place your answer inside the furnace door, to the right, and search there every morning for our messages. You need not grope around. Put your hand to the right corner of the furnace, and our parcel will be there. In case you can get out without our help, here are complete instructions :

" When you have crossed the marsh, keep straight on across the hill, at the foot of which, a mile from the prison, there is a narrow lane. Keep to the right on this lane till you come to the high road. Half a mile down this road to the left stands a cottage with a ploughed field behind. Go boldly into this house day or night ; the door will be left open, though latched. Once inside the cottage, unseen by the guards, you are safe. Trust implicitly on us for anything else."

Geoffrey read the letter many times before he turned to his miserable supper of dry bread and cocoa. He impressed every detail on his mind so that the writing might be destroyed. Then he began to eat and think together, and it was nearly morning before the thinking ceased. In his mind he must settle every difficulty, foresee and circumvent every danger before he made a move. Were it only his own peril he were considering he would have had small anxiety. But now he felt on himself the burden of the lives of his three friends, who would undoubtedly attempt to carry out his arrangements. At last he fell asleep, and it seemed that the vile roar of the waking bell began a few minutes later.

In the morning Geoffrey sat face to face with the first and least of his difficulties : he had no means of writing to his unknown friends. But the mind springs to experiment when it is left alone. In a minute he had paper, pen, and ink, and, stretched on the floor, with his only book, the prison Bible, for a desk, he was writing his answer.

The ink was on the floor, composed of the asphalt dust of which the floor was made. He had swept it into a little heap with his hard floor-brush, and mixed it with water from his washing basin. His pen was the wire-twisted end of his leathern boot-lace ; and his paper, whole leaves carefully torn from the Bible, across the small type of which he wrote in heavy letters as follows :

" We cannot possibly escape from within the prison. Our cells are on the third tier, opening into the prison, and two of our friends are old and infirm. We must escape from the guards while employed outside the walls, conceal ourselves till night, and then follow your instructions. To-day we shall begin our preparations. We cannot tell how soon we may make the attempt, or how long we shall have to wait. Wednesdays and Saturdays are the only days on which it can be done ; and we must wait for a very rainy or foggy evening on one of those days. The present weather is in our favor, so do not leave the cottage empty day or night for a few weeks."

Geoffrey concealed his letter, ate his breakfast when the six o'clock bell rang, and the bolts of five hundred cells shot back by one mighty stroke of a steam piston-rod, he paraded with his companions, and the four were marched off to their work at the monument.

Sydney and the Duke walked together in rear of Geoffrey and Featherstone. The Duke, in order to keep up with the regulation pace, secretly clung to Sydney's arm, which he dropped when the officer looked round and took again when the danger had passed.

When they came to the tool-shed, the prisoners went in one by one for their tools, which were piled up and taken away day after day, by the same men in the same order. The portable steam-engine was to the left of the door. Geoffrey went straight to it, opened the furnace door, and left his letter.

A few minutes later, when they were on the cairn,

Featherstone's anxiety spoke in his eyes, and Geoffrey told him the whole story, in a whisper, as they walked.

" Can it be done ?" asked Featherstone.

" Yes, I think so.   At any rate, we must try."

" What is your plan ?"

" We must escape from the guards outside the prison,"' said Geoffrey, looking down at Sydney and the Duke, who were doing cyclopean work under the eye of the Warder. " Those two could never escape from the cells, nor climb the walls if they did."

" True," answered Featherstone, with a despondent manner ; " but we are no nearer freedom than ever, if we have no definite plan."

" I have a definite plan," said Geoffrey, " and I think a good one.   We must remain outside some evening when the convicts march in.   On every evening but Wednesday and Saturday we go straight to our cells when we go in from work, and we close our own doors, so that if we remained outside on any evening but those two we should be instantly missed.   On Wednesday and Saturday evenings the prisoners are taken off work one hour earlier and are sent to school.   We want at least an hour's start for the sake of those two ; you and I could do with half the time. Therefore we must remain behind on one of those two days."

" But how ?" asked Featherstone, impatiently.   " The Warder walks beside us."

" We must manage to send him off or have him called away," answered Geoffrey.   " Can it be done ?"

Featherstone did not answer.   He went on working ; he even spoke about other things, as if he had not heard Geoffrey's question.   In about half an hour he said :

" I think it cannot be done. What do you think ?'

" I think so too," said Geoffrey.

" So that, even with our friends waiting for us, we are tied hand and foot."

" No," said Geoffrey, with a smile at his friend's gloom ; " but that is just what the Warder must say."

" What ! Seize him and tie him up ?" asked Featherstone, with a flash in his eyes that made the shaven prisoner a soldier again. " Bravo, Ripon ! It can be done. What a mole I am."

" Do you think it can be managed without hurting the poor devil ? With all his loud talk he has been kind to those two old friends. Just look at them now, pretending to turn that wheel, with no rope on the windlass, and he looking on ! I don't want to harm him, Featherstone."

" No, nor I. But we can take him gently and swiftly and gag him. That won't hurt him, will it ?"

" No ; but should he make a noise ?"

" Trust me, Ripon ; I could strangle him with one hand. I shall simply hold him by the throat while Sydney gags him, you tie his hands, and the Duke his feet. We shall do it any day or hour that you give the word."

The friends' hands met as they bent over the monolith, and Featherstone, perhaps to show Geoffrey what he could do, almost crushed his hand in a giant grip.

" Now, tell Sydney and the Duke as soon as you can. To-morrow is our first day of opportunity, and we must be ready. Should it rain heavily or should the mist hang, we shall take our chance. All we have to do is to secure the Warder just as the five o'clock bell rings, and lie down over there inside the wall of this little yard. No one ever looks over. They will think as they pass from the farm that we have marched in as usual."

Before night Featherstone had told the Duke and Sydney, and the manner of those convicts changed mysteriously from that moment. Their gloom vanished. They smiled at Geoffrey every time he met their eyes. They were constantly whispering to each other and smiling, and often they looked long at the Warder and measured him as a foeman.

The next day was Wednesday. It rained in the morning, and the hearts of the four political prisoners went up at the steady down-pour. But the sun burnt through the clouds at noon, and the moor glistened under his beams all the rest of the day.

"Don't fret, Duke," whispered Featherstone. "Our day is coming; we are young yet."

The Duke bowed at the kind words, and he and Sydney smiled broadly at Geoffrey to show him that they were strong-hearted, just as they looked serious to make the Warder think they were working very hard indeed.

The next two days were fine, and the Saturday opened with a smile that fell like a pall on the hearts that pined for freedom. But about three o'clock in the afternoon, as the two toilers on the windlass " heaved " laboriously, the Duke gave a little cry of joy, so low that only Sydney heard him. A large drop of rain had fallen on his hand, which he held toward Sydney. Five minutes later Geoffrey, who had been watching the clouds, bent his head to Featherstone, who was working in a cavity they had made in the cairn.

"To-night, I think," he said. "It promises splendidly."

Featherstone, who was quite concealed in his hole, laughed quietly, and pointed to his biceps.

Geoffrey glanced at the two below and found them watching his eye with a question. He gave a little nod, and they both smiled, and soon after turned their gaze on the Warder, who, to escape the rain, had crouched down in lee of the low wall.

When Featherstone saw him he said to Geoffrey, "Just look! The Duke alone could capture that fellow now."

Had the Warder looked closely at his prisoners he might have noticed something odd about their proceedings. Though it rained hard none of them had donned the heavy striped linen blouse furnished to Dartmoor prisoners for use in wet weather. The truth was that the blouses of all four were at that time being cut into strips, and twisted into stout cords by the big Colonel in his hole in the cairn.

At 4.30 the rain fell with sober steadiness, and there was no longer a doubt. In half an hour the bell would ring. The Warder still crouched under the wall.

Another quarter of an hour passed, and the machinery of escape began to move.

"Hold on!" shouted Geoffrey to the two on the windlass. They stopped and stood as if surprised at the tone. Geoffrey meanwhile spoke rapidly and excitedly to Featherstone, who was unseen in the hole.

"What's the matter there?" grumbled the Warder.

"I don't know. He says he has discovered something."

"Discovered something!" repeated the Warder, rising and coming toward the cairn, up the sides of which the Duke and Sydney had scrambled, regardless of rules. "What has he discovered?"

" What is it ?" Geoffrey cried to Featherstone.

" Tell the Warder there is something buried here which I can't lift. He had better come up here and see for himself."

¯ The Warder heard the words, and climbed the cairn. He knelt on the brink of the hole and leaned over to see the discovery. A quick, strong push from Geoffrey sent him headlong into Featherstone's arms, and before he knew what had happened the Duke had gagged him with his own woollen gloves and handkerchief, and Sydney had tied his hands and feet.

" Good-by," said Featherstone, as he left him securely fastened at the foot of the monolith in the hole. " If you had not been kind to our old friends you might have been hurt. You will be discovered before morning."

The Duke and Sydney also said " good-by" to the helpless officer, and then, as the bell rang, the four adventurers lay down in the lee of the wall just where the Warder had sat.

They heard the gangs march past on the other side of the wall. The sound of the warders locking the iron bridges on the canals came up to them clearly. In a few minutes the whole orderly closing of the day's work was over. They heard the lower gate of the prison slam heavily into place and the key turn in the lock, not twenty-five yards from where they lay.

As soon as the gate was closed, Geoffrey rose and cautiously looked all round. Not a living thing was in sight. He knew that they had a clear hour's start, and he gave the word :

" Now, friends, follow me."

They crossed the wall, and ran straight for the new tool-shed. Geoffrey forgot that his speed was much greater than that of the older men. Featherstone kept up ; but the Duke lagged, and Mr. Sydney, who ran lamely, was left far behind.

When the two latter came up to the tool-house they met Geoffrey and Featherstone shouldering a long new plank, and making for the first canal at the foot of the hill.

"Follow us," they said ; and, though awkwardly burdened, they far outstripped the Duke, while poor Sydney's pace grew slower and slower.

The plank was down and waiting for them when they came to the canal. They crossed, and Geoffrey and Featherstone pulled in the plank and set off for the next. There were nine canals to be bridged in this way.

The slowness of Sydney caused the loss of many precious minutes. At every trench they had to wait for the poor old fellow. When they came to the seventh canal, he stood on the prison side when all had crossed, and refused to move.

"God speed you, my dear friends," he said, with quivering voice. "I cannot go any farther. You will all be lost if I attempt it. I cannot run any more—nor could I even walk the distance you have to go."

"Oh, Sydney, come !" cried Geoffrey, with painful impatience.

"Dear Sydney, do not leave us," pleaded the Duke.

But Sydney did not move ; he only waved a good-by with his hand. He could not speak.

Without a word, Featherstone recrossed, seized Sydney in his arms, and carried him bodily over. Geoffrey pulled in the plank alone, and started for the eighth canal.

Mr. Sydney did not speak ; and now he seemed even to

gain new strength and speed. He kept up bravely, and even crossed the next canal ahead of the Duke. There now remained but one more.

"Fifty minutes gone," said Geoffrey in a low voice as Featherstone ran over the plank. "That bell rings at ten minutes to six."

"Bravo, Duke!" cried Featherstone, as the old man stepped from the plank. "Come, Sydney."

But Sydney did not come. Instead, when he came up to the canal, he bent down, seized the plank, and pitched it into the deep trench which ran rapidly and carried it off toward the marsh.

"Now go ; and God bless you all !" cried Sydney, and he turned back and went toward the prison.

There was no possibility of undoing Sydney's sacrificial work.

"No use waiting," cried Geoffrey. "In seven minutes we shall be missed. God bless you, dear Sydney !"

The brave old fellow heard their loving words, but he would not turn or speak, fearing they might delay. He walked on to the canal before him, and then he turned and saw them drawing toward the top of the hill. Then he broke down and sobbed. But his tears were not of grief, but of joy.

Next moment the fugitives heard the alarm bell clanging at the prison. They did not look behind, but Sydney looked, and saw the lower gates open and a crowd of warders rushing down the hill shouting. They had seen the escaped prisoners just as they reached the top of the hill.

Sydney's heart failed him when he saw the speed with which the pursuit crossed the marsh. The light bridges of the canals were easily opened and swung round, and in as many minutes half the canals were crossed.

Just then a light of genius entered Sydney's brain, and he turned and ran and shouted in his excitement as loudly as any officer of them all. The gout was forgotten. The years fell from him like cobwebs. He was a youth of twenty rushing for a football.

Straight toward the ninth and last canal he dashed, where his friends had crossed beside the locked bridge. He was panting like a hunted wolf when he reached the spot and sank down where the bridge was locked to the bank.

By this time the warders were at the eighth canal, howling like demons at sight of Sydney. They howled louder when they overtook him and found what he had done.

Mr. Sydney had filled the padlock of the bridge with small stones, and he stood aside with a grave face, looking at the warders as they tried to open it. When they understood the daring trick, one brutal fellow rushed at Sydney and struck him heavily on the face.

The old man reeled from the blow, and then recovering himself, turned from the ruffian and looked with disgust and surprise, not at him but at his crowd of fellow-warders.

" Stop that !" shouted one of them to Sydney's assailant. " That's no criminal ; and this is no criminal's trick."

There was no crossing this last canal without a bridge or a plank, for the further side was a brick wall considerably higher than the nearer, designed to prevent escape.

By the time the warders had cleared the lock from Sydney's obstructions, his three friends in Mr. Windsor's carriage, driven by Reynolds, were miles on their way toward that gentleman's steam yacht, which awaited them in the harbor of Torquay.

CHAPTER XVI.

MRS. CAREY'S HUSBAND.

OSWALD CAREY's father had just died and left him a great fortune made upon the Stock Exchange when the son met his wife for the first time at the country-house of his father's old partner and his then executor—Benjamin Bugbee. "Young Crœsus," as he was then familiarly called, fell head over heels in love with the beautiful daughter of the penniless and disestablished clergyman, and during the short space of his courtship and honey-moon he forgot the one thing which had previously absorbed his life—the gaming-table. If his wife had been a good woman, or if she had loved him, he might have stayed his hand from baccarat. But Eleanor had married him simply because he was rich and good-natured and she was ambitious and poor; and after their marriage she plunged into the gayest of fashionable society.

At first Carey yawned in the anterooms of balls, waiting for his beautiful wife, but after a while he tired of this; and, letting her go into the world alone, he betook himself to the Turf and Jockey Club, where the play ran very high, for there adventurers and gamesters of all nations congregated—the rich Russian met his great rival wheat-grower of America, and the price of great farms changed

hands at poker or at baccarat.   The hawks who infested the
club, eager for the quarry, speedily settled upon such a
plump pigeon as Carey, and while his wife wore his dia-
monds at gay balls, night after night, he sat over the green
cloth, throwing away his youth and his fortune to the harpies.
It began to be whispered in a few years that " Young
Crœsus," the beauty's husband, was cleaned out.   The
hawks found his I. O. U.'s were unredeemed, and his
gorgeous establishment in Mayfair was closed.   By some
influence Carey succeeded in getting an appointment as a
clerk in the Stamp and Sealing Wax Office, while his wife
went on in her career as a " beauty."

At the office Carey matched for half-crowns with his
fellow-clerks, read the sporting news, and busied himself
in computations, in connection with his " system" by
which he should infallibly win at cards.   Little by little
his system absorbed the wrecks left to him of his fortune ;
and he had nothing to live upon but his salary and the
money which his wife allowed him.

At last his habits lost him his place under government.

He had borrowed money from every man in the office,
and was in the habit of drinking brandy and soda during
hours, and of smoking upon the big leather sofa until the
janitor, at dark, shook him to his senses.   After this he
spent all his time at the Turf and Jockey, for he still kept
his name at this unsavory institution ; he led much the
same life there as at the government office, save that the
club servants let him sleep on the sofa until morning if he
chose, and he earned no pay while he slumbered.   As a
counterbalance, the brandy and soda was cheaper and
better than that which had been sent to him from the
public house opposite to the Stamp and Sealing Wax,

and he had all his time to devote to his system, while in the office he had occasionally a little writing to do.

Mrs. Carey had been living in her husband's lodging for three weeks after her interview with the King, in the night before Aldershot. All the world was wild over the attempted revolution, the trial of the state prisoners and the escape of the King to France—all the world but Oswald Carey, who gave no thought to what passed on around him ; he made deep calculations upon his "system" at the club between his draughts of "B. and S.," and played with other wrecked gamesters, until he lost his ready money, for his "system" worked to a charm conversely—his opponents infallibly won. Early in the morning he would stumble home to his lodgings cursing his luck.

On the morning of his wife's departure to join the King in France, she had informed him, as he sat at the breakfast-table, holding his aching head in one hand, that she was going to Paris to buy some new gowns, and that she would not be back for some time, but that during her absence her bankers would pay him $100 every week. He begged for more money, but his request was refused, and his wife coldly shook hands with him, and retired to her room to superintend her maid's packing. Oswald believed her story, and, finding that he could eat no breakfast, put on his top coat and crawled to the Turf and Jockey for a "pick-me-up." Fortified by this, he made up his mind that, since his "system" had failed because he had had always too small a capital to work with, he would allow his allowance to roll up at the bank for three weeks before he began play again.

Meanwhile he resolved to keep sober, and he spent his

time trying to perfect his "system" and watching the other players at the club.   His burning ambition was to win back his fortune from the sharpers who had fleeced him.   He cursed himself all the while for his folly in playing before he had learned the game.   He knew the game now well enough, he flattered himself ; all day long he pondered on the combinations, and at night myriads of cards floated through his head.   He dreamed that he held the bank, and that his old adversaries sat with pale faces opposite to him aghast at their losses.

One evening in April he appeared at the club and changed his accumulated dollars into chips.   Fortune favored him that evening ; his perfected "system" worked the right way.   He walked home early the next morning, exhilarated and happy, with his pockets stuffed with bank-notes.   He smoothed out and counted the crumpled bills when he arrived at his lodgings, and found that his pile had grown to $10,000, and for some days his dreams of success were fulfilled, and he was "cock of the walk" at the Turf and Jockey.   He ordered champagne recklessly at dinner for the other men, though he drank little himself.

He even wrote a little note to his wife in Paris, inclosing a thousand-dollar bank-note to buy some bonnets and a gown.

"Nell will be surprised," he had said to himself, as he slipped the notes into the envelope.   "By gad, when I get all my money back, I shall cut all this, and we will go to America on a ranch.   Poor Nell !   I haven't treated her right.   I fear I have made a dreadful mess of it all."

He went to the gaming-table that evening with a light heart, and with other thoughts than his "system" in his mind—thoughts which had not been his for years.

It happened that a young Oxford undergraduate was at the table, and the young fellow had drank freely and had consumed a great deal of the "Golden Boy," as he affectionately termed the club champagne. As a consequence of these libations and of his utter ignorance of the game, he played recklessly, and won from the beginning, although he was surrounded by the most astute players in England. Poor Carey's cherished "system" was powerless against the boy's absurd play and tremendous run of luck, and his pile of chips melted away like snow in April, until he had not a dollar left. He rushed down to the office of the club to get the letter to his wife which he had put in the box, but the mail had been sent away. He succeeded in borrowing $50 upon his watch from the club steward, and returned to the table. But it was of no use ; this soon followed the rest of his money. There were but two rules at the Turf and Jockey—"no I. O. U.'s were allowed at the card-table, and no one was permitted, under pain of expulsion from the club, to borrow or lend money." Carey had no alternative but to sit by the gaming-table and watch the play. He slept at the club on the sofa that night, and looked on at the play all the next day, drinking brandy all the while. The Oxford boy had left the club late in the night before, carrying most of the ready money of the establishment with him, and the broken gamblers played for but small stakes. The excitement of his losses and the constant draughts of brandy had made Carey wild and nervous. He paced to and fro in the billiard-room, racking his fuddled brain to find out a way for getting at ready money. His friends had long since ceased lending to him ; his wife had repeatedly told him that she would not supply him with money to gamble

with.   Finally he remembered that she had told him that
she had called upon the President to induce that wise ruler
to restore him to his place in the Stamp and Sealing
Wax.   If he could only get that task, he would in a few
weeks, with his hundred dollars' allowance a week and his
salary, have a considerable sum to give his system another
chance, taking care to avoid tipsy greenhorns this time.
He felt too rickety to face the President until he had
drank several more glasses of brandy.   This done, he
hailed a cab and drove straight to Buckingham Palace.
Immediately he sent in his name by the policeman ; he
was shown into the President's private room, where the
ruler of England was seated at a large desk looking over a
heap of official papers.   The President looked sharply and
inquiringly at him.

"Mr. Oswald Carey ?" he inquired, looking at the card
which he held between his thumb and forefinger.

"Yes, sir," stammered Carey, who felt his hand shaking
violently as he leaned against the President's desk.   "I
have come to shee about my reshtoration to Samp and
Stealing-Wax Office—I beg pardon, I mean Steal and
Sampling-Wax Office."   He twirled the waxed end of his
mustache with a trembling hand, and looked uneasily at
the President, feeling that he had taken more brandy than
was necessary to settle his nerves.

The President said nothing, but smiled a little scornfully.   Nothing gave Bagshaw such keen delight as to see
a gentleman, even such a wreck of a gentleman as Carey,
in a base position.

"Mrs. Carey spoke to you about it some t-time ago, I
be-believe," stammered Carey, who was sorry that he had
come there by this time.   "I was a useful public servant."

The President smiled grimly.

"We are under great obligations to Mrs. Oswald Carey," he said, "and I shall see that you are restored to your position, only you must not be so obstinate about your assessments in the future, as there is no Legitimate party now, thanks to your beautiful wife."

"Thanks to my beautiful wife! What do you mean, sir?" blurted Carey, staggering over toward the President and resting upon his two hands on the desk. "Thanks to my beautiful wife!"

"Come, come, sir," said the President, "be seated. You, of course, know what I mean. Your wife never spoke to me about restoring you to your office. She said that she would some time ask a favor of me in return for the information which she gave me. You have come to claim that return. I will keep my promise to her. However, if you do not leave brandy alone, the office will not do you much good."

"Damn your office," cried Carey, who had been a gentleman and a man of honor before the passion for gambling had seized upon him. Once he had dreamed of a home, of children who should be proud to own him as their father, and he still loved his wife. "What information did Mrs. Carey give you?"

Carey's hands nervously clutched a heavy bronze inkstand, which lay on the table in front of the President.

"The information which led to the suppression of the Royalist outbreak at Aldershot. Mrs. Carey is a government spy and informer," answered Bagshaw brutally. Then he tried to rise from his chair, for he saw a threatening look in Carey's eye.

He was too late, for Carey, crying, "You lie, you

hound !'' lifted up the heavy inkstand which his hands had been mechanically clutching, and hurled it at the President's bald head.

The missile stunned the President and cut a great gash in his head, and he fell senseless forward on the desk, a stream of mingled ink and blood dripping from his forehead upon the papers.

Carey looked at him disdainfully for a moment, and laughed derisively.

The policeman at the door said nothing to him as he went out ; there had been no noise from the private room.

Then he walked a little hurriedly to his cab and told the cabman to drive to the club.

On the way there he trembled violently with rage as he thought of what the President had said to him of his wife, but chuckled when he thought of the revenge which he had taken.

'' He will wake up with a cursed headache,'' Carey said to himself, '' and if he wishes to arrest me, he can do it. Even the President cannot slander a man's wife.''

He was quite sober now, and had forgotten all about his '' system.'' He thought of his wife, and wondered if she was pleased at the little present which he had sent to her in Paris ; he thought of the days of his early love for her, when she had seemed to him a goddess ; and this scoundrel had called her, his Eleanor, a spy, and asserted that he had come to claim the reward of her treachery. At the club he noticed that all the men whispered to each other and smiled. When he entered the smoking-room a group were eagerly reading the latest news, which rolled in over the '' ticker'' in the corner. He supposed that the other fellows were making merry over his losses, and, with a

hard laugh, he settled into an easy-chair and lighted a
cigar. It pleased him to think of the President's bald
head smeared with blood and ink. He felt himself more
of a man than he had for years. Just then a waiter
brought him a letter upon a tray. It was his letter to his
wife in Paris, into which he had slipped the bank-notes.
Her bankers had returned it to him, and it was marked
" Not found." He thrust it into his pocket, and wondered where Eleanor might be, and why he had not heard
from her all this time. He remembered now that she had
been gone a long time ; he had been so absorbed in his
play that he had not thought much about it before.
Looking up, he saw that the other men were all clustered
around the " ticker," and that one of them was reading a
despatch, and the others listened attentively, every now
and then glancing over to him. He could not imagine at
first what they were after ; then it occurred to him that
they were sending the news of his assault upon the President.

" What is it all about, you fellows ?" he asked, walking
over to them ; " it must be damned amusing !" The
men scattered as he approached, and left the " ticker" for
his use, looking uneasily at him as he lifted the white tape
in his hand and read the despatch which had so much interested them.

It was from Boston, U. S. A., telling of the arrival of
the steamer with King George the Fifth and Mrs. Oswald
Carey on board. The despatch darkly hinted that she had
been the cause of the King's failure to meet his adherents
at Aldershot.

The room grew dark to Carey, and seemed to whir
around him ; the other men saw his face grow deadly

white and his lips close firmly.   He did not seem to notice
them, but he pulled his hat over his eyes and staggered
from the room.

"God!" said one of the men.   "I believe that Carey
was the only man in England who didn't know what a
woman his wife was.   What do you suppose he will do?"

"Heaven knows," said a second.   "But, I say, boys,
let's have a drink."

Carey found in the office that there was time to catch
the next mail steamer from Liverpool for Boston if he
rushed to the next train.

"The cursed scoundrel spoke the truth," he said to
himself, "but I hope that I have crushed his head, just
the same ; and now I shall be in America in five days—
and then—"   He looked out at the landscape whirling by
the windows of the railway carriage and set his teeth.

CHAPTER XVII.

The news of the arrival of Mrs. Oswald Carey in Boston caused some flutter in social circles. Her precise relations to the exiled King became at once a subject for speculation. Men of the world, with a taste for scandal, shrugged their shoulders and laughed knowingly. Charitably disposed people, who did not believe in bothering their heads about their neighbors' affairs, preferred to give her the benefit of the doubt. The serious question was whether society ought to open its doors to her. Her reputation as a beauty had preceded her. The American public had long been familiar with her fascinating face. Should she be welcomed as a sister or treated to the cold shoulder, which the world regards as the due of Mary Magdalene?

Girls settle everything in America. Two married women and a maiden met to discuss the propriety of inviting Mrs. Oswald Carey to five o'clock tea. One of them brought the particulars of her life vouched for by the most charming attachés of the court. Her career had been peculiarly sad. She was the victim of a most affecting romance. The man whom she loved with all the passion of which woman is capable had discarded her for another. She had been left poor and friendless. She had supported herself by painting china and by the pittance derived from the sale of her photographs, the last not of course quite the thing, but pardonable under the circumstances. Then, and not until then, she might have been somewhat unconventional.

" Girls," exclaimed the maiden, " even if she has been a little indiscreet in the past, a grand, superb woman such as she ought not to be judged by ordinary standards."

" Besides, the King is old enough to be her father," said another. " I don't believe there is anything in these stories."

" It would be a pity to offend the dear old King," said the third.

And so it was settled. Mrs. Carey accepted their invitation. She came, saw, and conquered. Her charms were sufficient to deafen all but a few of the *jeunesse dorée* to the unsavory rumors still in circulation, notwithstanding the denial of their truth by the maiden and her associates. This trio took to themselves the credit of having overcome the squeamishness of society, and as a reward for their perspicuity they considered themselves entitled to intimacy with their idol. Very speedily, as may be imagined, the clever woman took advantage of these proffers of friendship. Before a fortnight had elapsed she had drawn tears from her three auditors by a narration of the story of her life. " How sad ! how pathetic ! how you must have suffered !" they exclaimed together, and Eleanor Carey, weeping with them, murmured in the intervals of her sobs, " It is almost worth suffering to have such friends as you."

The dear old King ! In the early days of his exile there had been much to flatter the pride of the deposed sovereign. On his first appearance at the theatre the orchestra had played "God Save the King," and a buzz of sympathetic interest spread through the audience. He had risen and bowed. For the next few days the Old Province House was beset with callers. The fashion and intelligence of the city paid their respects to royalty in misfortune. The Princess Henrietta, the King's only child, a stout, hearty-looking girl of eighteen, without beauty, made her *début* into society under these auspices. The first year, despite the change in their circumstances, had been passed happily and with comparative content by the exiles.

But time, in its craving for novelties, does not spare even potentates. King George the Fifth soon ceased to occupy the public attention, except in a minor degree. After their curiosity had been satisfied people began to laugh a little at the ceremonies and liveries of a court which existed only by courtesy. When the King went to the theatre the stage box was no longer at his disposal unless he paid for it, and on the opening night at the opera the claims of the family of ex-Senator Baggely, of Idaho, were regarded by the manager as superior to his. His exchequer, too, was low. He was said to be wholly dependent on what Bugbee allowed him. Rumors began to spread regarding the crown jewels. One of the best known hotel-keepers in the city was said to have a mortgage on them. The royal carriage was presently dragged by only one horse. The other, a magnificent bay gelding, was reported to have the distemper, a trifling ailment, which would last but a few days. The animal did not reappear, however, until a reporter discovered it months after among the blooded stock of a New York banker. So it went from bad to worse. Soon the King and his daughter walked upon ordinary occasions, and when they did drive made use of the public stable. A groom in livery on the box beside the driver alone distinguished the equipage. At last one day the King took the Princess Henrietta aside and said :

" My child, we must leave this place. I cannot afford to remain at the Old Province House any longer."

" What ! leave the Old Province House, the residence of the colonial governors ?" cried the Princess, who had picturesque and sentimental notions despite her portly appearance. " It is renouncing the last prestige of royalty. Oh, I hope your Majesty will not persevere in this determination."

The King shook his head mournfully. " Our present apartments are too expensive. Besides, I have—eh—eh— advantageous proposals from the proprietor of a South End establishment, who desires to improve the tone of his hotel and neighborhood. I think if I accede to them we may be able to have our carriage again."

" Oh, father, it is better to be poor and preserve our self-respect."

King George took a pinch of snuff and sighed meditatively. " It will be only for a little while. My party will soon restore me to the throne of England." He paused, and his voice trembled. He took out his handkerchief and wiped his watery eyes, which were blinking worse than usual. " If we do not move, Henrietta, I cannot see how we shall be able to pay the rent. You know I only have what Bugbee allows me."

" Oh, my poor father," cried the Princess, and she flung her arms lovingly about his neck, " has it come to this ? I cannot bear to see you in such distress. Let me earn something for our support. I have been idle long enough. I could be a good governess, I think, with my knowledge of modern languages. Very possibly, the Waitstill C. Hancocks would engage me to teach their children. They have been very friendly, you know."

" No, no, Henrietta, I will hear nothing of the kind. What! a Princess of the House of Hanover go out to service! This is the final stroke!" He repulsed her with indignation.

" But, your Majesty, consider. If I do not do something we shall starve."

" Not if we accept the terms to which I have alluded," said the King, mysteriously.

" Do you mean, your Majesty, that you have sold yourself?" asked the Princess. For an instant a suspicion passed through her mind, which she dismissed straightway. There were those about the court who declared the monarch was a miser and had a fortune hidden away in his strong box.

" It is merely a case of fair exchange," replied King George, doggedly. " The fellow wants to raise the character of his house. He will give me lodging in return for my patronage. I do not see anything out of the way in that."

" Oh, father! I will not be a party to such a degradation," burst out Henrietta, and she began to cry.

In the end, however, the royal exodus to the South End took place, and a new era of prosperity dawned upon the House of Hanover. By his arrangement with his new landlord, the King was enabled to keep up a more imposing state. He bought fresh liveries for his retainers and refitted his carriage. There was a report that he had made money in a grain corner. His anxious expression wore away, and he gained flesh. The public took little interest in him, to be sure ; but among fashionable people he was a great favorite. The coupés of the rich trundled over the pavements to his retreat at the St. James Hotel. The Court of St. James, it was called, with an obvious but happy pertinency. The King passed his day at the whist-table in the swell West End Club. He dined out frequently, and was a familiar figure at large entertainments. The Honorable Waitstill C. Hancock always treated him at his receptions (which were among the most elegant of their kind) with marked deference. It must have been very gratifying to the exiled monarch to note the courtly tone in which his host remarked, '' Your Majesty, will you take Mrs. Hancock in to supper ?''

Time passed, and one day the city awoke to hear that the King had gone off on a fishing trip to Florida. A splendidly furnished steam yacht, large enough, if needs were, for ocean travel, had come into the harbor in the evening, and sailed away the following morning with the royal exile on board. The Princess Henrietta had remained behind. There were rumors in circulation which tended to discredit the truth of the alleged destination of the yacht. Mariners from the docks declared her to be equipped for fighting. People remembered, too, that the King during the past few weeks had been seen to handle larger sums of money than was his wont. He had made purchases of army apparel and several silver-mounted revolvers.

A few weeks later the news of the insurrection at Aldershot and its suppression were flashed over the cable. The King, so the subsequent despatches said, was supposed to be concealed in London, and a large reward had been offered for his apprehension.   The good people of Boston were somewhat surprised, therefore, one morning to hear that the incoming steamer from England had a royal freight.   When the King was asked what luck he had had in fishing, he blinked his watery eyes and answered, mysteriously, "You will know presently." This was his reply to the friends who met him as he walked down the plank of the vessel.   A moment after all eyes were directed to the beautiful woman who emerged from the cabin and entered the carriage with the ex-sovereign.   All doubt of her identity was removed when the Court Circular of the following morning announced the arrival of Mrs. Oswald Carey.   Apartments had been engaged for her contiguous to those occupied by his Majesty.

One evening, about four weeks subsequent to the return of the royal party, the King was disturbed by the entrance of the Princess Henrietta into his *cabinet de travail.*   He was engaged in footing up his gains and losses at whist during the week, and the interruption caused him to glower slightly at his daughter.   But she was far too excited to observe his manner.

"Father," she said abruptly, "I can endure it no longer."

"Endure what, your Royal Highness?"

"The presence of that woman.   Either she must leave the court or I will."   The eyes of the Princess flashed angrily.

"I am at a loss as to your meaning, Henrietta.   Do you refer to the Lady Muriel Howard?"

"You know that I do not.   There can be only one to whom such language is applicable.   Mrs. Carey is not a proper person to remain at court."

The King scratched his chin thoughtfully. "What has she done?"

"Done, father? Is not her reputation in the past evil enough to disqualify her for the society of your daughter?"

"You have been misinformed, Princess. Mrs. Carey is a long-suffering and much-abused woman. I do not speak at random. I know her intimately."

"So I am given to understand," replied the daughter, with bitterness. "Lady Constance Percy inquired this morning if her Majesty was well."

"You do not choose your ladies in waiting with discretion. Mrs. Oswald Carey has a husband whose existence shows at once the absurdity of your disagreeable and unfilial suspicion. I have no purpose, Henrietta, to take another consort." The King wiped his eyes with a gentle melancholy.

"And you will send her away, will you not, father? I do not wish to be disrespectful, but I cannot endure her presence."

"Send who away?"

"Mrs. Oswald Carey."

"She amuses me, child. Her great beauty is delightful to gaze at." King George put a lozenge into his mouth and sighed reflectively. He was a victim to asthma. The east winds of Boston cut him to the bone.

"Do not compel me, your Majesty, to be more explicit. I repeat, either this woman or I must leave your court."

The late ruler of England wrung his hands. "I see you are resolved to drive me to distraction. This is the final stroke. My daughter wishes to desert me. Lear,"

he added, piteously, " was only a touch to me.   You are
Goneril and Regan combined in one."

He scowled angrily at her.   Just then the door was
opened, and a gentleman of the bedchamber announced
that dinner was served.

" Is the court in waiting ?"

" Yes, your Majesty."

" This is my birthday," observed the King, moodily.

" So it is," cried Henrietta ; " how remiss of me not to
have spoken of it."

But her father paid no attention to her words.   He was
fumbling in his pocket.   " How many will there be at
table ?" he inquired of the equerry.

" Fourteen, Sire."

" Humph !   Lady Constance Percy and Lady Rosamond Temple do not drink champagne.   Neither does
Paran Paget.   Lord Gladstone Churchill swore off yesterday."   He spoke as if soliloquizing, and went through a
process of calculation on the fingers of one hand.   He
handed a key to his retainer.

" Tell the Lord Chamberlain to have two quarts and
one pint," he said.   " And Lady Muriel Howard is on
no consideration to have more than a single glass.   Come,
Henrietta."

Dinner was always served for the royal party in the main
dining-hall of the hotel.   The large table in the middle of
the room was reserved for them.   First appeared the master of the household bearing the wand of office.   The
King came next, followed by the Princess and her three
Maids of Honor, Lady Constance Percy, Lady Rosamond
Temple, and Lady Muriel Howard, all alike duennas of a
certain age.   The first named were sober, prim-looking

persons, but Lady Muriel Howard, who wore low-neck, corkscrew curls, and carried an enormous fan, ogled the various occupants of the dining-room through her eyeglass as she advanced. The remainder of the retinue included the Duke of Wellington, an old nobleman of threescore and ten, and a half-dozen lesser peers, nearly all of whom were on the shady side of sixty. Lord Gladstone Churchill, Paran Paget, and Sir Humphry Davy, who were always in attendance on the person of the sovereign, were the only youthful spirits. It was the former of these who had furnished the romantic story of Mrs. Carey's early life to the society lady. As the royal party walked to their table a few guests of the hotel rose and remained standing until the King had signified by a glance that all should be seated.

The royal bill of fare was distinct from the *table d' hôte.* The proprietor of the house allowed under his contract with the King a certain sum daily for the cuisine. The King was entitled to save anything he could on that amount. To-day there was a boiled dinner. Boiled chickens at one end of the table and boiled corned beef at the other followed the soup.

" How good an *entrée* would taste," whispered Lord Cecil Manners to the Earl of Kildare, casting a glance at a neighboring table, where a *vol-au-vent* of sweetbreads was being passed by the servant.

" What was that you said, Lord Cecil?" asked the King, sharply.

" I was calling his lordship's attention to the champagne glasses," answered the peer, with a silly giggle.

" It is my birthday," explained the King. " You shall drink my health later on in the repast."

There was a flutter of congratulation around the table.

" How indecorous of me not to have remembered,"
said the Duke of Wellington, with old-fashioned courtesy.

" Many happy returns of the day," said Lady Muriel
Howard, and she whisked her handkerchief coquettishly at
her sovereign.

King George presided at one end of the table, and the
Princess Henrietta at the other. The nobility were seated
according to their rank. Lady Muriel Howard being the
eldest daughter of the Duke of Norfolk, the first peer of
the realm, sat on the King's right, and the Duke of Wellington in the seat of honor by the Princess. Midway
down the table was a vacant chair, and it was noticed that
the King glanced frequently with an air of impatience
toward the door in the intervals of the carving. He preferred to carve the dinner himself. Two servants waited
upon the company.

" His Majesty is out of sorts to-day. He has given me
only drumsticks," murmured Lady Muriel to the companion on her other side.

" Where is Mrs. Oswald Carey?" asked the monarch at
last.

" Here she comes, your Majesty," said Lady Constance
Percy, nodding toward the entrance.

Mrs. Carey, in a superb black velvet costume, cut square
in front, with a Maltese cross of brilliants resting upon her
bosom, swept grandly across the dining hall. She held a
small bunch of flowers in her hand. The head waiter of
the hotel, bowing almost to the ground, waved her toward
the royal table. Everybody in the room paused to gaze at
the superb beauty. The master of the household drew
back her chair, but she did not stop until she reached the
King.

"Sire," she said, with a profound courtesy, "pardon my tardiness, and accept, if you will, these roses in commemoration of your birthday."

The King looked delighted. "Yes, it is my birthday," he answered. "I was afraid you would come too late for the champagne."

Mrs. Carey was about to retire to her seat when the King exclaimed, "Lady Muriel, if it's all the same, I'll get you to change seats with Mrs. Carey. Am I not your sovereign?" he inquired, noticing the glum looks of the outraged maid of honor.

All through the rest of the meal Mrs. Carey and the King whispered together. "I have taken a great liberty," said she at last.

"And what is that? The only liberty that I should object to your taking would be taking yourself away."

"I have invited a party of friends to your drawing-room to-night. I had promised a sweet girl, who seems to have taken an interest in me, to chaperone a theatre party, and she is going to bring her guests here instead. Does this inconvenience your Majesty?"

"Nothing that you could do would inconvenience me," and he gurgled as he drank his champagne.

"She plays her cards well, *n'est-ce pas,*" said Lady Muriel to her new neighbor, Lord Gladstone Churchill.

King George caught her saturnine expression. He turned to the master of the household at his elbow. "Did I not order that Lady Muriel Howard should have only one glass of wine?"

"She insisted on more, your Majesty," groaned the major-domo.

"Am I not King?" said the monarch, and he pounded on the table so that the glasses rang.

This incident attracted every one's attention. Conversation flagged, and presently the Princess gave the signal for rising from the table. The ladies went out in advance, each turning as she left her seat and making a low courtesy to the King. Mrs. Carey was the last in the procession. As she passed through the door, her glance fell full on a man standing a little to one side, and gazing at her intently. She faltered, but only for an instant.

"Why, Mr. Jawkins, when did you arrive? Welcome to court," she cried in a cordial, conciliatory tone, holding out her hand.

Jawkins bowed stiffly, not seeming to see Mrs. Carey's hand. "Yes, I am come," he answered, "but small thanks to you, madam."

Dissimulation was not one of Jawkins's accomplishments.

"This is no place for a scene," she said, in a low tone. "If you wish an interview with me there will be an opportunity later. The drawing-room begins at ten. You will see me there." She smiled and showed her teeth ravishingly, despite the serious purport of her words.

"It is the King I wish to see, Mrs. Carey, not you," Jawkins replied significantly.

"Ah, indeed?" said the beauty, and she followed the Princess up the staircase.

The rest of the royal party remained only a few minutes in the dining-room. The King enjoyed a stroll through the corridor after dinner. He liked to chat with the habitués of the hotel and watch the billiard-players. To-night the Duke of Wellington and young Paget were in special attendance.

The King stepped up to the cigar counter. "Something mild and not too expensive," said he.

The attendant indicated several brands for his selection.

"Three for a quarter?" asked the ex-ruler, as he picked up three ten-cent cigars.

The man nodded, and the King, having presented a cigar to each of his companions, lit his own. His eye presently fell upon a pile of trunks, all of the latest and most improved manufacture, and marked with the letters "J. J." "A new arrival, I see," he said to a denizen of the hotel who knew everybody, and who derived pleasure from the prestige of conversing with royalty.

"Yes, your Majesty. A—a—a subject of yours, if I mistake not. He signs himself ' Jarley Jawkins, London.' Will your Majesty honor me with a light?"

"Jarley Jawkins!" cried the King. "It must be the individual caterer of whose wealth we have heard so much. His attentions to my friends during the interregnum deserve recognition. Several of them have been saved from absolute want by his generosity."

"That is the gentleman," whispered the other, indicating Jawkins, who was smoking in apparent unconsciousness and watching a game of pool. "I saw him just now talking with the famous beauty, Mrs. Oswald Carey."

"With Mrs. Carey?" exclaimed the King. "I have never heard her speak of him." The incident disturbed him little. He was too much absorbed by the idea of Jawkins's wealth. He hoped to be able to borrow some money from him. He turned to Paget and charged him to see that Jawkins was invited to the drawing-room that evening.

Meanwhile Mrs. Carey had retired to her own chamber, which she was pacing in some perturbation of spirit. The

presence of Jawkins was a veritable spectre at the feast.
The expression of his face haunted her. She felt certain
that he meant mischief. What was it he purposed to do?
He had asked to see the King. Probably he had discovered that it was she who betrayed the conspiracy to the
government, and was determined to revenge himself by
exposing her. She smiled at the thought, and the picture
rose before her of the monarch pouring out protestations
of love at her feet on the night when that band of gallant
gentlemen were laying down their lives at Aldershot to restore his throne. If this was all that Jawkins had wherewith to prejudice her with the King, she need not fear the
astute manager. But she could not feel wholly free from
dread. She was aware that Jarley Jawkins was not a man
to be trifled with.

She went down to the parlor where the royal reception
was to be held, so as to be in time to receive her own
guests. It was early, and no one had yet arrived. The
windows were open in order to cool the atmosphere. The
floor had been covered with white linen drugget. At one
end of the room, on a dais, stood a throne. A grand
piano was in a corner. A colored waiter put his head inside the door, and, announcing that the musicians had
arrived, inquired if they were to tune up at once.

"You must see the Lord Chamberlain," answered Mrs.
Carey. She felt sad this evening, and the tawdry character
of this entertainment was contrasted in her mind with the
traditions of drawing-rooms at Buckingham Palace.

A cornet-player, a fiddler, and a female pianist entered,
and the squeak of their instruments in process of recon-
struction soon jarred upon her nerves. She started to
leave the room, but encountered the Princess Henrietta

and her maids of honor at the door, who each regarded her with a haughty look. One or two peers were loitering in the corridor putting on their gloves. At its further end a group of chambermaids were ensconced to view the arrivals. The musicians struck up " Rule Britannia," and Mrs. Carey, looking back, saw that the ladies had seated themselves. The reception was about to begin. She joined the others, and the nobility speedily arrived. Before many minutes the King appeared, attended by the Lord Chamberlain, a fuzzy little man in red stockings and pumps, and mounted the throne.

" God save George the Fifth, King of Great Britain and Ireland, Emperor of India, Sultan of Egypt, and Defender of the Faith," cried the Lord Chamberlain, and the drawing-room began. It was the Chamberlain's duty to present to the sovereign each person who had never been at court before. Invitations had been sent to all Englishmen in the city and to certain carefully selected Americans. The guests began to arrive rapidly, and in half an hour the apartment was filled. All the English people wore regular court costume, but the strangers were permitted, as a special favor, to appear in ordinary evening dress. The duty of introducing the Americans devolved upon the proprietor of the hotel.

Mrs. Carey kept on the lookout for her friends. About 10.30 and an instant, among the names announced, she heard " Mr. Abraham Windsor, Miss Windsor." It was as if she had received an electric shock. She had neglected to inquire who were to compose the party. For an instant she was too surprised to think, then she looked and saw the King talking with evident admiration to her pretty rival. Her hate returned, and with it the wound of her despised love bled afresh. Stepping forward, she said in her most congratulatory tones, " How charming ! we meet again, Miss Windsor, but under different circumstances." There was a suppressed triumph in her tone. The young girl had to take the proffered hand, but it was plain enough to Mrs. Carey that if Maggie had known whom she was to encounter at court the meeting would never have taken place. Their eyes met, and in those of the American there was scorn and pride. " How do you do, Mrs. Carey," was all she said.

Her father came to Maggie's rescue. " Why, Mrs. Carey, your most obedient ! This is like old times," and he proceeded to monopolize the beauty.

" Isn't she entrancing !" whispered the æsthetic maiden, Mrs. Carey's friend, in Miss Windsor's ear.

" I have met her before," she said, quietly.

" Have you ! Oh, in England, of course."

But Maggie did not heed her words. The noise of voices at the door attracted her attention. The crowd was giving way before the wand of the Lord Chamberlain, and it was evident from the commotion that something unusual was about to take place. She looked and saw two men advance with eager step and fall on bended knee at the foot of the throne amid a buzz of excitement.

" My Sovereign and my King," they cried together.

" Rise, Duke, rise," said George the Fifth, wiping with genuine emotion his watery eyes, and he stepped down to clasp the hands of an old man with a bald head, whom Maggie recognized to be the Duke of Bayswater.

" Rise, Featherstone, rise," said the King to the other.

" Most Gracious Sovereign, I kiss your hand." Featherstone it was, and he pressed his lips against the

knuckles of the sometime King; but the words were
spoken coldly, like words of duty.   Lost in amazement at
this unusual scene, Miss Windsor had failed to observe a
young man follow soberly and even sadly in the footsteps
of the other two and stand aloof, though expectantly.
Her eyes and those of the King must have fallen upon him
almost at the same moment.   The heart in her bosom
leapt wildly.   Pale and worn as he was, she recognized
Geoffrey Ripon.

"Lord Brompton!" exclaimed the King, and he grew
confused, for the peer did not kneel as the others had
done.   "Lord Brompton, I am glad to see you," and he
remounted the throne.

"Sire, I have come to bring you a legacy from John
Dacre," said Ripon, and he drew from his breast as he
spoke a smoke-stained and tattered piece of the royal banner and laid it at the foot of the throne.   "This is from
Aldershot, sir."

A murmur spread through the room, and the color
mounted to the King's face.   "Sirrah, I do not understand you.   I am your King."

"As for myself," said Geoffrey, without regarding the
monarch's frown, "I return this, which my ancestor more
than a century ago first unsheathed in fealty to the House
of Hanover."   He took from its scabbard the sword with
which Maggie had girded him that day when he courted
her in the haunted chamber of Ripon House, and snapped
the blade in twain.   He flung the pieces on the ground
and turned to leave the room.   At the first step he encountered the glance of the woman he loved bent upon
him with an expression in which pride and tenderness were
strangely intermingled.   He bowed low to her, and was gone.

CHAPTER XVIII.

TWO CARDS PLAYED.

THE morning following the scene with Ripon, his Majesty was in an ill-temper. The events of the evening were not pleasant to remember ; then the King had lost largely at poker, and had passed a sleepless night. Mrs. Carey had sent word that she had not recovered from her fainting fit, and was not yet visible. Old Bugbee's promised remittance had not arrived. And the entire court joined in what seemed a deliberate effort to make things generally disagreeable. The pages who were on duty at the royal toilet came in for some bad moments ; and young Lord Gladstone Churchill privately confided to Paran Paget that he had never seen the old man in such a devil of a wax.

It seemed to the King that times had sadly changed from the regency of his grandfather. Nobody had ever ventured to argue with him about the desirability of the company he chose to keep. But now Wellington, the Lord Chamberlain, and the Archbishop of Canterbury had as much as told King George that he must break with Mrs. Carey. It was hard if he couldn't have his own way even in the little court at the South End. True, the papers had been full of Mrs. Carey these three months—the last

Sunday Globe had contained a grand plan of her own and
the royal apartments, and the *Advertiser* of the following
day had printed, without apparent reason, an editorial
upon Mademoiselle de la Vallière.   But the King considered it highly impertinent of American journals to make
any personal comment whatever upon majesty, and had
almost burst a blood-vessel when approached soon after his
arrival by an interviewer from the New York *Herald*.

Still, there was one ugly fact remaining—Mrs. Carey's
fainting fit.   What could have frightened her into that?
Not Lord Brompton, with all his rhodomontade—the King
liked to call it rhodomontade ; it soothed a certain uneasy
feeling he had had at times about his own part in the
affair.   Brompton was ardent enough, but he was not well
balanced ; he was impracticable ; he did not properly
sense the feeling of the times, but was eager to force an
opportunity.   Well, well—where was Mrs. Carey?   It was
audience time, and he meant to have her receive, with the
ladies in waiting.   He rang the bell, and a page entered
with a card.   The King looked at it, surprised ; the card
was something between an ordinary visiting card and a
tradesman's circular :

[COAT OF ARMS.]

JARLEY JAWKINS,

MASTER OF SOCIAL CEREMONIES

and

PURVEYOR OF GUESTS

TO HIS MAJESTY THE KING.

The King threw himself upon the throne—it was a fine old carved oak chair, one which had come over in the Mayflower—and waited.

Jawkins entered, bowing low. It was the first time he had ever met his Majesty face to face. As he slowly approached the throne his knees bent at their hinges, until with the last step they touched the floor with a heavy thud (Jawkins was a portly little man) as he kissed the royal hand that was kindly extended. When he rose, which was with considerable difficulty, he backed slowly away. As he saw no chair and did not dare to turn around, there was nothing for it but to continue backing ; which he did, until he brought up with a crash against a large photograph of Niagara that was hanging on the wall of the chamber. Here he stood looking at the King, but hardly within speaking distance.

" Mr. Jawkins, I believe ?"

" Sir, yes," said Jawkins, who did not like to say " Yes, sir," as being too colloquial.

" We have often heard of you, Jawkins, and favorably," the monarch went on. " I understand that several of our poorer gentlemen are indebted to your exertions for their —ahem—pocket money."

Jawkins smiled. " Well, sir, I flatter myself I have been the discoverer of retiring talent to some extent. But the money obligation is mutual, sir—mutual." And Jawkins so far forgot himself as to slap his pockets.

" Dear me," said George the Fifth, " dear me. You must be very rich. Is—is there anything I can do for you, Mr. Jawkins ?"

Jawkins's manner suddenly changed, and he became again the serious man of affairs. " Yes, your Majesty—

there is something I wish to—to suggest—merely suggest
to your Majesty." The King was silent, and Jawkins
wiped his bald head with a handkerchief. His small
head, ordinarily of the shape and color of a ripe cherry,
took a still deeper red as he stammered for words with
which to proceed. Finally he spoke ; humbly, in a manner almost servile, but fixed and cool.

"I have—to beg your Majesty—to consider—the propriety—of keeping Mrs. Oswald Carey at court."

The King stared stonily at Jawkins, who cowered close
to the wall, but went on.

"After what happened at Aldershot?"

"Aldershot !"

Jawkins saw that he had arrested the King's attention,
and went on, hurriedly. "The day was lost at Aldershot
almost without a blow. It was because the enemy were
prepared on all sides. They had known of the planned
rising for days. They were armed and ready at all points.
All the disaffected regiments were marched away, and with
them many of the officers who were in the plot. The
whole force of the government was at or around Aldershot
that day. The fleet was in the river. Worst of all, the
secret of the conspiracy was carefully circulated among all
the officers on whom they could rely, with instructions to
prepare their men, even to sound them in advance. And
it was Mrs. Carey herself who carried the information to
the government."

"Impossible." The King made as if to rise.

"One moment more, your Majesty—just a moment.
I knew all this almost at the time. Mrs. Carey was
staying at a country house in one of my parties when she
met the leaders of the noble attempt. It was she who bore

to Bagshaw the written evidence upon which Sir John Dacre was shot, and the others condemned to prison. Think but for one moment, your Majesty, the day might still perhaps have been gained at Aldershot, but for one thing—the King did not appear. Consider, sir. Who was it who prevented your Majesty from going to Aldershot that day?"

Jawkins heard the King mutter a curse to himself. He hastened to complete his victory, and pulling out a sealed document, unrolled it, and handed it to the King. It was the reappointment, signed by Bagshaw, of Oswald Carey to the Stamp and Sealing-Wax Office.

" This, your Majesty, was handed to me by President Bagshaw himself, to give to Mrs. Carey, as his private agent."

King George looked over it hastily, and then rising, paced nervously up and down the room. Jawkins kept silence.

After some minutes the King stopped in his walk. " Well—if this be true—Mrs. Carey is an agreeable woman. Suppose I chose, without trusting her, to permit her company—"

The King interrupted himself for a moment, as he caught Jawkins's eye. Then he resumed his walk hastily. " Yes, yes," he concluded, " I suppose you are right."

Jawkins looked carefully around the room, and then continued in a lower voice, " Does your Majesty know— what they say at court—that Mrs. Carey wishes to be the King's—" George stopped him with a look.

" Yes, yes—I know all that."

" The American divorce laws are very lax, they say," Jawkins went on, " and if the King were to marry her—"

" Marry her !" thundered the King ; " God, man, what do you mean ?"

" If I proved to your Majesty that such was her aim ?"

" She should leave the court this instant."

" Will your Majesty permit me to send for her ?"

Jawkins rang the bell for a messenger.

While this scene was going on between Jawkins and the King, the fair subject of their discussion was differently engaged. She, too, had passed a sleepless night. The sight of Geoffrey Ripon again had won upon her strangely, and his unworldly speech had struck some chord in the depths of her own heart now long unused. There is no greater error than to suppose the evil beings of this world all one consistent evil—that would be to be perfect, as Lucifer, the father of lies, alone is perfect. Every life is but a sum of actions, and in every action the good and evil motives are most nicely balanced at the best. A slight preponderance of evil or even some exaggerated habit of mind—a little over-development of pride, of ambition, of passion, a too accented doubt and an overcold analysis— suffices to throw the decision on the wrong side of every case, so that the outward life appears, perhaps, one consistent darkness and wrong. But no one knows how near at every step the noble impulse came to winning.

As Eleanor Carey strained her beautiful eyes in wakeful memories that night, the one memory that remained to her was Geoffrey Ripon. When she forced herself to close them, and tried to dream, the one dream was the dream of Geoffrey dying for his friend and laying his broken sword at the feet of his King. When she tried to think of his picture, the one picture she could bear to look upon was

Geoffrey Ripon. It had come to this. All the scheming and the passion of the world, and the hard ambition, the cold, worldly will that lifted her almost to a seat upon the throne—they brought her so far and left her at the feet of her old lover. This was all.

When Mrs. Carey rose her mind was made up—this time shall we call it for good or evil? Evil, yes ; but not the same evil as yesterday's, nor the evil of to-morrow. Her headache was feigned. Leaving this answer with her maid to any inquiries, she stepped out in the early morning into the streets. It was not hard for her to find out Geoffrey's hotel. It was a lovely morning in April, before the east wind had sprung up from the sea, and as she passed through the gardens the crocuses and the little blue flowers looked up to her as if they smiled—as if they, too, remembered other days. Mrs. Carey drew her veil about her face and walked the faster.

Geoffrey had got up that morning as one who arises in a world that is void. His mission to see the King was ended ; now there was nothing left. He owed to Margaret Windsor his liberty ; with that gift she had richly given all that his friendship could claim. And at the time she had nobly told him, frankly, kindly, like a true American woman, that here it all must end. She was to be married ; and he, Geoffrey Ripon, was left—free. But he loved her still ; he loved her, and there was no hope in it. What, then, was left to him? As he bitterly asked the question aloud, some one opened the door of his room. Mrs. Oswald Carey entered.

" Mrs. Carey !"

" Geoffrey !"

Both were silent, and each stood looking at the other.

Never had she been more beautiful than then. Her old
self-possession had gone ; there was a feminine weakness
in her attitude, or quiver of the limbs, a heaving of the
breast that made her seem different from the Mrs. Carey of
late years, and beneath the long, trembling lashes he saw
her eyes glorious with the glamour as of youth, tenfold
more potent. For a long time, it seemed, he stood looking at her. At last her strength seemed to give way, and
sinking into a chair she took his hand and kissed it.
Then Geoffrey broke from her.

" This is no place for you," he said, coldly.

" Geoffrey, I have come to tell you again how I loved
you. I ought never to have left you. You will not cast
me off from you now ?" She spoke pleadingly, and
stretched out one white arm as if to draw him to her.
" The American girl whom you thought you loved is married. We have only each other, Geoffrey, now. You
know you loved me once." She rose to her full height,
and looked deep into his eyes, her own on a level with his.
" See," she faltered, " I leave a king for you." And she
drew forth a little miniature of George the Fifth and flung
it on the floor at his feet.

If Geoffrey had ever hesitated, it was not now, though
Maggie Windsor was lost to him, and then she had loved
him. That was in the old, weak days of his, before
Dacre's death. " If Maggie Windsor is married, God
bless her !" he replied, simply. Then, walking to the
door, he rang the bell.

Mrs. Carey fell back upon the chair crying. Geoffrey
left the room. A minute after he had gone she rose, and
drying her tears, went to the entrance of the hotel, where
she called a carriage and drove back to the Court of St.

James. She went directly into the King's anterooms. No one was there but Jawkins.

"Ah, Mrs. Carey—just in time to remind you of our little compact," said he. As she looked at him, he stood, smiling grossly, vulgar, sensual, mean. All the years of her debasement came to her memory with a new sting to her wounded pride, and she swept on, ignoring him.

"Come, come, Eleanor—among old friends, this won't do, you know. Give me your hand. Let's see—what's the price to kiss it now? It used to cost five shillings." And Jawkins imprinted an attempted kiss, clumsily, upon the palm of the hand. "When do you leave the court? They don't like you here overmuch, I fancy. But you've been well advertised."

Mrs Carey lost control of herself for the first time that day.

"How dare you speak thus to me? I, who was—who am your—"

"Oswald Carey's wife," Jawkins spoke contemptuously.

"Your King's wife!" cried Mrs. Carey. Jawkins laughed and threw back a curtain. Behind it stood the King. He did not look at her, but waved her from him with his hand. She looked at him a minute or two, but then left the room. As the door closed behind her the King looked up.

"Well, Jawkins, it's done."

"Yes, your Majesty."

"She was a devilish fine woman." Jawkins started to go.

"Stay, Jawkins, a moment. Ah! you told me you had made a good mint out of— Are you in funds over here?"

"Quite, your Majesty."

"Jawkins, my bankers are devilish slow. I wish you could manage to advance me a few thousands or so."

CHAPTER XIX.

THE great café of the Trimountain Hotel is one of those interiors which can only be seen in America. Lit at night by a single electric glow, softened and unified in passing through the ground-glass ceiling, it is brilliant with mirrors and cut-glass and china. At one end of the room is the long bar, glittering with all that can make a bar attractive, served by a score or more of the prettiest of barmaids ; along the sides of the room are rows of little tables in carved oak and cherry, each unlike the other, each a work of art ; in the corners and upon the walls is a collection of paintings and statuary hardly rivalled in any of the private mansions of Boston. The centre of the room, save for a fountain playing in a jungle of flowering vines, violets, and rare orchids, is a polished expanse of inlaid floor, where one may walk and smoke.

As Geoffrey walked in he passed the news-stand by the door. Here are shown the photographs of the favorites or celebrities of the day, etchings of the latest pictures, play-bills of the theatres and operas, pictures of women and horses. Everywhere about that day he was met by the semblance of the woman he had just seen ; photographs in every size and attitude, in every dress, colored, plain ; taken in street dress, in house dress, in dinner dress, in *robe de*

chambre, full length and half length, high-necked, low-
necked, very low-necked ; on the handkerchief boxes and
the perfumery cases were still gaudier pictures, with the
Carey collar, the Carey perfume, the King's favorite ciga-
rette, and whatever else had any use or service for a pretty
woman.   Geoffrey noticed all these things as he passed
on, but was struck a moment later by the appearance of a
man he thought he knew.

The man wore the dress of a gentleman, but travel-
stained and untidy ; he was sitting alone at one of the
little tables, with head bowed down upon his breast ;
before him stood glasses and a crystal decanter half filled
with brandy.   Geoffrey started with surprise, and would
have turned back, but the man saw him and recognized
him.   It was Oswald Carey.

The two men looked at each other a minute without
speaking.   Finally Carey spoke, in a hoarse voice, not his
own of older days :

" Have you seen my wife ?"

Geoffrey started, less at the question than at the manner
in which it was asked.

" Yes," he said.

" Where is she ?   At the palace—at the court ?"

" Yes."

" Damn her," said Carey.

Geoffrey was silent.

" Where did you see her last ?" muttered the other.

" Here—in this hotel."

" In this hotel ?"

" This morning."

" Is she—is she not with the King ?"

" I believe—I do not know," answered Geoffrey.   He

turned to go.   As he looked at the other, standing there, white-faced, worn, with the glitter in his reddened eyes, this man whom he had scorned, there was something in him like the ruin of a man after all.   Geoffrey, too, was alone, and his heart warmed to him.   It was he who had married Eleanor Leigh, not Geoffrey.   "Carey," said he, "you can do nothing here.   I am going to the West. Come with me."

Carey looked at Ripon, puzzled ; then, with a broken sob, he grasped his hand and staggered to his seat.   Ripon noticed for the first time that the man was crazy with drink.

"Thank you," said he.   "I must stay.   I have something to do here first.   You know that she betrayed you ? that it was her treason condemned you and Dacre ?"

Geoffrey nodded.

"And you, Ripon"—Carey pulled the other close to his lips and spoke almost in a whisper—"you are the only man that woman ever loved.   I know it."

Geoffrey could make no answer.   Again he rose to go.

"Where are you going ?"   .

Geoffrey smiled and waved his hand vaguely.   "To the West."

"Why ?—I   thought—you   came over in   Windsor's yacht—"   The other stopped, embarrassed.   Geoffrey was touched by his interest.

"Carey, will you give me a glass of your brandy ?"

Geoffrey poured it out.   "Miss Windsor is married."

"Who told you so ?"

"Your wife."

Carey brought his fist down shivering on the table. "And you believe her ?"

"Miss Windsor told me almost as much herself."

"Almost!" Carey burst into a wild laugh. "Here's to her!" he cried, holding up his glass. "Ripon, you are the last gentleman who will ever drink with me. I suspect you are the only one who would now. And here's my last toast : Long life to your wife—and death to mine. Damn her ! Can't you see she lied ?"

Carey rose from the table and staggered out of the room. It was already the afternoon of a garish, shadeless day, and people stopped to look at Carey's terrible pace as he strode along the sidewalk. As Ripon had seen, he was insane with drink, or would have been but for one dominant thought in his mind.

As Carey walked along the busy street, hardly a shop window, not a bookstore, not an ignoble news-stand, but had displayed his wife's picture. It was *Mrs. Carey, Mrs. Oswald Carey, Mrs. Carey and the ex-King*, everywhere. One infamous pictorial publication had a bare necked portrait of the " notorious Eleanor Carey" side by side with that of " Jim Dingan, the Lynn pugilist." As he entered Washington Street, the newsboys were crying, " Horrible crime in New York ! Scandal in high life ! Mrs. Carey leaves the court !" and Carey read the caption outlined on the bulletin boards.

He felt in his coat pocket, where he carried a small revolver he had purchased, and hurried along more rapidly. His gait was quick and firm as an athlete's on the course. No trace of intoxication now.

He reached the St. James and asked a page to be directed to Mrs. Carey's apartment. The boy grinned at first, but was silent at a word from Carey and led him the way. When they reached her door, at the end of a long series of corridors and stairs, the page wished to announce him, but Carey pushed him aside roughly and opened the door. His fingers were clinched upon the pistol in his pocket; his plan was to ask her one question, and then, while she was hesitating about her answer, to kill her.

The drawing-room was a large apartment, vulgarly furnished in a style gone by. A marble clock was on the mantel, and a photograph of the King. Carey pressed through into the bedroom. No one was there. Bits of lace and muslin were scattered about the floor, and one or two garments lying on the chairs as if hastily thrown aside. Carey thoroughly examined the rooms and then turned back to the page.

"Where is Mrs. Carey? Do you know?"

"I do not. I heard that she was about to leave the court."

Carey turned away, and, leaving the hotel, took a carriage and drove to the railway station. A train had just left for New York. At the news-stand was the usual collection of her pictures on sale. Carey spoke to the boy in charge, pointing to a photograph.

"Have you seen that woman go by here to-day?"

"Yes, sir; I see that woman go by here not twenty minutes ago. That's the beauty, Mrs. Carey, that is. There was another woman with her, and a man."

Her maid, probably. But who could the man be? Carey found the next train for New York did not leave till evening. He waited in the station for it, and arrived in that city at midnight. It was too late to get any trace of his wife that night.

Early in the morning he began the search, but it was all of no avail. His wife had apparently stopped at none of the hotels. A certain lady looking like her had been seen at a small hotel on the Fifth Avenue, but she had been with a gentleman, and their names were registered as Mr. and Mrs. Copley Hutchinson, of Boston.

Carey wondered whether she could have left the city. Several European steamers had sailed or were to sail that day, and he spent an hour or two at the docks searching them. All the papers, all the shops, were full of his wife and her movements ; he alone knew nothing of them.

As he walked back, up Broadway, he looked at the bulletin boards. He had a habit of doing this now. In front of the *Herald* office they were changing the bulletin, and he waited a moment to see. The first line on the new broadside he read aloud :

" *Mrs. Oswald Carey sails for Brazil.*"

Carey went in and bought a copy of the newspaper. In it he found the sailing-list of the City of Rio, and there the first name was " Mrs. Oswald Carey and maid," and then, just below, " Jarley Jawkins."

Carey stood on the sidewalk several minutes, like a statue. Then, slowly crumpling up the newspaper in his hand, he threw it in the gutter. That night he was a passenger in the emigrant train for the North-west.

CHAPTER XX.

" Mr. Windsor," said the Duke of Bayswater to his host, as the two were sitting in the library of the latter's house in Boston, " I have received to-day a letter from our poor friend Sydney from my late residence, Dartmoor Prison. It is exceedingly interesting to me."

" Poor fellow," answered Mr. Windsor. " What a pity it was that we could not effect his escape with the rest of you. How does he bear up ?"

" Ah ! pretty well, pretty well," answered the Duke, rubbing his gold-bowed spectacles with a white silk hand-kerchief. " But still, I must say that the poor fellow seems very down-hearted. Shall I read you his letter ?"

Mr. Windsor bowed assent, and the Duke adjusted his spectacles to his sharp aquiline nose, and read, in faltering tones :

" Dartmoor Prison, 198-.

" Dear Duke : I was delighted that you all made good escape on that eventful night of the fog. It is foolish to complain of fate, or rather of the life of free living, which made me have a tendency to rheumatic gout. As I sat on the edge of the canal and watched you then, as you suddenly disappeared over the hill,

I cursed all French cooks and vintages, and my roystering old grandfather to boot. But I led the guard, who were hot on your scent, a devil's own dance when they found that the lock of the last bridge was filled with pebbles. But I am delighted that you others escaped; I could not bear to imagine you, dear Duke, whose magnificent hospitality I had enjoyed in days gone by, cramped in a narrow cell, or mopping up the corridors of this jail."

The Duke broke down completely as he remembered his life at Dartmoor, and Mr. Windsor looked out of the window to conceal the smile which this picture of his venerable old friend brought to his mind. The Duke, after vigorously rubbing his spectacles and clearing his throat, remarked :

"Excuse my stopping, Mr. Windsor, but poor Sydney's handwriting never was good. I remember I used to tell him, when he answered my invitations, that I should have imagined that a fly dipped in ink had crawled over the paper." He laughed for a moment at his former moss-encrusted and ducal witticism, and continued reading Sydney's letter :

"However, I have become resigned. I was born under an unlucky star, and the uninvited bad fairy at my christening, after the others had given me beauty, riches, and wit, hopped in malevolently upon her crutch and shouted in a disagreeable falsetto : 'He shall have all these, to be sure, but he shall have a poor digestion and the gout!' and whirled away on the evening wind astride her broomstick."

Mr. Windsor laughed out loud ; the Duke seemed annoyed at this, and, begging not to be interrupted again, continued his reading in a rather offended tone :

"Since your escape I have been under the strictest surveillance, and as I have recovered from my gout I have been set to

work upon the ignoble task of breaking stone into small bits with
a hammer.   I am known as No. 5, and am called by no other
name.   Imagine me, who found it so difficult to look out for
Number One, having to care for No. 5.   Indeed, I should find it
well-nigh impossible were it not for the assistance which I have
from the warders and turnkeys, who look after me with a touching solicitude.   No physician could have kept me to a regimen so
suitable for my health as strictly as they.   You remember how I
used to enjoy lying abed in the morning.   What a pleasure it
was to wake up, to feel that the busy world was astir around you,
and lie half awake, half asleep, stretching your toes into cool re-
cesses of a soft, luxurious bed.   But it made me idle, very idle.
But now I must be off my hard cot, be dressed and have my cot
made up by half-past five ; then I breakfast off a piece of bread,
washed down with a pint of unsweetened rye coffee innocent of
milk, drunk *au naturel* out of a tin pail.   And how I miss my
after-breakfast cigar and the *Times,* as I put my hands upon a
fellow-convict's shoulder and march in slow procession to my
task.   The work of breaking a large piece of stone into smaller
bits with a hammer is not an intellectual one ; but it has got me
into tolerable training ; I have lost twenty pounds already, and
am, as we used to say at the university, as ' hard as nails.'   I
am afraid that my old trousers, which my tailor used to let out
year by year, would be a world too large for my shrunk shanks
now.   I dine at noon, as you remember, and for the first time in
my life I do not dress for dinner ; indeed, a white cravat and a
dress coat would be inappropriate, when one sits down to bean
porridge and boiled beef served in the same tin plate.   But I
have a good appetite after my pulverizing of the morning, and I
am not compelled to set the table in a roar under duress.   I am
surprised what good things I think of now that I am not expected
to and have no one to whom to say them.   Jawkins would double
my salary could he get me out.   Rye coffee is a poor substitute
for Chambertin, but it does not aggravate my gout.   After
dinner I return to my stone-breaking, and feel with delight my
growing biceps muscle, and after my supper, which is monotonous-
ly like my breakfast, I tackle the tracts, which are left with me by

kindly souls. They are of a class of literature which I have neglected since childhood, having, as you may remember, a leaning toward 'facetiæ.' In fact, since my great-aunt's withdrawal to another world, where it may be hoped that the stones are more brittle and the coffee better, I have seen none. I cannot say that I have been comforted by the tracts, but I have been interested by them, and I spend the brief hours of leisure which are vouchsafed to me in annotating my editions. And yet, my dear Duke, unfortunate as my situation is, I would not exchange places with my old self, a hired jester at rich men's tables, selling myself for a dinner which I could not digest, nor with that wretched monarch, in whose cause we all suffered, who left his gallant gentleman to die for his cause while he pursued his selfish pleasures. If it were chance that I get out of here, I shall strive to earn my bread, in the appointed way, by the sweat of my brow, and to work with my fellow-men. Present my kindest regards to our good friend Mr. Windsor, who has dared so much for our sake, and believe me, my dear old friend,

"Yours faithfully,

"No. 5 (*né* JAMES SYDNEY)."

The Duke, when he had finished reading the letter, folded it carefully, and returned it into his pocket. His eyes were full of tears, and his voice broke as he read the quaint, pathetic words.

Mr. Windsor slapped his bony knee energetically, and arose from his chair.

"I must try to set the poor fellow free," he said energetically. "I do not believe that a forcible prison delivery would be successful again, when our former attempt is so fresh in the mind of the prison governor ; but the presidential election in Great Britain and Ireland is approaching, and if I judge the signs of the times aright, the Radicals under Bagshaw will enter the campaign heavily weighted. If the Liberal-Conservatives put up such a man as Richard

Lincoln they will re-elect him, and if the administration is changed, diplomacy and entreaty may accomplish a general release of political prisoners. The cause of the House of Hanover is so dead that, as Mother Goose says :

> " ' All the king's horses and all the king's men,
>   Couldn't set Humpty Dumpty up again.'

By the way, I believe they call George King Humpty Dumpty in the comic papers."

The Duke smiled ruefully ; in his heart he despised the King, and faintly saw that his class had lost their privileges, but he could not get used to it. He knew that he was a broken old man, an exile from home, and dependent upon the kindness of Mr. Windsor ; and he sighed deeply, wishing that he had died before the deluge which had gulfed all that was holy and precious to him.

Mr. Windsor saw that his thoughts were too sad and solemn for an alien intrusion, and left the old gentleman, still motionless, looking vacantly at the wall. The old Duke saw no Mount Ararat rising from the troubled waters ; all that made life worth living for him had passed away, and he lagged superfluous on the stage ; a supernumerary with a pasteboard coronet ; laughed at and ranted about in the pantomime at which the world had laughed, " King Humpty Dumpty."

That afternoon Maggie Windsor had gone for her usual walk upon the Charles River embankment, a fine esplanade stretching for seven miles along the river-side. It was a beautiful day—one of those rare days which gladden the drear northern spring and remind dwellers in Boston that they live under the same latitude under which Naples idles. A turn of the Gulf Stream and the descendants of the Puritans would lose the last vestige of their inherited consciences and bask in the sun like happy animals. But though the sky was violet, the bright sunlight was cold.

Maggie walked briskly along, by the water park, out by the great houses in Longwood, to the light bridge which swept over the river to Cambridge. There were but few people walking on the embankment this cold day; a stream of carriages bright with glistening harness rolled by. A barge, filled with a merry party, and drawn by four horses, aroused Maggie from her thoughts, which had been of Geoffrey. She had not seen him since the evening of the King's drawing-room, when he had broken his sword before the monarch, and had returned his empty title to the dry fountain of honor. Her suspicions of him had died away long before she had received his letter by Reynolds's hand. She had heard of the *émeute* with an aching heart, and from her distant home in America she had watched the proceedings of the trial eagerly. Her life had died away within her when she read of the sentence of the prisoners, and knew that the man she loved was shut up from the world for fifteen years, like a common felon. And he owed his liberty to her, and yet he did not know it. He should have known it, by instinct, she thought. She had fancied that she knew the moment when he had made good his escape. Of a sudden, one day, during her father's absence in the yacht, the load from her soul had rolled away. She felt that he was free, and speeding over the sea to meet her. Now that he was arrived in America, she had seen him but once, and he had not spoken to her; he had bowed, with a stern, set face, and left the apartment. Had her cruel words there on the cliff by Ripon village cut away his love for her? Then the message which she had sent to him by his servant : " Tell your master that I am to be married." She had almost forgotten that. But his heart should have told him what she meant by that, she argued. " She was to be married, if only he wished it." Why did he not come to her ? Could it be possible that he thought she was to marry another ?

Such thoughts the rush and jingle of the great barge had interrupted. The barge rushed by, and looking up the strait she saw coming toward her, his form dark against the red sunset, Geoffrey Ripon.

He saw her at the same moment, and he took off his hat. She walked up to him and offered him her hand.

" Miss Windsor, Maggie," he said as he grasped it.

" You received my message ?" she asked, looking into his eyes.

" I did. Is it true ?"

" I do not know," she answered, looking down at the river, which gleamed below rosy with the sunset ; a happy omen. " It depends—"

" Upon what ?" asked Geoffrey, eagerly.

" Upon you, Geoffrey," she answered. " Did you not know it ?" And the sun, which just then disappeared over the Brookline hills, did not in his circuit of the world look upon a happier pair than these two lovers, clasped in each other's arms.

CHAPTER XXI.

NULLA VESTIGIA RETRORSUM.

So they were married, and the alliance between simple hearts and Norman blood was complete. It came to pass before many months that the millionaire, pleased, it may be, to find his homely patronymic transmitted to his grandchild, bought back Ripon House from the mortgagees and gave it to his son-in-law. Mr. Windsor knew it was the secret desire of his daughter that Geoffrey should return to England and devote himself to aiding his countrymen in their struggle for liberty. But Geoffrey was too content with his own happiness and too appalled by the confusion which still overspread his native land to evince much enthusiasm in this regard. "Wait a little, Maggie," he said, and Maggie was shrewd enough to understand that this was the better way to attain her purpose. She remembered how her husband had broken his sword and renounced fealty to the perjured King. Give Geoffrey time, and he would work out his own salvation.

But while individuals wedded and were happy and begat children, and while patient women tarried for God's word to awaken in their lovers' hearts, the great world, which is never happy and which never waits, rolled on remorselessly. England still knew perilous days, but the hope of better things to come glimmered through the mists of evil rule.

The bulwark of the nation's safety in that hazardous time, as history well knows, was Richard Lincoln ; and though we who have faith that God is ever working for man's good, know that human nature must in the end evolve into higher grades of truth and power, and that even the sublimest soul is but a cipher in the eternal scale ; yet England had need of a rare spirit in that time of her sore distress to save her from the rocks of revolution and anarchy. She found this in Richard Lincoln, whose name will be ever famous in the gratitude of his countrymen.

In strange contrast to the career of which we have just been speaking stands out the final pageant of the once splendid court of Britain. George the Fifth died, leaving no son to inherit his foibles and his title. The House of Hanover was shorn of male heirs in the nick of time, for it is doubtful if the populace would have permitted exiled royalty to indulge in the mimicry of another dynasty. But for the purposes of our story the King is still alive, since his death took place, as many of us know, in his eightieth year. There were but few of those whose vicissitudes we have followed able to tell the tale when the last Hanoverian, tenacious of vital breath as he had been of everything else, descended to his fathers. *Le roi est mort*, but the old world cry, "Long live the king," is silent forever.

Perhaps one of the keenest strokes at the self-esteem of the unfortunate monarch was the matrimonial apostasy of his daughter. The Princess Henrietta, contrary to the long-cherished traditions of her race, wedded in her thirteenth year a commoner, as it was described at court. She became the wife of L. Pierson Dana, a prominent dealer in hides and leather, and a man of culture and standing in the community. King George, with a senile confusing of terms, always insisted on speaking of the marriage as morganatic.

Concerning those who composed his court little remains to be said. The Duke of Bayswater was joined by his wife shortly after his escape to America. They never returned to their native country, but lived very exclusively in apartments near to the royal suite.

Colonel Featherstone, lured by hopes of fortune, organized a successful corner in lard, and invested the proceeds in a vineyard in California. The famous blue seal dry Hanover, which is even to-day regarded by connoisseurs as a grand *vin*, is a monument to his reverence for royalty as well as to his talent as a vine-dresser.

One day in late November, when little Abraham was about five years old, signs of great activity were noticeable about Ripon House. For a week past the environs had been rife with rumors concerning the return of Geoffrey to the house of his ancestors and the wealth which had accrued to him through his marriage with the daughter of the rich American who had once rented the manor-house. London mechanics had been repairing and furnishing the old-fashioned pile, striving withal to retain the flavor of antiquity which hung about its towers. There had been employment, too, for the artisans of the neighborhood, and even to-day, when the guests were to arrive before sunset, a bevy of the people were running hither and thither at the bidding of an old man with white hair and bent figure. He was evidently merely an upper servant, but the expression of his face betokened one whose joy and sorrow are an echo of his master's fortune.

A few hours later a carriage drew up before the threshold. A young man leaped to the ground and grasped with both of his the hand of the aged servitor.

" How are you, Reynolds ?"

" God bless you, Mr. Ripon ; God bless you."

" And here is my wife, Reynolds. You remember her."

The old man doffed his hat with a respectful formality. It was still a little against his grain to see an American his master's bride. " Welcome to Ripon House."

Maggie shook him by the hand, and her father's bantering voice now startled his dignified mood.

" So this is where you have been hiding all these years, Reynolds ? You look like the wandering Arab, with your gray beard !"

Mr. Windsor doubtless referred to the Wandering Jew, but he was no scholar, as he would himself have been the first to acknowledge. All laughed at the mistake, and none louder than the fourth member of the party, a tall, middle-aged man, with a noble but genial countenance.

It was Richard Lincoln, to whom time had been generous during the six years which had flown since he was last at Ripon House. Despite the cares which had weighed upon his spirit, his brow was scarcely furrowed. He had come to be Geoffrey's guest for a few days and enjoy the tranquillity of the country. There were business matters also to be talked over with his friend, for Geoffrey had promised to take an active part in the public service of the country.

The friends sat long that evening around the dinner-table. There was much pleasant talk, but every face wore a thoughtful look. The intervening time since last they

had gathered here was too full of incident to be passed over
lightly. Recollection stood beside the hearth, and yet with
a finger on the lips, as though loath to jar the atmosphere
of revery with a word. And yet there were references
made to the past. Lincoln asked what had become of that
strange man Jawkins. But no one knew further than that
he had fled with the splendid beauty.

" Is that woman's husband still living?" inquired
Maggie.

All shook their heads in doubt.

" And dear old Sydney, do you know anything of him,
Richard?" said Ripon.

" Yes. Only a few weeks since he married an attractive
little widow with a snug property. I had him pardoned,
you may remember, among my first acts as Prime Minister. Prison life seemed to have agreed with him. He
had lost his dyspeptic air."

" That old scoundrel Bugbee had a curious end," observed Mr. Windsor. " To think of being bitten to death
by a tarantula. Ugh! It seems he used to keep spiders
under. glass in his apartments, and this was one that
escaped. And what an enormous fortune he left!"

So the conversation proceeded, and by and by they all
adjourned to the library, where a wood-fire lighted up the
huge fireplace. Richard Lincoln seated himself in a deep
arm-chair beside the hearth, and rather avoiding talk gazed
at the sizzling logs. His own thoughts sufficed him.
Maggie, whose seat was next to his, watched his expression, where a shade of sadness lingered when his attention
was not engrossed by others. At a moment that Geoffrey
and her father were out of the room she leaned forward
and said :

" Where is she buried ?"

" They sleep side by side," was the quiet response. " Their love to-day laughs alike at peasant and at noble. I try to think of it as a symbol of what is to be," he continued. " Theirs is the first alliance in that reconciliation between the few and the many on which the hopes of posterity depend."

THE END.

STORIES BY AMERICAN AUTHORS.

*For sale by all booksellers, or sent, post-paid, upon receipt of
price, by*

CHARLES SCRIBNER'S SONS, Publishers,

743 AND 745 BROADWAY, NEW YORK.

EDWARD EGGLESTON'S NOVELS.

Mr. Eggleston is one of the very few American novelists who have succeeded in giving to their works a genuine savor of the soil, a distinctively American character. His "ROXY," "HOOSIER SCHOOLMASTER," "CIRCUIT RIDER," and the rest, are home-spun and native in all their features. The scene of the stories is the Western Reserve, and the characters are types of the pioneers in the territory now comprised in Indiana and Ohio.

ROXY. One vol., 12mo, cloth, with twelve full-page illustrations from original designs by WALTER SHIRLAW. Price, $1.50.

"One of the ablest of recent American novels, and indeed in all recent works of fiction."—*The London Spectator.*

THE CIRCUIT RIDER. A Tale of the Heroic Age. One vol., 12mo, extra cloth, illustrated with over thirty characteristic drawings by G. G. WHITE and SOL. EYTINGE. Price, $1.50.

"The best American story, and the most thoroughly American one that has appeared for years."—*Philadelphia Evening Bulletin.*

THE HOOSIER SCHOOLMASTER. Illustrated. 12mo. Price, $1.25.

THE MYSTERY OF METROPOLISVILLE. Illustrated. 12mo. Price, $1.50.

THE END OF THE WORLD. A Love Story. Illustrated. 12mo. Price, $1.50.

COMPLETE SETS (IN BOX) $7.25.

THE HOOSIER SCHOOL BOY. With full-page illustrations. 12mo. Price, $1.00.

THE HOOSIER SCHOOL BOY, as its title shows, depicts some of the characters of boy life, years ago, on the Ohio; characteristics, however, that were not peculiar to that section only. The story presents a vivid and interesting picture of the difficulties which in those days beset the path of the youth aspiring for an education.

⁎ *For sale by all booksellers, or sent, post-paid, upon receipt of price, by*

CHARLES SCRIBNER'S SONS, Publishers,

743 AND 745 BROADWAY, NEW YORK.